SAPTARSHI

NARAYAN

ATLANTIC
PUBLISHERS & DISTRIBUTORS

Published by
ATLANTIC PUBLISHERS AND DISTRIBUTORS
B-2, Vishal Enclave, Opp. Rajouri Garden, New Delhi-110027
Phones : 25413460, 25429987, 25466842

Sales Office
7/22, Ansari Road, Darya Ganj, New Delhi-110002
Phones : 23273880, 23275880, 23280451
Fax : 91-11-23285873
web : www.atlanticbooks.com
e-mail : info@atlanticbooks.com

ISBN 81-269-0131-4

Printed in India at
Nice Printing Press, Delhi

Dedicated To

Tapaswini

OTHER BOOKS BY THE AUTHOR

1. *Wheel of Life* (1990)
2. *Ashwini* (1991)
3. *Blossom in the Blaze* (1993)
4. *Reminiscence* (1994)
5. *Quest* (1996)
6. *Ritual* (1998)
7. *Beginning of End* (1999)
8. *Transformation* (2000)

THE ATTITUDE OF AN AWAKENED INDIVIDUAL IS TO RETURN TO THE SOURCE.

PREFACE

Tapaswini is at the centre stage of this novel. I met her in Kutch when I was young. I was caught up in a dimension of vibrant conscious energy and was unable to retrace my steps to land firmly on the terra-firma. Tapaswini appeared before me and initiated me. She vanished as soon as her work was accomplished. This brief interlude changed the course of my life.

In this novel, an attempt has been made to unravel the core of the subliminal world, the vast potentiality of the spiritual dimension and the possibility of enacting vital role to set right the world.

Taking a global view, this is a macho world. Women are suppressed since the beginning of time. Our literature, epics, philosophies reveal male supremacy; characters are created in order to assert male chauvinism. Our marriage customs, conventions are parochial favouring the male. Women have become a commodity for sale. They are exploited for man's comforts. Women are being treated as secondhand human beings.

There are saptarishis, three God heads, all male. In times of crisis, Female Shaktis came to their rescue and established the universal order.

Truth is the only thing, beyond sex. The great initiator, the hierophant is neither male nor female. The true representation of Shiva is ardhanarenateswara.

In this novel, there is an attempt to create an order with female ambiance where they will come upon the essence, the core of creativity and work out their destiny. Tapaswini has taken up this task to set right the imbalance. It's a noble cause. The devotion earnestness and unmotivated work of these women make them adept in the sphere of spirituality. They have become aware of the world situation socially, politically and accidentally discovered a way to alter the psychological structure of important key persons who are capable of changing the course of world destiny.

The novel is a spiritual manual and contains glimpses of secret teachings of tantra and a few hints on undisclosed tenets of spiritual practices.

64 A, Block II
21st Cross
Rajajinagar
Bangalore-560010

NARAYAN

1

"Dear Sanath,

The bearer is my son Chandra. I have kept reliance on you. Take care of my son. I have kept Rs. 50,000/- in his name authorising you to draw, and spend. Take him as yours. Greater is your task because what we cannot give, you would be giving and that is 'love'. Chandra lost his mother when he was only one year and now it's my turn. I might not repay your debt, what you would be doing all the years, eternity for me, but I trust in my blood, Chandra under your guidance will amply repay your debt.

This letter will probably reach you after my death.

With love, Nithish."

Sanathkumar lifted the face of Chandra. He had a striking nose, slanting eyes, strong jaws. He was fair and looked intelligent. He asked him taking inside, "When did your father die?"

"Last month".

He wondered why he was not informed. The only reason was that his family members were angry because of his marriage with a Tamilian girl who came from Adidravida community.

When he conveyed the news to Yogini, she took it calmly and accepted the boy in the family. She was pregnant completing eight months.

Sanath admitted him in a Convent, the best in the city. Within only a few days, Chandra picked up health. He studied tirelessly but always found time to assist Yogini in the house. She liked him. She fed him with her hand lovingly. He was her son who gave her good company. In her, he found a mother, who he had lost long ago.

Yogini gave birth to a female baby, Kumudini. She was a lovely baby. As a one year old, she wanted Chandra to feed her, kiss her. Chandra treasured the baby. Yogini was carefree, attended to the household work and supervision of the ever changing pattern of servants.

A visitor once came enquiring about Yogini. He was dark, short with squint in his left eye. Sanathkumar had not seen him in the past. "Who are you?" he asked.

"My name is Shanmuga. I want to see Yogini."

Sanathkumar instead of inviting him inside went upstairs to inform Yogini.

"Somebody by name Shanmuga has come. He wants to see you."

Yogini was changing saree. She asked, "Have you invited him inside and offered a seat?"

Sanathkumar instead of keeping quiet told in good humour, "You have not informed me that you have somebody by name Shamnuga with a squint in one eye, short and dark?"

Yogini after delivery had developed an irritable temperament. Suddenly she lost temper. She slapped him so hard that the sound reverberated in the entire house. He was stunned. Unmindful of consequences, she ran down. Sanath realised his mistake. A visitor who had come to meet his wife should have been treated with respect. Instead, making fun was not proper.

After about an hour, she came up. Sanath was sleeping on the cot. He was awake. He had no thought about the incident. He did not feel insulted. Yogini came near him, caressed his cheek and whispered, "Sorry, I lost temper. Are you angry?" Sanath dragged her into his arms and told, "why should I be?" Yogini was puzzled. She wondered what made Sanath so innocent, childlike? He was not hurt, never acted out of a bruised mind.

"Have you excused me?" Yogini asked pathetically.

"I do not understand what you talk. Why do you suffer unnecessarily?"

"Have you no manliness?" She asked seriously.

"What do you mean? We are having a baby."

She laughed. "Not that, a wife beats you and you keep quiet."

"If a husband beats wife, will it make any difference? Man and woman are equal in status. Moreover it's over. Why should I worry? That too when you have already expressed regret. Come on, forget and be free."

Living with Sanathkumar, she felt a thrill, a feeling of being transformed effortlessly. Sanath remembered the past when on the first day he had contacted her. It was evening. He had driven to the estate in his new car. The vast farm had a backdrop of green mountains. It was a lovely spectacle. More than income, he loved the breathtaking view. When he was thus lost in communion, Sarangapani, the supervisor came on the scooter accompanied by a young woman. He was an elderly man, tall, hefty and dark. He had been looking after the farm for nearly twenty years and before him, his father for another twenty years. He was provided with living quarters on the estate. He was responsible for everything.

Sanath looked at the young woman. She was there standing with her back to him. Of medium height wheat complexion, long hairs below her shapely bottom, wearing high heeled shoes. She appeared to be oblivious of him. It was not deliberate. He wanted to see her face. "Changpa all this you manage?" She turned to look at her uncle. Sanath was talking about labour problem, when he stood transfixed by her face and voice. She was beautiful with large sparkling eyes, straight nose and pearl like teeth. Sarangapani was embarrassed. "Yogini, meet our landlord." She smiled. "Sorry to disturb." She moved away, as if unconcerned, ignoring him?

Sanath called her, "Yogini, I am not disturbed. Please come and Join us".

She hesitantly moved towards them. “This is a beautiful place. I love to be here Changpa.” She was talking with her uncle, not looking in the direction of Sanath.

“All this belongs to him.” Sarangapani spread his hands to show the estate.

Sanath was pleased by her graceful bearing. She appeared proud.

“What do you do?” he asked politely. Sarangapani told, “she has completed M. Com., she wants to join some Bank. She is my niece.”

Sanath liked her. “Will you till then assist me in the office?” he asked gently.

She turned and looked into his eyes. Sanath felt subdued because she never winced when she looked. She held her gaze steadfast. As if to measure him. Sanath felt disturbed by that look. On attainment of explosive awakenment, he was aware that ‘self’ was not a source of trouble. It made its appearance only when necessary. ‘Why then am I feeling subdued? Is there still an image left? This is the first time I am feeling like this,’ he thought.

Yogini asked softly, “What kind of work?”

“Financial management. I have two clerks. I am not satisfied nor have I time to supervise.”

She was thinking. Sanath mentioned hesitantly, “I will pay you Rs. 5,500/- per month. You will take lunch in our house. I do not want to trouble you, going all the way to your house and coming back.”

Sarangapani was bewildered. The remuneration was what he was entitled after a service of twenty years. He told her, “Yogini, accept the job.”

Sanath mentioned soberly, “Yogini, you will be helping me. You are free to leave any time.” She looked up and stared at Sanath. Again he felt subdued and wanted to find out and experiment whether he had conjured up an image about himself unknowingly.

“When should I start working?” She asked him directly.

“Tomorrow by 10 a.m.”

It was settled. She came, saw the house-cum-office and waited on the verandah. Sarangapani went inside to inform Sanath. Yogini was wearing a silk saree of golden colour. She was beautiful like a bride. When Sanath invited her, she entered the main hall. It was a large room opening to the outside through floor to ceiling glass panes. The outside view from the main hall was splendid. The floor was made of black and blue gleaming stones. The Cook brought tea and snacks. Yogini gracefully gave a cup to Sanath and then to Sarangapani who was dumbstruck. She doesn’t belong to me, he thought. After tea, she asked Sanath, “May I go round the house?”

Sanath got up timidly and took her inside. He showed her the study room, bedrooms, dining hall, kitchen, bathroom and toilet. Everything was modern. She hesitatingly once or twice remarked that the rooms required thorough cleaning. “Take one vacuum cleaner. Such a house needs one,” She suggested. While returning to the Drawing room she told casually, “thank you.” She did not say ‘Sir’.

Within only a month, Sanath proposed to marry her. It took place in a Registry office without much fanfare. Virtually she came, saw and conquered. It was destiny, thought Sanath.

“Why was she named Yogini?” Sanath had enquired. Sarangapani’s brother had no children. Once a Yogini came for alms, blessed him telling that he would get a daughter who would rule over land and water. She was named Yogini as her prediction had come true.

Once Sanath asked Yogini after marriage, “You agreed without any courtship or troubles. Why?” Yogini looked at him stealthily and told, “That evening when I saw you, I knew you are mine and only mine. Specially born for me. When I saw the estate, an uncanny feeling persisted that the entire estate belonged to me.” She smiled, came near him and took him in her arms. “I do not exaggerate. I feel as if I have lived with you since ages.”

Sanath was surprised. Yogini was like a proud animal. Even when she undressed, she kept that animal grace and came to him without submissiveness. A class by herself, thought Sanath.

For Sanath, it was an opportunity of a life time to be with this woman. She was unpredictable. She wanted everything to be straight, good and noble. Sanath was flexible. He wanted her to continue in her natural state. Never wanted her to change influenced by the opulence of the house or be grateful to him for having given her the status of wife. She also did not express even once that he was generous. She remained whole, a superior entity. She rejected everything awkward, immoral, cruel and obscene. Untimely sex even in the initial period was abhorring to her. She was scrupulously clean. Before going to bed with Sanath, she would have grasped his attitude and her own mood and prepare herself elaborately. After food, she would take bath, scent herself, wear clean clothes and wait for him. He would come with reverence as if entering a sacred precinct and take her with care and love.

Sanath as a child rarely played any game. He busied himself with books or during leisure spent alone staring at the sky, the people around, the mountains, the trees and flowers. He shunned company. At the age of twelve, once when he was not traced till next morning, he was found finally sleeping on the edge of the estate below a Banyan Tree.

When his father asked him what made him remain alone, he told that he was engulfed by an all-encompassing power who was a living Entity.

From then on, care was taken not to leave him alone. He was very mindful of studies and did not feel unduly elated when he got through with a first class first. His efforts were not the outcome of a sense of competitiveness. It was an inborn quality within him to study anything that came his way perfectly. He was not interested in food like his sister. Not craving for dress. Not accepting the Gods found in temples. The profound experience had silenced him for the rest of his life.

His father died of a heart attack when he was still in the college. He had to manage the estate. He did not show any negligence. He had an uncanny power to unearth falsehood, disband unworthy parsons. He managed the farm well. At the same time in his dealings, he exercised profound discretion so that the workers did not feel harassed.

During the day, he managed to keep atleast two hours to himself. Yogini knew well his aloofness and rarely intercepted in his moods. However she watched him from a distance, Sanath sitting cross-legged, eyes half-closed, meditating. Silence pervaded the terrace where she rarely ventured to step in. She felt drawn to him whenever he was there. She wanted to look at his countenance lost in otherworldliness. Sanath did not feel the need to go and consult anyone nor seek shelter in books. He read occasionally; sometimes voraciously but never to rely on its authority. He found it increasingly interesting to delve on the unknown, to trespass into that dimension where words fail, where human knowledge has no role, where thought lingers only momentarily and retreats to a state of 'not knowingness.' In this state, he became aware of undeciphered thoughts making appearance from their hideouts, the snowy creaks of brain matrix where millions of brain cells acted as store houses for memories. He seemed to remember happenings which had no relevance to his time and place. He was bewildered whether he was turning insane. In the amazing scintillating silence, memories emerged like living entities, some of them were dwarfs, ugly goblins, some were winged fairies and Angels! It was at times difficult for him to keep awake, remain critically alert. He felt relieved only when the river of joy came rushing towards him driving away all the phantoms of memories.

Yogini would wait for Sanath to emerge out of his trance and come down from the terrace. Looking at his transfigured face, she would hesitate but taking it as her duty, she would lovingly bring him to the realities of daily life. Her role was of paramount importance because she knew in her heart, he would otherwise become unbalanced. A mean had to be struck between the dimensions, the known, the unknown and the unknowable. Unless one grasped the significance of the 'mean' there was no possibility of coming upon truth. When one was lost in the grandeur and beauty of the unknown or engrossed in the known, one was likely divorced from the 'mean'. The 'mean' appears to be the living force lurking between seeing and not seeing, hearing and not hearing, feeling and not feeling. Sanath knew in the core of his heart that the moment was not very far when he would be blessed with the presence of the 'Other'. Faith in its coming is also an impediment, he thought.

2

Chandra lived between two extremes, Sanath, the unknowable passive principle and Yogini, the active ever vigilant principle. She seized the elusive Sanath and lived the role of a woman.

Chandra was destined to imbibe supreme qualities. When he was doing his post-graduation, Kumudini entered the Medical College. She was a college beauty, fair, tall, slim and shapely with silky brown hair at the level of neck. Chandra always accompanied her, keeping an eye on her and drove her back home. She was attached to him, expected utmost devotion from him and he naturally loved her. He had learnt to ignore her aberrations. She was convinced that he was her benefactor who would be obliged to ensure her safety and well being. Chandra waited till her classes were over, she finished her rounds with her friends, and brought her home reminding her of time, Yogini and Sanath.

Surendra was Chandra's classmate. He was an womaniser. He was engaged to Supriya, a wealthy girl and they were expected to marry within a couple of months. Supriya, and Kumudini were classmates. Kumudini liked Surendra who was tall and handsome. She liked the way he dressed, his boyish ebullient nature. He had unique ways to arouse the interest of a woman. Kumudini admired his jokes and liked his company. Surendra being sure of Supriya strayed far and wide. He liked Kumudini who displayed extensive sex appeal. Bold and proud like her mother, she challenged every man who happened to cross her gaze. Chandra knew the intention of Surendra who was also his friend. He cautioned Kumudini a few times but he was met with a sneer from her. "You mind your business" she would tell and shun him. He became more and more vigilant. Supriya also noticed the way Surendra behaved with Kumudini but she took it jovially without suspecting any ulterior motive. She did not know nor had occasion to notice that Surendra craved to touch Kumudini. Supriya was a charming girl who wanted to lead the life of a conventional housewife. Surendra craved for the money that would come on marrying her. But at the same time, he wanted the bizarre Kumudini, stunning specimen for flirtation.

Two days before the marriage, Kumudini went to Surendra to congratulate him. It was not necessary. He told "My dear Kumudini, I love you, even though, I would marry Supriya, you occupy my mind all the while. I am helpless."

Kumudini was dumbstruck, she laughed nervously and assured. "I shall treasure your words. After all the world is not very vast. We shall meet."

The marriage was a grand function. The hungry eyes of Surendra hunted out for Kumudini even when he was tying the mangal sutra to Supriya. Chandra disliked the way Surendra behaved. To his plea that he was the most undesirable person, Kumudini did not agree and persisted in her ways. "What is wrong? He is after all having Supriya as his lifemate. I am just his friend." If Chandra tried to convince her, Kumudini would suddenly recoil like a cobra and glare at him shouting. "Shut up. Who are you to me?" To his prolonged silence, she would make fun and tell, "That's really gentlemanly. I love you Chandra." She would start laughing. Chandra took her words lightly knowing that she was joking. She knew that he would not dare to disclose to Yogini and Sanath about her. He was an addition to her family after the death of his father. She did not refer to his past, as he was held more than a son by her parents. He was looking after the estate and managing all the financial affairs. He had in his name a deposit which had steadily grown to Rs. 4 lakhs. Sanath had not touched the deposit. Yogini kept more reliance on him. If any money was required, Kumudini had to ask Chandra who would never part without questioning the purpose. She would take it as natural and give all the particulars. Yogini at time observed the episode and loved to listen to the children. Kumudini always got more than she asked because Chandra considered more eventualities and increased the quantum demanded by her. "Generous Chandra!" she would laugh, praise him and pat his cheeks.

Yogini underwent tubectomy after the birth of Kumudini. Sanath was surprised. "Why not get a son"? he asked. "No, Chandra fulfils the role." Sanath was satisfied. He did not venture to question her wisdom. She declared, "I want Kumudini to marry Chandra."

Sanath thought that it was not proper to plan in advance. Much would depend on Kumudini. Chandra, he knew would leave everything to them to decide. He was a Mirror image of Sanath. Since the time he was united with the family, he rarely felt alienated. Rather he was aware of greater love, greater harmony and accomplishments in the new surroundings. Sanath was more dear to him than his own father who had other preoccupations, like the sickness of his wife and then his own. He was aware that his father and mother were not free to give him love. There were times he had to serve food for himself and eat. Generally cold food after coming from school. It was not so in this house. He was taken care of in all the possible ways-good food, clean clothes, good school and love. He forgot his past. Once or twice in a year he had to perform the annual rituals of father and mother. Then he remembered that he belonged to another family. On these occasions, he would feel sad, forsaken, morose, heartbroken. Sanath and Yogini would attend to him with special care so that the occasion did not bruise his mind. The little deeds of kindness by Sanath and Yogini had transformed him into a devoted son who was prepared to do anything to preserve the honour of the family.

Thus Kumudini had come under the special care of Chandra

who wanted her to grow into a healthy individual. No harm should come to her from anybody and she should not suffer, he always prayed. Sanath and Yogini knew that Chandra took care of Kumudini and had already started repaying the debt.

Yogini had ample time now to devote to Sanath. He was undergoing a spiritual crisis. He spent greater time meditating. Yogini had made it a rule not to confront him when he was having his spiritual exercises. At times during night, she would find him awake struggling to adjust to some imaginary stress and pain. Yogini would try to understand him, come to his rescue but he would not talk on such occasions; by the gesture of his hand tell her to wait. She would keep awake by his side, watching like a mother without touching him, his face contorted with suffering. Yogini would be terrified, unable to call the Doctor because Sanath had told her that it was not for them to help him. Her very presence was a solace. He had also begun to teach her the rudiments of spiritual Sadhana, about the grave dangers of trespassing into that dimension. She knew that Sanath was undergoing a process of transformation with the awakenment of Kundalini Shakti. At times his face radiated a brilliant glow. He did not take usual interest in sex. Not that he was indifferent to her. He loved her more. Yogini knew that it was an alien sphere where her discretion would not prevail much. But she wanted him to realise his responsibility on the mundane plane, where she inhabited and was supposed to be his wife. She would not tolerate anyone to usurp that, even Sanath. So she planned intelligently so that Sanath came down from the great heights of spirituality to her terra firma, looked at her alluring figure and came to bed. This was absolutely necessary, otherwise Sanath would be carried away, unbalanced, insane, totally unacceptable in society. Yogini had a role to play, an important role which had something to do with the Divine Plan. She was virtually a tyrant terrorising Sanath to move away from that dimension which held him in captivity.

Sanath had to be coaxed to take adequate quantity of food, devote some time at least to the supervision of office work as before. She would force him to come and meet Chandra and Kumudini, chitchat with them. Even though initially he did not evince that much interest, as days passed, he realized the significance of living intensely on both the planes, of being critically alert and not be carried away. It was not easy to realise that there was no contradiction between these two dimensions. It was a real problem demanding tremendous discretion and meditation. This meditation had no beginning and no end. Sanath had begun to grasp the alphabets of that dimension.

3

Surendra had money, position and influence. With the alliance of Supriya, he had acquired not only greater position and wealth but also within only one year, a son. His father was greatly pleased. So also his father-in-law who gave him a Nursing Home as a gift. He had two cars at his disposal. He was in the habit of arranging lavish parties. He made it a point to invite Kumudini often, who much against the wish of Chandra attended invariably Chandra was also forced so that he could atleast remain near her, watch and ensure that no harm came to her. These parties came in the wake of Supriya's delivery. She was not available. Therefore the party meant that Surendra was determined to entice Kumudini. He danced with her, talked, promised her better parties, convinced her that he was really in love and that even begetting a son through Supriya was only a marriage obligation. She became confused, spent sleepless nights and craved for greater intimacy with Surendra. When Surendra took Kumudini in his arms while dancing, when his fingers moved down her slim waist and spacious bottom, Chandra would watch losing a heartbeat. Kumudini would not discourage Surendra. Chandra thought whether women liked to be courted by the undeserving, the lusty and the wicked. In the middle of the party, he would force her to come away reminding her of time, Yogini, who was very strict. He wondered how Kumudini came to like Surendra, a married man with a son. He had no explanation.

Chandra was a mute spectator because he was not prepared

to take the extreme step of bringing the facts to the notice of either Sanath or Yogini. He knew that Kumudini would not excuse him if he told the truth. He had nevertheless confidence to steer her away at the right moment.

Surendra was under the impression that Chandra was her brother. He had to his records many girls who came from every background; they were of all shades, colours, shapes and caste.

At home, Supriya lived comfortably. She had everything. Her sister-in-law Bhagya who was a graduate and waited for her would-be groom to return from States gave her the much needed company. She would constantly remind Supriya about her brother, to keep an eye on his activities as he was fond of women. Much harm however would not come, she would mention and laugh.

Surendra spent lavishly as no one was there to restrain him. His father Shri Muthuraman, a well known businessman of the city lived in Tamil Nadu where he had set up an Industrial House. He visited home rarely, once in two or three months and stayed for a few days. Surendra imbibed the qualities of his father. Muthuraman loved his son and daughter. He had faith in his wife who spent her time in religious activities. He satisfied her needs by taking her once in a year to all the sacred places in the country. She knew of his clandestine affairs. The house was everything for her. It was a big house with a dozen rooms spread over on the ground and first floor.

Kamaxi and her mother lived in the servant's quarters. Kamaxi attended to the cleaning of the floor and keeping the furniture in fit condition. She was seventeen, completely black, clever, careful in dress, slim in body with specially good teeth. She had hairs on her hand which attracted the attention of Surendra. She had otherwise charming features with a delicate nose and speculative eyes. A perpetual smile played on her wet lips. She kept herself clean and never forgot to wear flowers. Whenever she came for cleaning the room, Surendra would watch her movements with amorous interest. In his imagination, she was also a thing of beauty. He wanted to come near her, talk to her like a benefactor and lover. He had to exercise discretion because Bhagya would every day make it a habit to visit him whenever Kamaxi came for cleaning the room. Surendra would fidget in his seat, cursing his sister. Kamaxi took special care of the room and was aware of the attention bestowed by Surendra.

Supriya lived on the ground floor after the birth of a child. The baby was only two months old. Surendra rarely failed in his duties. He would dutifully spend some time with the baby and the mother. He liked to tease Supriya touching her at sensitive places, test whether she continued to desire, kiss her when she avoided him assuring a lively future and depart. She was not bothered to restrain him at home because she did not think, he could be so mean as to even flirt with Kamaxi.

It was 9 p.m. Chandra was driving home. Kumudini as usual sat in the front seat. She was staring at the moon. Chandra was serious. "Are you angry with me" She started probing. "No" Chandra turned towards her, looked into her eyes. She was mischievously smiling at him. "You are angry", she confirmed.

Chandra looked straight and carefully maneuvering a curve told, "Yes, Kumudini. Surendra is not a desirable person. He is a confirmed womaniser".

Kumudini became alert. She did not like the topic. "How do you know?" She asked vehemently. "He is a married man with a son. Why should he take so much interest in you?"

"I am his wife's friend. What is wrong if he is intimate?"

"People will talk," he stopped abruptly.

"I don't care." she answered.

She turned and looked at Chandra who was hurt. She wondered at her conflicts. She wanted Chandra to remain near her, even when she flirted with Surendra. She would make sure that he was within her range of gaze. Sensing that he was not in his mood, she came near him, placed her head on his shoulder and whispered, "Ah, are you angry?"

Chandra loved her, not like the usual lover who would be jealous and quarrelsome. He patted her shoulder and drove on.

“We are late today,” he told her.

“If you are with me, I am not worried.”

“That does not mean we should be indiscreet.”

She was nervous. “Sorry.” She reached his neck and planted a kiss. “Will you excuse me now?”

Chandra wondered at the ways of women. He smothered a smile which she noticed and was satisfied. She had won the day. Kumudini was not required to toil for his company, the quiet solace and security which she got with Chandra. At times she would think, ‘Is it not true love?’ Whenever there was confusion, sorrow, she would seek his shoulder to rest her head and forget. Whatever she might do, there was an assurance and a certainty that he would always be there waiting. Even on days she behaved rudely and ill-treated him, unhesitatingly she sought refuse in him, begging before him to excuse, telling that she was immature, most undeserving and searching for that kind smile radiating his face. Then he was sure she would kiss him either on his face, cheek, neck and sometimes tenderly even on his lips. She would laugh away heartily at his plight. Her heart fluttered at his name. She waited for him before taking food, tea and going out. He was her guide, Guru and benefactor. She would take care of his dress, arrange them in order. Chandra would call her if he wanted anything which could not be traced because he was sure she should be keeping his things in safe custody.

Kumudini often wondered why she was attached to Surendra? He was not supposed to be a man of good character. She felt sexually aroused by his looks, occasional touch during dancing. She would be caught up in wild desires. In his presence she was afraid whether she would become a slave to his passion. She wanted Chandra to be near so that he would snatch her away at the right moment.

Supriya resumed her college when her child was six months. She had already lost one year. Before she could complete, again she was pregnant. Surendra wanted her to bear two children and then stop. Kumudini felt a wave of jealousy. She continued to keep contact with Supriya so that there was no misunderstanding. Supriya knew that her husband had taken keen interest in her friend but she thought that it was not unusual with him. Surendra was an adept in enticing young girls. He would sneak in taking all opportunities and whisper endearing words in Kumudini's ears, words like, "I love"; "You are the most beautiful flower", "I treasure you"; "I dream about you". Kumudini would smile and crave for his proximity for listening to those words reaching her in whispers, his hot breath on her neck. He was sure of his progress and waiting to strike.

At home one day when his sister was not near, he quietly dragged Kamaxi and gave in her hand fifty rupees for taking a nice dress. She was surprised and asked him, "Should I tell my mother?"

"You may if you please."

Next day, he came and stood behind her took a deep breath. The scent of jasmine flowers, the coloured cheeks of Kamaxi and her total willingness to submit made Surendra mad with anxiety and lust. She eagerly waited and turned to look into his eyes. He embraced placing his hands firmly on her bottom so that she would feel him. He touched her firm breast and caressed her body at all the sensitive places, using his skill either to press firmly or lightly depending on the area. Kamaxi enjoyed his touch, the first man in her life. For Surendra, the first black girl and maidservant. Her mother was a willing partner. Any woman near him was not safe. Surendra had to exercise great caution because Supriya had moved upstairs. But Surendra knew that Kamaxi would also be careful, co-operate in defeating the vigilance of others. Wherever he ventured for his amorous episodes, he built up an enduring relationship so that the victim would knowingly cooperate in indulgence. In order to enjoy unbridled sex, with the consent of Supriya, who was in advanced pregnancy, underwent vasectomy operation even before her delivery. Supriya was surprised but Surendra clarified that he was very sorry to see her plight in pregnancy.

Supriya was in her eighth month. Her mother-in-law wanted

to take her to a temple before sending her home for delivery. It was 9 a.m. Bhagya also volunteered to accompany them. Surendra was at home; deliberately refusing to accompany them. Bhagya drove them at 10.15 a.m. Halfway they realised that they had forgotten to take God's money. They drove back at 10.25.

Surendra knew that Kamaxi would avail of this opportunity. As expected, she came upstairs and purposely came to another room expecting him to notice her. He did not call her but came behind, lifted her and took her to his room. "Please leave me. My mother wants money." With his breath stuck up in his throat he asked, "how much?" "One hundred".

He jumped to the almirah, snatched a hundred rupee note, gave her and even before she took it, he started undressing her, kissing her all over the body. The door was open. He never expected anyone to come so soon.

Supriya returned home to get God's money. She enquired with the cook why the front door was kept open. She informed that Kamaxi was cleaning the furniture. Instead of rushing to the car, on second thought she went slowly upstairs. There were whispers, heavy breathing and laughter. Her heart fluttered. There was something amiss. She looked at the open door of Surendra. She slowly approached the door. It was unbelievable. Surendra was having sexual intercourse with Kamaxi who was by then giggling with joy. She slowly went inside. Both of them jumped apart. Hurriedly started dressing. Supriya packed her clothes in two suit cases and told Kamaxi to bring them down.

Bhagya and her mother were surprised to see the suit cases and Supriya going towards her car. She went and took her son and told her mother-in-law "I am going home." "Why?" her mother-in-law asked fumbling for words. "Go and ask your son and Kamaxi." She drove away.

4

News reached Yogini that Sarangapani was admitted in the hospital as he had lost appetite and was not taking food for about a month. He had also developed chronic constipation. His stomach had become bloated and he had become lethargic. It was only when he cried that he should be given poison instead of food, he was admitted in the hospital. He had developed a tumour in the stomach and it required urgent operation. Sanath was much concerned with the well-being of Sarangapani because he had rendered faithful service for twenty-two years. Therefore he took the entire responsibility of providing the best medical assistance. After operation, the diagnosis revealed that the tumour was malignant. It had enveloped the whole of the stomach and in removing the tumour the stomach would be automatically removed completely. The time for survival was only two months with or without operation.

Yogini was deeply upset. She was very much attached to him as he had brought her up and was instrumental in bringing her first to Sanath. He had only one son Kumar who was employed in the Telephone Department at Rameswaram.

The end came unexpectedly. Only after a fortnight of operation. Yogini was deeply shocked. Sanath provided all the financial assistance for the last rites and attended the funeral. With the death of Sarangapani, Yogini became moody. For the first time in her life, she felt that fate was unpredictable. To a large extent, it was not within the control of man. A deep mystery shrouded the end of life. In the face of such uncertainties, all acquisitions had no meaning. Only one thing was relevant and that was love. Everything else seemed a trifle, irrelevant. She examined her life closely. 'Whether she loved Sanath? Whether she loved Kumudini and Chandra? Was she more concerned about herself? What does love mean? Has Sanath touched the orb of love? He appeared compassionate but he did not come near anybody. He remained aloof, inaccessible and like God, unknowable. Her inquisitiveness moved her in the proximity of Sanath. He wondered what she wanted. Yogini had started visiting when Sanath meditated alone on the terrace. She would come and sit on the terrace at a distance, first observing his eyes, looking at his face lost in contemplation. Then she would close her eyes and meditate. At times Sanath opened his eyes and looked at her face, serene, serious and beautiful. In the bottom of his heart, he blessed her that she might also come near that dimension where beyond time, space and causation Truth abided. He thought that her name was coined rightly, she was Yogini. Otherwise why should she come and live with him? Why should she take care of him?

One day when she was looking at him in wonderment Sanath opened his eyes. He smiled at Yogini and called her to come closer and sit. She was pleased. "I hope, I am not disturbing you," she murmured. "Not the least. Now you are not my wife." Yogini asked, "what is the meaning of this life?" Sanath maintained discreet silence. Yogini continued. "This life, myself, yourself, this farm, wealth, Chandra and Kumudini, the stars, planets, the vast cosmos! What is the meaning of this existence?"

Sanath wondered at her insight.

"What is the meaning of death? What is Love? Are we in love? Do we love our children?"

Sanath looked at her with great compassion and told, "I do not know. Really I do not know".

She wondered whether Sanath was telling the truth. She searched his face for an answer.

"Yogini, that sense of wonderment which you have is the way, the path to come upon the answer. The answer should come to you. It has no verbal content. It's not an explanation. The answer is a living thing, a deep mystery. Truth is the only answer." He placed his hand on her head, she had closed her eyes and was meditating. It was a blessed day!

Kumudini was in the third year M.B.B.S. Chandra was working as a Doctor in a Government Hospital. Kumudini wondered why Surendra had lost interest in her. He was busy with the Nursing Home. The Nursing Home given by his father-in-law was managed by Supriya. She had completely dissociated from Surendra. He had also not shown much concern because he was still obsessed by Kamaxi. He had become a dangerous point of contact. Kamaxi continued to hold great attraction and he was not capable of coming to the end of this relationship. For him the charm of her ebony body was unfathomable. He wanted more and more of her. Both mother and daughter exploited Surendra to their heart's content.

Kumudini had also heard the alarming news that Supriya had left him. She was living with her parents. She had also discarded her studies. Kumudini wanted to find out the facts by contacting Surendra. His Nursing Home was outside the city. Chandra would not come to know if she bunked a few periods and visited him.

Surendra was surprised to find her. He had not seen her for nearly four months. Her presence evoked in him memories and an urge to take the best opportunity coming at the door step uninvited. Kumudini was under the impression that Surendra would be a heartbroken man being deprived of the company of children. Instead he was more energetic and adventurous. He took her into his posh chamber equipped with a computer, an intercom and telephones. He sat near her on the sofa and felt that he was not intelligent in having ignored a virgin beauty.

Kumudini with downcast eyes with great anguish told, "You have forgotten me". Surendra felt excited seeing the victim in readiness to succumb and murmured in a meek tone, "My fate Kumudini. Supriya is not living with me. Four months are over. She wants a divorce".

She wanted to know the facts. She became serious, thought that she had the right to know everything about him. "Why? Will you tell me? You don't seem to trust me."

He was an adept in concocting stories. "I am ashamed to disclose, Kumudini. No, you are an innocent girl. I won't disclose. It's not proper."

She was restless, anxious. She got up from her seat went near him and told looking into his eyes, "Trust me. I need you."

"She had an affair with her cousin."

Her curiosity was aroused. "Tell me all the details. Do not hide."

He held her palm, slowly dragged her near him and told, "I found in my bed both of them kissing each other."

Surendra hungrily stared at her body, her silky hairs, shapely breast and murmured, "I have missed you." He put his arm around her slim waist and planted a kiss on her neck. She felt his hot breath. She wanted to go and sit on her sofa but Surendra forced her to sit near him. He lifted her face and kissed her lips, softly at first, then with passion again and again. She succumbed. She wondered whether she wanted him more than he asking for her. She was mad. After some time she was afraid. "Let me go now."

She was lucky that he considered her request. He wanted to have an enduring relationship so that the victim came willingly.

Even before Chandra had come to pick her up, she had reached. During journey back home, Chandra became suspicious. She was unusually alert, excited. invigorated. There was a charm that enhanced her brilliance. She was dreaming. A smile lingered on her lips which was very sensual. Kumudini noticed that Chandra was minutely observing her. She asked hesitantly, "Why are you staring?"

"There is something."

"What's it?"

"As if you are reborn, you got your treasure."

She chuckled, came near him, placing her head on his shoulder kissed his neck. She was happy. She wanted him to share. Chandra was shocked. It was not those cold lips. "You are hot today!"

She jumped apart. He asked wondering, "Why sudden dislike?" "Constitution."

Rest of the journey, there was silence. Kumudini went to bed after reaching home. She did not turn up for food. When Yogini came to her room to enquirer, she pretended to be asleep. "What is wrong with you Kumudini?" She opened her eyes and pleaded, "I want rest Ma. I do not want food today."

When Yogini went to fetch milk, Chandra sat by her side and caressed her hairs. He asked lovingly, "Are you really all right?"

"How innocent", she thought. By gesture she assured him, closed her eyes and opened with an alluring smile. He was caressing her hairs, when Yogini returned. She thought that Kumudini was love sick. The time is auspicious for their marriage, she thought of telling Sanath.

Kumudini craved to be alone. She had lot of thinking to be done. More than thinking, she wanted to enjoy, remembering the sensual episodes, committing to memory every word, breath, whisper, treasuring the beatitudes, imagining the future rendezvous. Sex is a great accomplishment, communion she inferred. What is sinful in it? She questioned.

What is love? Chandra. He cares for me. His touch has a sense of solace, security, comfort and an assurance like the love of mother, father, brother or sister. Is it Love? Is Surendra an womaniser? Is Supriya capable of an affair?

She was pregnant; a homely type of girl who never mixed with any boy in college. Will she indulge in sex with her cousin? She doubted the statement of Surendra. She wanted to contact Supriya and get at the root of this problem. She knew that she was caught up in a spider's web. There was no scope of escape, 'Will he divorce Supriya? A man with two sons, is it advisable to make an alliance?

Her moral well-being was eclipsed. She was doomed. 'Yogini and Sanath! How noble, good and loving! What should I do? She spent the whole night without sleep, brooding, playing with her body which had transformed into an instrument of pleasure. She marvelled at her sense organs. Morning she got up late when others were taking breakfast.

Yogini discussed with Sanath and they decided that the marriage of Kumudini and Chandra should be arranged without further delay. When the decision was announced to Kumudini, she was shocked. She protested "Chandra is like my brother. How can I think of marrying him?"

Yogini corrected her. "You love him. He has right to marry you. It's not only my wish, your father and his father have willed it. You can certainly be happy with him. No further arguments Kumudini. Marriage is not mere sex; you seek love, protection, security and faith. No other man would give so abundantly."

"Have you asked Chandra?"

"Yes, he has left it to you."

5

Kumudini was in a dilemma. She wanted to arrive at a quick decision. Chandra was her benefactor. She never wanted to shun him, hurt him. Still the big question remained troubling her. If Surendra is serious about me and Supriya is determined to seek separation, I might have to take a momentous decision. To break away form Chandra; it would imply breaking away from home, Sanath and Yogini. The vast estate. Is Surendra reliable? Or a profligate womaniser? If so, I would be also like Supriya.

She kept on brooding. She spent many sleepless nights before succumbing to the temptation of seeing him again. The hidden purpose was to get herself mauled sexually even though it was camouflaged as another, to elicit his views on her engagement. So far she had not disclosed her mind to Chandra. She evaded the topic intelligently, remaining cordial, loving as before. She was confident that in whatever state she might eventually be found, he would accept her as an inevitable choice, taking it as his sacred duty. She knew he would suffer even ignominy, defeat and malice for her sake.

She went to Surendra. He was not particularly worried hearing her, even though he took care to make it appear so.

"Oh Kumudini, I love you. I thought you would think of me before deciding." "So I am here. Do you doubt me?" Kumudini asked him seriously.

The faculty of discretion was already impaired. She was incensed by his lips, wanted him to take her. Surendra, got up, came near her, lifted her from the chair and guiding her to the inner chamber murmured, "It's like this. I would take divorce. It takes time, say one or two years. By that time, you might complete M.B.B.S. We cannot marry till then. Of course we would be living together."

She was overwhelmed by the experience. He was supreme, the first man who took her before marriage.

On her way to college, she became thoughtful. 'Knowing that Surendra would force me, I went to him. I wanted him, not the other way. Why I am like this?'

Chandra was waiting. He was shocked seeing the car of Surendra. Kumudini waved and by gesture told him that she was above suspicion. Chandra got a clue form her recent attitude. She was meeting Surendra. He wanted the facts not because he was engaged to her; even if she were to reject him, he wanted her to be away from Surendra. Her well-being was uppermost in his mind.

She came after nearly half-hour. She was nervous, guilty of something. "Where did you go?" She did not respond. It was the first time her reaction in many years and it meant many things for him. Great troubles were ahead. He thought of Yogini and Sanath, their confidence and trust in him. He should tackle this case single-handed; he was not prepared to seek their help, hurt their feelings. "Where did you go Kumudini?" His voice was sober, affectionate, responsible.

"Surendra"

"Why?" He stopped the car near a tree. There was much traffic on the road.

"Why have you stopped the car? Move on."

She was angry, offended. He obeyed; asked again. "Why did you visit him? Since how long are you keeping contact?"

"Is it important to you?"

"Very much. Oh God, what should I do! Kumudini, what has happened to you?"

"Are you worried about you?" Kumudini asked abruptly.

“No Kumudini, if you do not want to marry me, all right. Still I am concerned about you. Your happiness is my happiness.”

Words choked in his throat. Tears streamed down his cheeks. Kumudini was shocked. She came near him, wiped his face with her palm, kissed him on the neck and assured him.

“Listen Chandra, I shall tell you everything. I want you. I cannot proceed alone. But not today. Give me some time.”

His hand came round her, his cheek on her cheek, he told her, I love you Kumudini, even when you want another, you remain mine. That is my destiny.” The next day Kumudini unhesitatingly told Chandra “I want to meet Supriya. Will you take me?”

Chandra was not surprised. He knew something was going on. There was still uncertainty. He only prayed that Kumudini would come out unhurt.

Kumudini told Chandra to stop the car a little distance away from Supriya’s house. She went alone. It was a big house. She waited for her in the drawing room. “Kumudini, surprise!”

Supriya had grown slim; appeared worried. She took her inside. Her two sons were playing with dolls. They were lovely, with striking resemblance to Surendra. Kumudini was nervous. She wondered why she should be affected by the two happy children. She lifted the youngest and kissed him, “Lucky you are.” She declared.

After exchange of formalities, Supriya confidentially asked, “What brings you here, Kumudini?”.

“I have a problem.” She stopped, hesitated and then spoke,

“Why is Surendra keeping away from you?”

“Didn’t you ask him?”

Kumudini was aghast. ‘She knows already.’ Gathering courage, she pleaded “Supriya, I want to know the truth. I am afraid…”. She stopped.

Supriya knowingly smiled. “Is he pestering you?” Kumudini hung her head in silence. “Careful Kumudini, he is a flirt.”

She narrated the whole sordid tale and added, "I shall never return to him. He is still sleeping with Kamaxi."

Kumudini was heartbroken. Supriya told "He wants the children, wants to fight in the court. I will face him with facts. Let me see how he survives?"

What a fool I am! Another victim of his overtures. Chandra was right, Surendra a confirmed womaniser. I Shall never see his face again? She decided.

Kumudini asked in a feeble tone. "Have you got any cousin with whom you are intimate?"

"So, he is building up a story for your benefit. None here. They are all married, decent men settled outside the state, some abroad."

Kumudini returned to the car. She was walking as if she was drugged. Chandra was worried.

"Any problem Kumudini?"

She kept silent. After some time she asked, "Are you free?"

"Chandra took her to his chamber. She told slowly in a pathetic voice, "Chandra, I have been duped by Surendra. He is an womaniser. You are right." He was all along knowing. He asked, "Why did Supriya leave him?"

She narrated the facts. "Will you excuse me?"

"Do not worry. Whatever has happened in the past, fortunately it has ended on a lucky note. I have won."

He took her in his arms tenderly and led her to the car. Kumudini and Chandra were married quietly. Sanath and Yogini were happy, decided to devote greater time for spiritual quest.

Kumudini was not sure whether she would disclose about her sexual involvement with Surendra before marriage; Whether she was already pregnant? She had agreed for marriage in a dejected mood on hearing Surendra's affairs with Kamaxi. Moreover Chandra, she knew would accept her under any circumstances. She belonged to him and him alone. Yet if she was pregnant, she wanted to tell him the truth for the invaluable trust he kept in her. She wanted to wait atleast a couple of months before going to bed with Chandra. Would he cooperate? It was not proper to tell him in advance. What purpose would it serve? Suppose she was not pregnant? She had to play it cool, try not to get laid by Chandra. It was for his good.

She was afraid of the approach of the first night. Not because she was a novice but she had a mission on hand. She wanted to accomplish it at any cost. Chandra came late at 11 p.m. He was busy with his friends. It was the first time he had to shift to her bedroom because it was provided with a double bed. It had all the modern amenities. Kumudini was dressed fully in silk with the Mangal Sutra displayed prominently on her breast. She gave him the glass of milk and blushed in spite of herself. He was in dhoti and a silk kurta. He looked handsome a little taller than her, strong and well built. He took it from her hand and with the other dragged her near him. "Atleast permit me the liberty today."

She wanted to tell him something, it was too early she thought. After drinking half, he made her sit by his side and held the glass of milk to her lips. Some magical feeling exploded in her. She resisted and then succumbed. She forgot to mention about her decision that she wanted to wait for two months before having sex.

Yogini and Sanath unexpectedly planned a tour round the country to visit all the sacred places. Sanath had a natural allergy for temples. He held the view that they were built on the edifice of belief and conventions and inhabited by greedy men. He wanted to find out whether there was anything sacred behind the facade of phenomenal existence. Gradually he had turned over a new leaf, when he came upon an experience of absolute stillness; death itself it was, he thought, coming out of it. In that sacred moment he was aware that he decided involuntarily to 'let go' everything, even the hope to continue, the instinctual pull to survive. Then out of that undecipherable spell of nothing, a state beyond words came. This experience had come to him when he was still a boy; he didn't question, doubt, analyse, struggle. It had altered his outlook on life. The values held by society had less appeal for him.

Kumudini felt perplexed at her predicament. Whether she had become impregnated by Surendra? She was not sure. If she was pregnant what should be done? There was no easy answer. At the same time, she had decided not to deceive Chandra. She would not mind getting away from home or taking an abortion in the alternative. In any case, she knew that cooperation of Chandra would be needed. Without him, she would be lost.

6

After touring all the southern places, Sanath and Yogini reached Varanasi. Sanath was thrilled in the presence of the sacred river Ganges. People came here to die, perform the last rites of their relatives, wash away their sins. They travelled for miles to have a glimpse of the river.

When they were returning from the Viswanath temple, they were attracted by a sanyasini wearing an ochre robe. She was slim, appeared to be middle-aged with a weather-beaten face. Her eyes were half-closed, face radiated a peculiar glow of silence and austerity. She looked at Sanath coming down the steps and stood still exchanging glances. A beatific smile lighted up her face. Sanath came near her. Yogini wondered whether she was an old acquaintance. "I am glad to meet you," she told smiling knowingly. She led them under a peepul tree and told by gesture to sit.

"Where do you come from?" Sanath asked.

"I have no abode."

Sanath asked hesitantly, "May I ask your name."

"Okay call me Tapaswini."

Sanath sat quietly for some time looking at her queer features. At times he saw that she appeared to be aloof but at times very near. Observing an intimate smile, he asked, "I have a problem haunting me since ages. Anger, lust and greed are taken as undesirable and a person who is not freed from them is held as impure, immature on the spiritual plane. What is purity?"

"Anger, lust and greed are natural qualities of body like hunger and thirst. The presence or absence of any of these qualities do not contribute to integral purity of the individual."

"What is purity then?" Sanath argued.

"Why do you need it?" Tapaswini asked slowly.

"Without it how can any one reach Truth? An individual with an impure mind is disturbed; he has no authority, eligibility to approach Truth."

Tapaswini did not speak. She waited for Sanath to talk. Sanath told, "A disturbed mind cannot reflect Truth."

"You talk like a parrot, Sanath. If you are really serious earnest to know Truth, no means are necessary, no purity, no effort. It might come unexpectedly, uninvited."

Sanath wondered how she knew his name. What she told was lost in this incident. He asked with wide eyes, "How do you know my name?"

Tapaswini smiled. "I am sorry, it just came to my mind that you are Sanathkumar. Is it important?" She laughed. "Sanath, your name is not important. What is your question?"

"What is purity?"

"We do not give answers. Experience is the only food for those who are hungry for Truth."

Sanath insisted, "What is purity?"

"Dichotomy, duality are not accepted by us. Living in non-division is purity. Innocence is purity. Our normal natural way of life reflect purity. When there is no self-importance, there is purity."

"How is anger relevant here?"

"When you are angry, if you suppress, there is division. You are then separate from anger, a superior entity, then your state is impurity. Effort to change is the basic ingredient of division.

Truth alone can release mind form the evil influences of anger, lust, greed and jealously. Duality, the self is evil."

Sanath was thinking and talking "Can I put it like this? Non-acceptance of nature creates duality. Ego emerges alive."

Tapaswini smiled looking at the thoughtful face of Sanath. "You define very well. Yet it is defective. Ideas, ideals, definitions are the stuff of the ego. Instead, recognise animality. Be rooted in the centre. Otherwise you remain on the periphery." Yogini who sat listening attentively asked in a trembling voice, "Madam, does it imply that no discipline is necessary, no mending, no control?"

Tapaswini looked into the eyes of Yogini. "I forgot you exist. Very well. What you say is correct. No control, no discipline, no guidance. In the Universe, order is inherent. Also in yourself, there is order. You cannot create it. Discipline comes automatically.

Sanath ventured to explain himself. I am lust, I am anger, I am greed, animality is my nature."

Yogini fumbled for words in the middle, "I feel terrified. I am losing my gravity, my individuality, self-respect, self-importance."

Tapaswini smiled and told. "Sanath, please continue further."

"I accept what I am, not verbally, actually. I feel that is the end. Authentic and real."

"It means your ego trembles." She told looking at Yogini. "It means throwing away your ego which has accompanied you; rather yourself and be nothing. The ego-image gets dissolved. Effort ceases and with it time. You come to the Sacred."

Yogini asked doubting, "In this country there were Mahatmas, Mathadhipathis, Jagadgurus, who taught pursuing ideals of non-violence, non-greed and non-sex. This country has witnessed centuries of struggle to come to this Ideal State. Do you mean to say they do not attain Truth?"

Tapaswini was staring into something very far. It was as if

she travelled back to meet Yogini. "When you think of the opposite, the ideal, you are deliberately escaping from the present. You like to have violence, greed and lust. Therefore you want to avoid facing it. When you are violent with yourself, you do not become anything. Not a sage. It's sin. Truth alone can free the mind. Therefore first step is to see what you are and this is the last step."

Yogini ventured a question, "Madam...." She then stopped. Tapaswini looked into her eyes caressing her in looking. Yogini became emboldened. "Madam, I feel it would mean sex is not an impediment."

Tapaswini looked at Sanath who was shy, looking at his palm.

"Sex in mind is an impediment. Mind must dissolve in sex. Be just body which must become the centre of sensuality. Sexuality. No hesitation. No ideals. Move deep in sex. It's the abode of love, where duality ceases."

Yogini looked confounded. She blurted out, "I have not understood."

"When you are loving, being loving itself not you loving another. Lose yourself totally in sex. That's pure existence. The participants are unimportant. Of course it's convenient to have this Sadhana between husband and wife. Some prefer other partners to break away from inhibitions. When the participants get lost, there is a blissful state."

Tapaswini looked at the Viswanath temple and conveyed by gesture the eternal blissful state, the base beyond the powers of constellations.

Sanath and Yogini sat silently meditating and after some time, Tapaswini got up. Sanath asked, "Can I be of any help to you?"

Tapaswini smiled lovingly and told, "Yes. My work is over after meeting you. I am going to the north."

Sanath offered her one thousand rupees which he had drawn that morning. She accepted in customary style by taking the money and touching her forehead. She took out two hundred rupees out of it and gave the rest to Sanath.

"This is my contribution to you. Whenever there is crisis, utilise this money." Sanath took the money and stooped down to touch her feet. She withdrew telling him. "No, I am not your Guru. We do not believe in guidance. Walk on your feet."

Tapaswini slowly started moving away without even once looking back. Sanath and Yogini sat there for a long time without talking. He told atlast, "Yogini, nearly a month is over. It's time to return. I have gained much having accompanied you." The mighty Ganges flowed remorselessly towards the ocean.

Sanath and Yogini arrived home. Kumudini and Chandra were happy to see their parents in the best of spirits, jovial, healthy and energetic. Then it happened suddenly on the next day. Kumudini who was going out with Chandra fainted in the drawing room. Yogini was shocked. A lady doctor who arrived announced after examination that Kumudini was pregnant. Yogini ran to Sanath who was luxuriating on the terrace and told, "Look my prayers have been fulfilled. Kumudini is pregnant."

Sanath's smile widened looking at Yogini's Joy. Yogini declared, "We will again visit Thirupathi with my grandson. What do you say?"

"I shall also come. You think, you can avoid my company? Never hereafter."

Kumudini was shocked. She never expected that it would come true. 'Surendra has succeeded in impregnating me', she thought. She did not go to college. Chandra went away hearing the news, glad that he had succeeded in his first. He was not sure whether Kumudini would excuse him. She wanted to avoid pregnancy for a few months. Perhaps till she completed her studies. Kumudini however was heartbroken. 'How can I bring up another's child remaining married to Chandra? It's improper, a crime to deceive a man like him. What can I do?' She closed the door, covered her face and cried.

Yogini was shouting at the door. Kumudini had not heard in her anguish. At last she opened. Looking at her tearful face, Yogini asked surprised, "Why are you crying?"

Kumudini hesitated. She was afraid. "Bearing a baby is a great joy!" Yogini told. Kumudini murmured. I wanted to remain for sometime till I finished my studies."

"Studies can wait Kumudini if it comes in the way of a child."

An army of thoughts raged a severe battle in her mind. What she should do? She thought of telephoning Surendra and informing him, seeking his advice. She was alone in her room. She dialled his number and then dropped. Again she dialled and waited. The young lady, the P.A. was on the line.

"Surendra?" Kumudini waited on the line.

"Who is speaking?" her clear voice.

"I want to talk to him."

"Who are you?"

"Kumudini."

"Please wait."

Surendra came on the line. His familiar voice. "Hello Kumudini, what's the problem?"

"I am pregnant."

"Congratulations to both of you". A jeering tone came on the line.

Kumudini felt exasperated. What kind of a man I did stupid thing in contacting him, she thought. "Any new idea?" he asked in a hurry in a mater-of-fact business tone.

"Surendra, you are cruel, senseless. I committed a blunder in coming to you. It's your child."

A laughter big enough to explode reverberated the phone. "My baby, is it? I have only two sons. God bless you. Good-bye."

He abruptly disconnected the phone. Kumudini was shocked. It was a slap on her face. Her immature childish deeds amounted to only flirtation. 'I have erred and now flaunt the baby whose parentage is between Surendra and Chandra. Bringing him up all my life, facing him till my death, reminding me of my foul deed, of unfaithfulness, mistrust and perfidy. If I resort to abortion, Yogini would never excuse. Chandra would grow suspicious. Should I disclose everything to Chandra?

This is a crucial question and how can I face myself? The ugly flirting bitch; What should I tell Chandra? How should I confess? I kept on visiting Surendra week after week to get laid by him, without taking any precaution relying on him, that even if I became pregnant, he would be there willing to marry. A married man with a charming wife and lovely sons; Should I tell him? I enjoyed Surendra every week in his arms, playing with him, talking in whispers, kissing getting kissed in spite of the facts that Chandra gave repeated warnings that he was an womaniser, not a worthy person. What would be his feeling towards me? He truly loves not only now but from the very birth. He fondled me, played with me, took care of me, married me. Perhaps to save my honour, of my family. Should I offer him an abominable gift? If I commit suicide? A bottle of sleeping tablets and dream about the baby and the father; proceed to hell to join them. What would happen to my parents? Would Chandra excuse me? Have I the courage to disclose before him, before God, like a sinner, seeking his compassion? 'I am like this, do whatever you want to do, kill or take care of me. I surrender unconditionally. What would be his reaction?'

She did not get sleep. Chandra had taken her in his arms, consoled her telling that everything would end up on a happy note and not to think of any extreme step.

Chandra woke up at 6 a.m. He became suspicious looking at Kumudini. Out of curiosity, he smelled her lips. The medical chest was open. The bottle of sleeping pills was on the floor. He was shocked. He felt her pulse and ran down to inform Yogini.

Kumudini regained consciousness in a Nursing Home. Gradually she realised what had happened. Wantonly she had taken more than three pills.

"Ma, I never intended to die. I didn't get sleep." Slight

indiscretion perhaps. She scanned the room and asked "Where is Daddy?"

"He is outside. He cannot face you, see you suffer."

Kumudini started crying.

Chandra was busy. He came with a glass of fruit juice. He wiped her tears and held the glass of juice to her lips. She looked at him wondering, swallowing him. With a pathetic tone filled with emotion, she asked, "Will you excuse me?"

He smiled with relief and told, "Okay"

"Ma, I am not a good girl, troubling you all."

Yogini placed her fingers on her lips and whispered, "You talk like a good girl."

She was brought home the same day. Kumudini was not happy when she noticed that the medical chest had been removed. She waited for Chandra and when he came after food asked, "You still think I wanted to commit suicide?" Chandra sat with a thousand questions in his mind "You are a medical student. How many tablets you have swallowed?"

"I could not sleep thinking, thinking about my predicament. Thinking I forgot, might be more than three."

Chandra became alert. She appeared to be not in the room. Very far, still in her thoughts. She was held captive by an army who pursued her relentlessly. He came near her, took her face in his hands, stroked her beautiful hairs, kissed her. He wanted her to unwind, "Kumudini, a tryst with you, with my destiny. Tell me everything, whatever it might be. Tell me as if you are telling before God."

She did not know how to begin. What to tell? What to do? Her heart cried with every beat. "I love you Chandra, I love you" she murmured. She was helpless, unable to proceed further. Looking at her, Chandra out of desperation prayed for the first time in his life, "Let Kumudini survive this crisis." Holding her like a doll in his hands, he asked, "Kumudini, do you treat me as an intruder in your life?" Chandra looked pathetic. Kumudini awakened from her groove and pleaded, "No Chandra, give me some more time."

"Kumud, no more time. Whatever it is, I will bear. I assure you, we will always be together."

Kumudini felt that postponing, might be dangerous. Meeting Surendra, might complicate the whole thing. 'Nothing is greater than life. She remembered the words of her father. Chandra was caressing her checks with his lips. She moved a little distance away and asked him, "Will you bear what I am going to tell?"

"Undoubtedly."

"Chandra, inspite of your warning, I went to Surendra for nearly two months till it was disclosed that Supriya left him because of his affair with Kamaxi. In all probability, I am carrying his child."

Chandra was unruffled. He got up, came near her, lifted her face, planted a kiss, long and passionate. "Fool you are mine, your baby is mine. This I tell it honestly," he assured her. She steered away from his grip. "No, why should you suffer?" she asked seriously. He smiled a measured smile and told "If I suffer, your question is relevant. I do not." She was staring at him perplexed. "You must be suffering. You are also human."

"No, it's different in my case. I suffer if you suffer, not otherwise. I know your plight. You suffered ignominy with Surendra. Never mind, let us face together." He took her in his arms. Her eyes pools of tears. She was looking at his blessed face.

"Are you human?" she asked disbelieving.

"Very much Kumud. One condition but, because I am human. Hereafter, you will not reject me. We shall be husband and wife."

"What about the child?"

"It's my baby, it's yours. We shall bring up as a token of our love, eternal bond."

He kissed her passionately, really in love for the first time.

Undressed her in a hurry. He wanted her to drive away all her worries. He caressed her as if he and she were caressing till they were lost in deep sexuality, the blessed state where sin got washed away. In the morning they awoke to a new day. A great day had begun!

7

The young attractive lady in the Nursing Home was Shailaja. She was a doctor by profession. Surendra was greatly influenced by her disciplined attitude. She had proportionate model like features. She had cropped her hairs like a boy. She never used lipstick. No cosmetics. A naked face which revealed austerity and purpose. She had large breast and slim waist. She was conscious of her largeness and felt awkward in the presence of prying eyes. She held every man immoral who looked at her longer than necessary. She was cautious and unpredictable. Surendra tried all his knacks to court her and having failed, out of desperation promoted her to the rank of Special officer who was expected to know where and why doctors were required to function. She was provided with a computer in which she filed all the relevant particulars. She was Specially trained for the purpose. In return for her duties she was paid twice of what she was entitled. She also managed his telephone calls exercising discretion. So that Surendra was not overburdened. She managed every affair.

In having taken her within the range of his manoeuvres, Surendra wanted to assault and fondle her body for his exclusive pleasure. She did not express any gratitude to Surendra for having elevated her to the rank of Number Two. At times when she was in his chamber, he would call her near to explain a particular point and watch her breast. Once he tried to finger touch her buttock and she withdrew so suddenly and so far away, Surendra was surprised. It was time for her to tell him clearly.

"Surendra, you have not spared any women, attractive or otherwise, in and out of the Nursing Home. You have used your chamber for fornication, atleast you will spare me, if you want me to continue here. We will reach a solemn resolve: You will never come near me. We will have a cordial good relationship. Let there be efficiency. If you agree, I remain or I quit."

Surendra was nervous, despondent. "Have you anyone in your life?" he asked. She smiled a cryptic smile and told "I cannot tell you but with you I want to remain like this. Do you agree?"

She was indispensable. He had made her position so inviolable that there was no scope to leave her now. With this, Surendra got a new lease of life. He was learning a,b,c of relationship. He felt in her presence, a sense of stepping into clean quarters. By and by he felt that her presence was weighty, whole and invaluable.

Shailaja did not avoid him. She strived to understand him, probe into his intentions, moods and good points. She rarely interfered in his distractions. If she noticed that he was closeted with any woman, she would put a red light with the sign, 'Do not disturb'. It was done without any instructions from him.

However with her entry into his life, Surendra started thinking and meditating about his life. As time passed, there were moments when he preferred to be alone. He had not so far opened his heart before any body. Not before Supriya who was engrossed with two deliveries in a span of two years. Not with Kumudini who ventured foolishly to enter his heart but ended up on his bed. Shailaja occupied supreme position and communed with him.

Once he asked her, "Will you mind sitting with me for some time. I am in a bad mood."

She readily agreed and asked softly, "Any particular problem?"

"Many Shaila, I remember my children, I feel, I have not seen them in years. I feel like killing myself. There are only amorous indiscretions!"

"Did you try to contact them?"

"No, I haven't the face nor courage."

Shailaja was curious. He was certainly in a rare mood. “Surendra, what made her drift away?”

“Shailaja, she will never come, never,” he told looking outside through the large windows at the distant horizon. His long wavy hairs moved in cool breeze.

“Why? What have you done to your wife, forever to forsake you?”

He covered his face. She saw for the first time Don Juan breaking up before her very eyes.

“She found me sleeping with the maid servant and that very moment walked out. She was pregnant, in her eighth month.”

She was shocked. She almost saw him vanishing before her eyes. “What do you propose to do?” she asked.

“I do not know. I want my children back.”

She felt sorry for him. “Does she insist on divorce?”

“Yes, she was so much devoted to me. Now it is quite the opposite.”

“Do you still love her?”

He laughed cynically and told, “Shailaja, I do not know what is love. Those who came loving me, I took liberty of their bodies. I was determined to destroy them. The latest Kumudini, I think, she survived.”

She was astonished by the frankness of Surendra. She looked at his face.

Surendra asked, “What is love?”

“Have you loved your mother, sister, father?”

“Most of the time, I was with Aya. My father was at Madras.”

“Did your Aya love you?”

He recollected the past, cryptically laughed and disclosed, “Her love is still playing a havoc in my life. She was middle-aged woman, unmarried, good looking and educated, assuredly my father’s favourite. She stayed with us till I was fifteen when my mother dismissed her.”

"What happened?"

"From the age of six to fifteen, she nursed me. Rather she laid the foundation for my present lasciviousness. She used to play with me, excite me with stories, fondle me, teach me the art of love and even the first intercourse. My mother discovered us once and then dismissed her."

Shailaja felt polluted listening to him. "If you are so sure of Supriya, why don't you marry again?"

He looked at her, spread his hands helplessly. "I do not wish to marry again. Never. Moreover I cannot get children. I have undergone vasectomy which is irreversible soon after Supriya became pregnant the second time with her consent."

Shailaja was surprised and asked "But why so soon?"

"My fate Shailaja. I wanted to flirt with women without any liability."

He slowly looked at her, probing her mind. "I am so ugly, I am lust, at time I feel like destroying myself." He murmured. Tears welled up in his eyes. Shailaja did not console him. She had nothing to offer him. It's good for him to talk and empty himself she thought.

"You are like a pendulum gathering momentum at the extremes. It can be dangerous."

"Shailaja, these days often I keep awake beyond midnight brooding, utterly desperate."

"Who are all in the house other than you?"

"My mother, she is invalid, arthritic and asthmatic. None."

Then after some time, he added, "Kamaxi."

"Who is she?"

"The maid servant who was responsible for my predicament. I have taken her to bed."

He sat quietly for sometime and then told, "Shailaja, thank you. I have thrown all the rubbish at you. I feel now relieved, so light, so free."

Muthuraman was disturbed when he heard about the impending crisis. No one disclosed to him why Supriya deserted his son. She had maintained discreet silence. She was not of a mean type. She restrained from scandalising her husband. Only Bhagya knew the reasons. She swore after her marriage not to come back unless Supriya returned to the house.

Muthuraman wanted his son to get remarried but when he came to know that he had undergone vasectomy operation, he became heartbroken. What would happen to the vast fortune amassed, he was worried. He tried to get back the children but Supriya's father refused to entertain the idea stating that the children were in need of mother and any such move atleast now was unthinkable. He was helpless to take further steps and retreated to his abode at Madras.

At home Surendra had become a slave to the machinations of Kamaxi. She enticed Surendra and made him crave for her company. Both mother and daughter were snatching away around Rs. 10,000/- per month. The mother wanted Kamaxi to get pregnant so that she could systematically blackmail Surendra and extract the maximum. They were surprised why it never happened. Slowly the mother introduced other customers to Kamaxi without giving room for suspicion to Surendra.

Kamaxi became pregnant. Her mother had planned with utmost care. After making sure of her pregnancy, Kamaxi disclosed her condition. She started crying pleading for protection. Surendra became alert. "So you have started accepting others?" Surendra asked suspiciously. She was shocked. She ran to her mother. Her mother was nervous. Still mustering courage, she told, "You are responsible. What should my daughter do? I will tell your mother."

Surendra laughed heartily. "God bless you. Good-bye. I do not need your service hereafter."

Her mother was defeated. How could it be that Surendra knew about the misadventure of her daughter? Still gathering courage, she went to his mother. She was amused by the story and told emphatically, "How can it be? Your daughter might have been pregnant by others, not certainly my son who cannot get any children. He has undergone operation." Both mother and daughter realised their mistake and had to vacate the quarters.

Surendra was disillusioned. He had to swing back to normality. Change his style of functioning. He started living like a recluse at home. He needed very much now Supriya and children.

Shailaja knew Supriya personally. However for the last few months with the desertion of Supriya and the rift, she had not met her. She decided to find out the state of her mind, the latest moves and if possible save the marriage. Perhaps save Surendra!

It was a cloudy day. Drizzling. Surface winds were strong hinting at the possibility of heavy showers later in the day.

Supriya was cordial, rather happy to see her. Shailaja was once her trusted friend. Supriya knew that she would never fall a prey to Surendra. The children were lovely, growing happily. Supriya had bestowed her undivided attention. After exchanging courtesies, Shailaja settled down for a serious talk.

"Supriya, I have come with a purpose, not as an accomplice but being an observer for nearly ten months."

Supriya became serious and asked, "What is it?"

"Surendra has changed. He wants to meet the children. He is not like before. Believe me, he does not flirt. Even at home, he has sent away Kamaxi."

Shailaja exercised the highest discretion and tact in breaking the defenses of Supriya.

"He remains yours Supriya. He has expressed before me everything. He has broken down while talking about the family and children. He has shed tears. He has expressed that he is ugly, a man without character. He doesn't want to come near any woman. He treasures your devotion. He wants to meet children." "I cannot send my children away from here." Supriya mentioned emphatically.

"I know. Will you mind if he visits them here? I propose this for the sake of his mental condition. He might kill himself one day. You know he is not touching alcohol. No escape since he started keeping aloof from women. Naturally he is helpless."

"Are you exaggerating?" Supriya doubted.

"No. I have not told him that I am proposing to meet you. I have come here without his knowledge."

Supriya thought over for sometime and told "Let me think."

Shailaja was determined to clinch a victory. "I am afraid, I will fail him, if I do not take your consent today. Supriya, he is my brother. He has not come near me, that was the understating we had when I joined him. Please save him", she pleaded.

Supriya cautiously took a tentative decision. "Let him come and meet the children."

8

Deepavali. The sound of crackers and the laughter of children rent the air. On this occasion, Kumudini and Chandra evinced great interest in decorating the house with coloured electric bulbs and paper lantern. Light classical music was put on the tape for the pleasure of Sanath and Yogini.

The day began with Kumudini and Chandra taking bath early and distributing sweets to the parents. Kumudini was blown to full size, nine months. She was expecting baby anytime. After breakfast, she was climbing the stairs, she complained of pain. Chandra accompanied by Yogini rushed her to the hospital. As expected, as if in fulfillment of the prayer, a son was born. The baby was healthy, beautiful. Kumudini was however curious to verify whether any of the features resembled Surendra. To her astonishment, none. He was a replica of Chandra. Yogini remarked, 'Junior Chandra;' Looking at the baby, hearing the comments, Kumudini was relieved. Chandra also listened to the comments but kept discreet silence. His attention was on Kumudini who was in need of care and love.

Kumudini was haunted by the shadow of doubt. She was not certain of the identity of the baby. Chandra knew her plight. He was therefore cautious.

The days passed. The baby was named Deepak. Under the vigilant care of Yogini, the baby came on the threshold of her first birthday. Chandra was very much attached to the boy. However Kumudini was not happy. Even as the boy become one year old, she was carefully tracing whether there was any resemblance to Surendra. But she failed.

She invited Supriya to attend the birthday. She came with her two children. Kumudini left her son to play with them and watched. Supriya congratulated Kumudini and remarked, "Your son just like Chandra. None of your features."

Kumudini asked hesitantly, "What have you decided Supriya?"

Supriya appeared adamant, "He has changed of late. It appears he wants to come and meet the children. So far he has not turned up."

Kumudini asked, "Can you not excuse him?"

"It's not a question of excuse. I want to see whether he has really changed. I am not sure."

Kumudini also wondered whether he would at all change. "If you drag on, he might marry some other woman," she mentioned.

Supriya chuckled, "I am not bothered. He doesn't want to marry. He cannot get children." She mentioned amusingly.

"I have not understood. Why?"

"Do you know he underwent vasectomy with my permission, immediately, I became pregnant the second time."

Kumudini was stunned. She blurted out, "Why?"

"He wanted to save me from troubles. Perhaps he thought of enjoying women without any liability."

Kumudini realised why Surendra had laughed when she had telephoned and had categorically declared that he had only two sons. "What a fool I am! I had even tried to commit suicide," she thought.

Chandra came late. By that time Supriya had left. Finding

Kumudini in an unusually good mood, Chandra was surprised. The gloom which hung on her face since the day she became pregnant had suddenly dissolved. There was freshness, a sense of purity. He wondered and asked. "Anything special? You appear relieved of all your tensions."

She blushed and told, "Yes, Chandra, I have something definite to convey."

"What's it?" he asked wondering, preparing himself for another surprise.

"Supriya came with her two sons."

Chandra didn't expect Kumudini would invite them. "So?"

"While she was talking, she disclosed that Surendra had undergone vasectomy immediately after she became pregnant. My worry is over. Deepak is really yours."

Tears came down her cheeks. Chandra took her in his arms and murmured, "Okay even otherwise Deepak is mine, you are mine. That doesn't make difference.

"But for me it's very important. I never wanted another's child."

Chandra wiped her tears and told, "I knew about it a week ago."

Kumudini was offended, "How? Why did you keep it a secret?" she asked accusingly.

I prepared a list of persons who underwent vasectomy and his name was very much present. I wanted to give the news as a birthday present."

Surendra was hesitating to come and meet Supriya. After much persuasion by Shailaja, he accompanied her to Supriya's house. She remained in the car and sent him inside. Surendra met Supriya's father in the drawing room.

Surendra was crestfallen. He didn't expect her father. Just then appeared Supriya. She was dressed for the occasion, and came accompanied by two sons. He stared at his wife in surprise even when her father watched him. She had grown slim. Her face austere beautiful, she was serious. On her lips played a truant smile that she had succeeded. "Daddy he wants to meet my children," she told blushing. "Very well, his sons."

Supriya giggled. Surendra felt humiliated. Supriya's father left the room. She went and sat at a corner, in the spacious drawing room looking at a magazine. A thousand thoughts ran through her mind, a thousand images of married life, clouding her heart. The children started playing with the toys. Everything was prearranged. He sat with them, looked on with a sense of joy, deep compassion and love. Feeling intensely jealous of his wife, angry. 'Why should I be punished?' He was thinking. 'What can I do to make my children happy? To make my wife excuse me?" 'There was no solution. He gave up. Looking at the tiny tots, his own flesh and blood, he totally lost himself, forgot his wife even. Slowly he approached them, sat on the coir mat folding his legs, crouching, kissing their lovely cheeks. They felt a magnetic attraction. They smiled at him, beat him, fell over him. He took out the costly colourful toys out of his packet and displayed artistically like a conjuror. They liked the toys, laughed with him heartily. He lifted the eldest and kissed him. Then the younger.

She observed with delight. 'This is not the one who I had married, flirted with the maid servant. He is reborn during the interregnum.' She wondered at his childlike nature, innocence which she had never noticed before. The seriousness had dissolved. She walked out and almost galloped to the car, when the maid who brought tea whispered in her ears that a lady was waiting in the car outside. Shailaja in her usual jeans sat like a statue. Supriya affectionately told, "You think you are not welcome?"

Shailaja woke out of her reverie. "How is he? Am I right?"

"But why do you wait here?"

"I do not wish to meddle in your private communion."

She was triumphant and before Supriya wanted to stop her, drove away.

She walked back to the drawing room. Surendra had not touched tea. She came and stood a little distance away with her heart throbbing audibly, her checks flushed, eyes a cloud of tears. "Have some tea," she told softly.

It was a trembling voice. He was in a tense mood. He did not respond, as if he had been ill-treated. She took the tea cup, came near him and offered. "Take it now," she told.

He lifted his face to look; unbelievable, her eyes were tearful. He kept the tea cup by the side, dragged her down. "What are you doing?" she asked and was afraid as if a stranger was about to molest.

"I love you Priya, I love you. What a fool I was so long;" he kissed her lightly on her lips. "Sha, my father is inside," She told and moved away. Deliberately she rubbed her lips.

"So what?" He was trying to drag her again.

"Stupid, still the same." She ran away and stood at a distance, smiling.

Life had changed suddenly and splendid days ahead, thought Surendra. She went inside to fix lunch. Surendra observed her lovely stride, the body which he had known so intimately but which held now an irresistible appeal. The eldest boy was curiously observing the episode. Surendra touched his hairs lovingly and murmured, "I am your daddy."

Supriya who came just then overheard, remarked. "Do not teach them and spoil." She had a naughty smile on her lips while making a request, "Let us have lunch, come on."

"Me?", "Yes, you."

"Do you excuse me?"

"No, come on."

Surendra took the elder boy in his arms and Supriya the younger; both came to the dining hall. To his surprise her father sat at the dining table. "Welcome home, come on boy," he told with a smile that was a solace to the troubled soul of Surendra. He was grateful to Shailaja who he remembered just then, “Oh, I forgot my car!” he exclaimed, wanted to run outside. Supriya laughed and told, “The car has left long ago. Do not worry.”

After food, Surendra went and sat with the children. The younger had slept. The eldest was playing with the toys. Surendra took him on his shoulder and tried to put him to sleep. Supriya was delighted to see him accomplish the task with ease. She sat with the sleeping children waiting for him to speak. “Priya, I do not know how to make you happy. Will you excuse me for my indifference?”

“Do not open the same topic.”

He wanted to tell her to come home but he was afraid. She might say no, then what?

She was playing with her hairs. The kiss had rejuvenated her, stirred and incensed a thousand desires and both were anxious to touch each other.

He got up. She was afraid he might mistake her silence. She looked up anxiously. His eyes were pleading. There was a heavy downpour of love. He came near her stroked her hairs tenderly, bent down and pressed his lips on her cheeks. She did not object. He started walking away. She remembered he had no car. She came behind and gave him the key. “My car is in the shed,” she told. He didn’t take the key but took her and kissed her passionately, telling “Thank you Priya. Of all days today, I will sleep. Remembering this day, a blessed day!”

The telephone rang. Supriya took it. Shailaja was on the line. She joked, “My brother is missing. Should I inform police?”

“He has left in my car. Thank you for everything.” Shailaja disconnected the phone. She was not for verbalisation. Action appealed to her.

9

December. The night was cool. The leaves of the peepul tree fluttered in the breeze. It was peaceful. A half moon shone in the sky surrounded by silvery clouds. On the terrace, Sanath was lost in deep thought, remembering the words of Tapaswini. 'You like to have lust, greed, violence; you want to avoid facing it. Truth alone can free the mind. The first step is to accept what you are and that is the last step. Living in non-division is purity. When there is no self-importance, there is purity.'

Doubts assailed his mind. His whole background revolted. 'How can sexuality detested by sanyasis be synonymous with spirituality.' How unnatural the path of Tantra! Tapaswini wanted more of action than verbal explanation. To him she had pointed to the Viswanath Temple, the mysterious God in Linga form emerging out of the genital of the Goddess. The bliss of that union was supreme transcending all limitations imposed by the Wheel of life. For Sanath, spirituality meant gradual withdrawal from sexual attitude, practice of austerity, time consuming control of greed, lust and anger and the quick moving desires. According to Tapaswini, nothing is unholy, no control is necessary, no discipline. Everything is sacred; in other words normal. So be aware, free of guilt, sadhana, of time. He doubted her words; whether the path suggested by her was sane? She overruled even guidance. In a way she rejected the concept of Guru which acted as an insurmountable barrier.

Yogini had restrained him from the path of control and helped him to understand the contradictory attitudes. He was in two minds, a broken soul unable to reconcile his burning conflicts.

Yogini came on the terrace wearing a single piece of nightie. She had unwound her hairs. She looked sober but unusual. She was surprised seeing Sanath sitting like a statue unmindful of the cool breeze. She approached him. His eyes were not closed. He turned towards her. Not a whisper escaped his lips. He was surprised. Whenever he was on the terrace which was exclusively their possession, she was expected to behave like a visitor. When Sanath was obsessed with doubts, when he was in deep anguish to probe into the whirlpool tormenting him, she came and spread her buttocks on his laps and kissed his lips. Not only once but repeatedly. He was invigorated, felt refreshed, in a way he was grateful for her discretion.

“Are you so overcome by sex?”

“Is it abominable?”

“I do not know, I was thinking about it when you came.”

“You cannot understand by thinking.”

She kissed him again. Long and silently. Sanath felt a sense of oneness, a non-division. His doubts seemed to vanish. Tantra meant action.

“Yogini, you have taught long ago, even before I met Tapaswini that sexuality was not abhorring. It’s more a spiritual exercise.”

“Not exercise. It’s natural. It has the potentiality to open the doors to Truth.”

She closed his mouth with her mouth and merged in him. Sanath felt deeply that his thoughts about sex and sexuality were not only a distraction but amounted to self concern, an anathema to the seeker. He became aware of centuries of sexual suppression which actually had resulted in a neurotic state. There should not be condemnation, negation nor a positive involvement. Every act should be spontaneous, natural and not an obsession. It should not be a state of cogitation. Even a feeling of oneness is a diversion. He looked at the beaming face of Yogini with her half-closed eyes in deep embrace. She had transcended both body and mind. To be different from the ordinary, exceptional, he was under the impression that sex should be suppressed, attempted in times of only emergency. It was inconceivable for him to think that sex should have a role in his life to make it appear as a way of reaching the highest and at the same time, not to feel a sense of guilt.

He became aware of sex-allergy in him and realised that it should be eliminated. Humility should become a natural state for being exposed to the other dimension. However when he separated from Yogini first he felt polluted.

“Is it the result of centuries of conditioning?”

He asked Yogini, “Do you also feel like me?”

She wondered and asked, "Why should I?"

She was still blissful and slept peacefully.

He decided from that moment to pursue the guilt feeling and past conditioning and dissolve in explosive sex. He thought of Linga and Yoni in that unprecedented union where 'self' was annihilated. There would be love beyond the stirrings of the wheel, he guessed.

In deep sleep, Yogini entered the portals of death and with the elimination of 'self' she was reborn but Sanath remained thinking : awake!

2

1

Every day when he reached the nursing home, he found Shailaja engrossed in work and she didn't forget to wish him. Surendra was surprised that day, she was not there. In every matter, he consulted her. He kept complete reliance on her discretion. She had become indispensable. He wondered whether he had fallen in love with her.

After about an hour, she came on the intercom, "Surendra, I have work." Never that demand was made anytime in the past. He wondered. "Come at once," he pleaded.

When she came, he got up and offered her seat. "So I am V.I.P. today?"

"Shailaja, you have united me with my family. Because of you, for the first time in my life, I have felt the sublimity and perfume of love."

"Will you do me a favour?"

"What's it?"

"I am quitting this job!"

He was shocked. He sat spellbound.

"Why? Have I misbehaved?" he asked abruptly.

"I am going to California, Surendra."

"Alone?"

"I am engaged to Dinesh."

Another shock. "What is he?"

"A computer engineer."

"When are you leaving?"

"Soon, today." After some time, she told "I hesitated to disclose all these days Surendra. I am sorry"

He ordered tea. He wrote a cheque for Rs. 50,000/- and handed it to her.

"What's this for?"

"You have earned more Shailaja. You may need it now."

She looked at him lovingly. "Thank you Surendra. I shall meet you again whenever I come back."

Tears collected in her eyes. She slowly got up and went away. Surendra was dumbstruck. Change is inherent in life, never there is a moment of stability, he thought.

Shailaja and Dinesh sat side by side on the plane. Dinesh stared at her. She was always in jeans without cosmetic, with short cropped hairs. Unmindful of appearance. It gave her animal grace. People turned to look at her twice.

"I am still puzzled Shailaja, why did you not agree to marry and then accompany me?"

She smiled knowingly and told "I do not trust anybody Dinesh. Let me get used to you sometime."

"This shows you do not trust yourself. Am I right?"

She was serious. After some inexplicable silence, she confessed, "I think, you are right. There was a time when certain events in my life forced me in this predicament."

Dinesh was curious. "May I know what these events are like?" he asked.

She lifted her eyes and looked at him speculatively. "Have you the courage to face the facts?" she asked.

"I am not like others. Past is past. Tell me. Moreover you are not yet married. Free, come on."

"Past is not past in my case. It's everything, my very life."

Thus she narrated her past.

'Shailaja came from a very poor family. Her father was head

constable. She had two sisters and a brother. Her brother after marriage, left them and settled at Bhadravathi. No help came from him. Shailaja was not surprised because from the very beginning, he was selfish. Her elder sister was a teacher and was married to a Keralite. They had settled at Cochin. She did not visit them even once in a year. They were financially sound. Another sister was a bank employee and had married a Christian. He was employed in the Railways. She stayed in a separate house and her husband visited her once in a fortnight. She ignored her father, mother and Shailaja. After S.S.C., Shailaja insisted on going to College though her father wanted her to work as a clerk in his office. He was due for retirement that year. He yielded to Shailaja. In the P.U.C., she passed with distinction and got a merit seat in a medical college. Her father reluctantly agreed. He fell ill; it was diagnosed as lung cancer. He expired within only three months. All the savings were exhausted in his treatment. What should she do?

At this critical moment carne to her rescue, Pathi. He came from Orissa, the only son of a rich businessman. He was fascinated by her simplicity. She never brought lunch. She sat in the library reading books. Pathi followed her very closely. He gathered full particulars about her. He knew she was in need of money, love, protection and good food. He wanted to see that she completed her studies with his assistance. He wanted to make her his friend and if possible, life partner.

The first approach was difficult. She refused to entertain him. It was the month of her father's death. Fees had to be paid. How would she collect? She knew none. She could not tell her mother who was a widow. 'Begging, borrowing, stealing?' She started crying. No one was there in the library. Pathi came unexpectedly. He knew during lunch time, she would be there. Sensing that somebody was around she wiped her face and concentrated on writing. Thoughts raced through her mind. 'Oh god, why are you so cruel? If I do not pay my fees today I am going to be removed from college. My brother has not responded nor my sister.' She wanted to run away from everything, home, college and even mother. She clutched her hairs and tears trickled down her checks.

"Shaila!"

Pathi, dark, boyish, handsome, of medium height stood before her. He was an embodiment of humility. She wiped her face and sported a smile in vain.

"Yes" She looked up at him hoping he would vanish from her sight soon. He did not speak. He was hesitating. "What do you want Pathi?" she asked.

"I have a problem. Will you help me Shaila?"

Her heart fluttered. She became alert, nevertheless keeping her discretion awake she asked with a forced smile, "Help from me? What is it I can do for you?" She wondered.

Pathi smiled almost relieved as if he got help.

"Will you come out? I shall narrate," He asked hopefully.

"He is luring me to go out with him. Careful!' she thought. "No, Pathi tell me here. Do not be shy."

Pathi swallowed two gulps of saliva and proceeded to clarify. "For the last one year, I have followed you Shaila. I know your family history, your predicament, your plight. My father is a very rich businessman in Orissa. He sends me a lot. Shaila, I Love you, Permit me to help you till you get through the medical course."

There were tears in his eyes. He was waiting for his salvation. Shailaja was astonished. 'Has God listened? But how can you trust him?' She asked, "What do you expect from me in return?"

"A smile from you when you meet me! Next, accept me as a friend! Just a friend, nothing more!"

Her circumstances were such that she was unable to refuse him. Still she asked him one final question. "Do you do it out of pity for me?"

"No I am not a philanthropist. I Love you. If you do not complete your M.B.B.S honourably, you shall cause me distress.

In return I do not seek anything. I swear." He touched his neck.

She hesitated. "You know my need, how much you will have to spend and how long."

"I am not counting. I will meet your mother and explain."

"Okay, but I am not like others. No parties with you, no picnic. I won't come in your way, you are free to go with other girls."

"Will you remain atleast a friend?"

"Let me see!"

Pathi took her in his car to her home. On the way, he gave her the fee receipt which he had already paid in her name. She was surprised. She noticed that there were tears in his eyes. 'Is he really in love? Can I rely on him? Already he has trespassed into my heart. Am I lucky or a victim of a grand design? Let time decide. My fate at present is critical!" she thought.

Pathi looked at the old house which required extensive repairs. There was a big compound with coconut trees. Shailaja went inside and explained her mother why Pathi was there and his good intention. "Shaila, be careful. He might try to spoil you."

"No Ma, I am careful. He appears to be genuine."

When her mother came to meet him, Pathi touched her feet. She stood back surprised. "Ma, take me as your son," he told.

Pathi not only came to be respected in the house but he had become a member of the household. He didn't trespass the limit expected of him by Shaila, never touched her even once casually and strangely dissociated from other girls who were vying for the maximum attention from him. Pathi and Shaila were always together coming to college, taking lunch, attending library, studying together. Shailaja however did not change her habits; she remained in jeans, without cosmetics, without resorting to any excesses. There was an inherent discipline in her. Pathi felt overwhelmed by her charisma.

Shailaja passed in first class whereas Pathi failed. One day Pathi went away when he received the news about his fathers illness and never returned nor contacted her. That was three years ago.

Dinesh was disillusioned. He was free, not engaged at all; all his castles were built in the air; no substance. He wanted to know.

"Do you still love him?"

Shailaja remained silent.

"Have you not contacted him?"

"No, he didn't leave his address. I kept such a reliance on him."

"No letters from him?"

"None so far"

"Do you love him?" He repeated the question.

"I had trusted myself that I would never be involved but he has stolen my heart forever. I cannot think of any other man."

Dinesh sensed now why she had mentioned to his father that she would not mind if some other girl was found for Dinesh, if marriage was to be performed before departure abroad. She had secured a foreign scholarship purely on merit. Dinesh however craved for her company and was prepared to wait.

"How long I might have to wait?"

"I do not know. Perhaps till I am sure he doesn't need me; he is out of my way."

"Is he not already out?"

She kept mum; her heart murmured, 'He is very much around.'

Within only a few months, even before she settled down, she met Pathi. It was a surprise of her life when he came to meet her in the Hostel. He was in the lounge, dressed immaculately in the western dress. He had remained slim, agile alert as before. He appeared confident, capable. She could not believe her eyes stood transfixed in the middle.

"Pathi!"

Tears rushed down her cheeks. Words failed to form. Her vocal cords had frozen. Pathi took her firmly in his arms breaking the old code and made her sit by his side. "I have followed you all along, everyday."

She didn't believe. "How?" she staring at him blindly.

"It's possible. I will tell you some other time."

"What do you do here?" she asked gasping for breath in his presence.

"My father is no more. I am looking his business. I am the only son."

"How long you are here?"

"I am leaving tonight."

She was heartbroken; like a dumb child forsaken by her only guardian.

"Do you love me?" Words escaped from his lips for the first time.

In answer, she was looking with tearful eyes as if confronted by God.

"What happens to Dinesh?"

"I have nothing to do with him. He knows about us."

"Are you prepared to come along with me today?"

She nodded.

"Your studies?" he asked pointedly.

"I want you Pathi, I want you, I want you," She was crying covering her face.

Pathi and Shajlaja were married in a grand ceremony in Orissa. Their honeymoon tour after a fortnight ended in California.

The wind whorled the leaves round the ward. Pathi was sitting with Shailaja in her Hostel on the last day. He whispered, "I love you Shaila." A wistful emotion briefly clouded her eyes. She was overcome by a struggle of emotions within her so intense she could hardly breathe, speak. He felt an overwhelming passion at seeing her beautiful face before leaving. He had no words.

2

Sanath led a vigorously circumspect life. He was nearing sixty. His hairs had begun to grey. Yogini was twenty years younger than him. She retained a youthful appearance. She practiced yoga regularly and spent sometime in meditation. Not excessive like Sanath who at times went out of bounds to become unbalanced. She was discreet in her approach to every problem. She rarely overworked. However she kept herself busy with work, maintaining sparkling cleanliness around, getting food ready with the assistance of Kumudini who had become a housewife. She had discontinued her studies. Chandra had opened a dispensary in the city.

Sanath was increasingly becoming aware of the futility of efforts on the spiritual plane, of a disturbed mind anxious to achieve results and gain experience. 'Dying is the key; it is not the outcome of positive efforts.' He was aware at times that his mind was relieved of the burden of thought, effort and attained tranquility. He was overcome by a sense of resignation to let go of desire. During such moments the stream of consciousness lingered near his heart clearing thoroughly of all the past contamination.

He had several doubts about birth, death and living. None of these doubts were cleared. Stray glimpses of that dimension did not settle the raging storm in his mind. He wondered how Yogini kept a quiet composure. She was not struggling. It was a quality ingrained in her. Once she mentioned to Sanath; 'I was sitting closing my eyes. A point of light came gliding through space and I moved through it. Not me. The self was like a shadow. When it dissolved, the seed memories of the cosmos seemed to disappear in a strange nothingness. But the spark moved away. I felt I was being guided by Him, Shiva!'

Sanath was surprised listening to Yogini. "Your previous efforts are blossoming perhaps," he told.

"Previous, what do you mean?"

"Past life."

"Is there birth, death? It appears to be timeless, immortal, unborn and therefore not subject to birth and death."

Sanath smiled in appreciation. He did not deem it fit to comment. Her face appeared illuminated. Like her name she was truly Yogini!

He saw a dream. He was standing on the bank of Ganges in Varanasi. A boat was moving towards the other shore. Yogini and Tapaswini were in it. They did not return. It was his impression that he remained alone on the other side of the shore.

"Yogini!" He woke up sobbing, calling her. "Why? What happened?" Yogini asked keeping an arm around him.

"You are with me?" He opened his eyes wide and stared disbelieving her presence.

He clasped her palm firmly and slept like a child.

It was a cheerless day. Overcast with drizzling. Sanath remained indoor reading. After breakfast, he went to the dispensary of Chandra.

"Uncle, how are you?" he asked lovingly.

"Okay my boy, carry on."

He kept on looking at Chandra with his patients. Chandra felt uneasy at the queer behaviour of Sanath. He was certainly in an offbeat mood. After nearly half hour, he got up, went to Chandra, patted his cheek and went away.

Sanath was met at the door by Kumudini who was pregnant, in the sixth month. He hugged her tenderly and told, "Careful, do not exert."

Then he searched for Deepak, "Dad, he is in the school".

"Oh, I forgot."

He went to his room. Yogini sat on the sofa reading a book. Sanath went and sat near her. He took her palm in his hand and held it firmly, affectionately. "Why, you look different, remote like a distant mountain. What is wrong?" she asked doubting.

He reclined on the sofa as if weary. "Get me some water," he asked as if exhausted. She rushed inside and came back within minutes. Sanath appeared to be asleep. His mouth was open. She held his head in her arms and gave him water. It dribbled away. Sanath had left the world.

Chandra and Yogini took the ashes to Varanasi to perform the last rites. When they were coming down the steps of Viswanath temple, Yogini was glad to meet Tapaswini who had not much changed during the last ten years. She recognised Yogini and smiled. She became instantly serious, came near her, took her by the hand and led her to the peepul tree. A decade ago, they were there listening to Tapaswini. Chandra sat at a distance wondering how Yogini knew her. "I am sorry, Sanath was moving very fast. He has to don a new fabric. Rather I would prefer to wait like a flowering tree taking my own time, yielding to Nature's laws. Overcoming, controlling and struggling are not our way."

Yogini sat with tearful eyes. After some interval, Tapaswini suggested. "Yogini, will you come with me?" Her eyes, those orbs of light held a mischievous glint of invitation. It conveyed the message of a daring warrior marching ahead undaunted by crisis for a rendezvous in the other dimension.

Yogini told, "Yes, I want to come."

She turned to Chandra who was curious at this confrontation. He was bewildered. "Who is this sanyasini?" Why did Yogini readily agreed to go with her? What is happening?"

Yogini interrupted his thoughts and told, "Meet Tapaswini, Chandra. We met her ten years ago. I am going away. Take care of Kumudini and your child, good-bye."

He was speechless. He faltered and asked, "When will you come back?"

"I have not yet reached the other shore. How can I predict about my return?"

Tapaswini smiled, called him to come near, patted his cheeks and told lovingly, "Yogini needs a new life."

Chandra stood aghast looking at the two women moving away. When they disappeared from the view, he realised that he had not taken her address; Yogini had not taken her suitcases. The episode was steeped in mystery; it was beyond comprehension!

On the train, Tapaswini and Yogini occupied seats opposite each other. Tapaswini was silent either absorbed in the scenery outside or at times, lost in contemplation. She was observant of everything. She was aware of Yogini who sat with a sad face, a heavy heart.

Yogini remembered all her past, taking stock of everything; the passing away of Sanath, the family life consisting of Chandra, Kumudini and Deepak; the house and the farm. In her resolve to accompany Tapaswini, everything was washed away making her empty. She was alone. Her childhood days and poverty compared to the startling affluence in which she was abruptly placed with the coming into contact with Sanath, the first impulse of love and attachment lingered in her mind. She started crying secretly, wiping her tears hurriedly. Tapaswini looked at her lovingly but didn't try to pacify her. Looking at Tapaswini, she felt that she belonged to another dimension, not this planet. Even though she looked at her lovingly, took care of her, she didn't belong to anything around. She was alone with her sorrow.

Tapaswini seemed to be in a transcendental mood. She was not participating with the people around 'I am alone with my sorrow. No one to share. Me and my sorrow are one.' Yogini carried it in her heart like a baby, a part of herself. She was unable to throw it out nor do anything about it, apart from living with it. There was no other escape. She slowly looked at Tapaswini who was comprehending something extraordinary. She was in an ecstatic state. A bewildering smile pervaded her face. Yogini looked in the direction where Tapaswini was staring. She saw vast fields blazing with coloured flowers. Tall trees swaying in the breeze; the clear blue sky with few white fluffy clouds afloat, "What is my relationship with Sanath? In essence it's love. Unfathomable feeling of peace; she felt the same love, peace spread around, alive, vibrant, eternal. It was not gone with the death of Sanath. It was not a mortal fabric. She wondered why she mourned. 'Am I sobbing for Sanath, or for my own sake? Am I feeling sad because I lost a companion in whom I kept reliance for giving me sexual pleasure?' A smile pervaded her face with that understanding. She became overwhelmed by love. Ecstatic!

Tapaswini looked at her. She was surprised. Yogini was reborn with the elimination of sorrow. Their eyes met and both of them lifted their hand in unison to acclaim the gorgeous spectacle around. They laughed at their common insight and communion.

Yogini became withdrawn again. It was the habit of mind to get back into the crevices of the past and suffer. Having left home and heading towards an unknown destiny, have I done the right thing? Perhaps Tapaswini lived in some corner, a cottage on the out-skirts of a mountain. She lived probably on alms and led a hard life, full of austerity and simplicity. Probably, I will also have to get into an ochre robe and wander from place to place. Her life with Sanath, Deepak, Kumudini and Chandra was slipping away, vanishing like thin fog under the bright sunlight of reality. There is no going back, she thought. She remembered her father telling the story of her birth. She was named as Yogini in remembrance of a Bhairavi who had predicted her birth. 'Whether that time has come?' She had apprehension about her real intention. Tapaswini was sophisticated except for that hair style. She had neatly combed and tied a knot on her head. The hairs were not neglected, had good lustre, black except for a few white hairs at the temples. The ochre robe was of quality fabric. It was scrupulously clean, probably ironed. She wore flat healed chappals. She carried a suit case which was not of cheap quality. She had a canvas bag hung on her shoulder in which she carried the essential items like towel, handkerchief, purse, a mirror and a comb. Yogini felt inwardly that she was not used to walk from place to place. Her age could not be assessed. She was slim, still carrying a good figure. Her skin appeared fairer this time. Previously she thought that it was wheat complexion. There were a few lines below her eyes and forehead. Eyes specially emanated innocence. There was a sense of perpetual wonder at everything she observed. Every time she turned to look at Yogini she felt whether she had taken time to recognise. Because Tapaswini smiled at her with a sense of wonder. 'Why did she ask me to accompany her? Have I taken a wrong step? Irrevocable step?' At this thought, Tapaswini, as if Yogini talked loudly told, "Yogini, you are free. If you want to go back, you may."

Yogini was puzzled. "No, I want to come with you. I have nothing left behind," she told assuredly.

She wondered at the statement made by her without second thought. Tapaswini smiled and looked away at the distant mountain. It was 2 p.m. Tapaswini called the caterer to bring lunch for them. Before touching the food, she looked at the various items, closed her eyes. Yogini thought that she was praying. Then with a smile she beckoned Yogini to take food. Tapaswini ate with contentment as if food was an immortal recipe.

The taxi took them outside the suburb about ten kilometers and then stopped. She accompanied Tapaswini inside the gate. On either side of the gate tall trees swayed in the cool breeze leading to a white house about a furlong away. The house was surrounded by a well kept garden. The house which appeared to be small from a distance was actually quite spacious with a portico supported by eight pillars. There were a few chairs here and there. The house was unusually quiet.

Yogini sat on the chair staring at the modern look of the house which overlooked a vast farm. She remembered her house and strangely, there was not much difference. She was swallowed by a peculiar silence which appeared to be a living thing. Not Yogini listening; silence was aware of Yogini; she was a mere shell like the chair on which she was sitting.

When she opened her eyes, Tapaswini was sitting by her side waiting for her to wake up.

"Sorry, I slept away."

"Were you sleeping?" Tapaswini asked doubtfully.

Yogini did not venture to answer. Tapaswini smiled and told," Do you know, how long you were meditating?"

Yogini looked at her watch. "Two hours!" she exclaimed.

3

Kumudini sat alone on the verandah. She remembered her father who was an embodiment of nobility, intelligence and spiritual strength. He knew about his death. During the night time when light went out she used to be scared. Alone without Chandra, it was an ordeal. A new experience. She dreamt on the previous night that she was waking up in a burning house, aghast at the thought that her family might be in grave danger. She prayed that Chandra and her mother would return safe.

Being alone, she remembered her past days. As a child playing with Chandra, bossing over him and the loving attention bestowed by mother and father. She was pampered too much to the extent of spoiling her. She looked down with chagrin at her own unstylish dress. 'Why did I discontinue studies? If I had continued for another two years I would have become a doctor like Chandra. I was perhaps frightened to go out. She cursed herself looking back with shame on past amorous escapades. 'I have ruined my career. Now it's too late. Another pregnancy and in another two months, second baby to worry over. Surendra is living with his family. What a fool I was to pursue a married man.' She felt disgusted.

Just then a taxi came and stood before the house. She got up and approached the gate. Chandra had come alone. She was afraid. When she saw the suit cases, she flinched from thinking about her mother.

"Where is Ma?"

She was anxious. Chandra came inside with a heavy heart.

"What happened?" She asked.

"Kumud, she met her Guru Tapaswini at Varanasi who took her away."

She was visibly shocked, "No, it can't be true. Her suit cases, you have brought back. Tell me the truth."

Violent feelings broke out into uncontrollable expressions, Chandra went near her and taking her tenderly in his arms tried to pacify her. "Kumud, there isn't any calamity. She is alive. Believe me. She went away with Tapaswini."

She gave a grim look at her husband. "Why her suit cases have come here?" She asked like a school teacher before an errant child.

"Come inside, I shall explain."

As soon as he took her inside, he tenderly caressed her hairs and tried to kiss her. She moved a little distance away and hissed like a snake, "Give me just the bare facts without any embellishments."

He sat on the sofa. She kept standing. She had never shown such an agitated demeanour. "Kumud, I cannot offer any explanation. I have not grasped why she went away. Tapaswini is a strange woman wearing an ochre robe. She told Yogini to accompany her and she readily agreed. It appears she knew Sanath and your mother ten years ago. I asked her when she would return. She gave a strange answer. 'I have not yet reached the other shore. How can I predict!' Tapaswini called me, patted my cheek and informed that she needed rest. They went away. When they disappeared, I realised that I had not taken their address; the suitcases were left behind. Everything in Varanasi was steeped in great mystery."

Kumudini was frightened. She was aware of a calamity that threatened to wipe out her family. She started sobbing covering her face with both the palms. It was beyond her comprehension how such a thing could happen to her.

She was coming through the room of her father. He kept a

diary in which he recorded all the important events. She went through it carefully right from the beginning.

Two years before meeting Yogini, he wrote; 'Is there God? This is the key question. I have not found an answer. I want to devote my life for this investigation.'

Ten years ago, the following entry was found: 'We met Tapaswini accidentally. I am lucky. She is a great soul. She initiated me into meditation, cleared my doubts troubling me since childhood.'

Three months ago: 'I am struggling to come upon that dimension which is life, consciousness, beauty and ecstasy. Sex has been totally eliminated. Yogini doesn't agree. According to her, it's unbalanced attitude.'

4

Yogini looked at the calendar. 'Two months since I have left home. Not a thought about home. This place makes for forgetfulness. Tapaswini doesn't impose herself on me. I am left to myself. She sensed instinctively what to say and what to leave unsaid, often practicing restraint. Everything moves effortlessly here. No worry. Perhaps this is my destiny.' She thought unable to believe her mind.

Tapaswini taught yoga to school children who came by bus once a week. She was busy with the students all the days of the month, as most of the schools took advantage of the yoga class run by Tapaswini.

Yogini evinced keen interest in the farm. She plugged the loop poles and managed it with a firm hand without being harsh. She was tactful, made purchases for the farm under her personal supervision. Thereby the expenditure was reduced.

Yogini woke up frightened. There was a single bed lamp at the corner of the room. In the dim light, she looked at Tapaswini. She was sleeping with her back to Yogini. Her cot was nearly ten feet away. At the foot of the cot, a translucent fog like figure, human in form looked over Tapaswini. Yogini kept on staring at the figure to make sure it was not her imagination. She pinched herself, she was not dreaming. She was afraid to call Tapaswini. She closed her eyes and pretended to sleep. When she woke up, it was morning. Tapaswini had already left the bed.

It was 2 a.m. Yogini woke up listening to a hissing sound. To her astonishment, she found Tapaswini sitting in the middle of the room naked. She was doing pranayam. After some time she started meditating. Nearly after one hour, she got up, went to the mirror and then she put on her nightie. She looked young without clothes with a good figure and lustrous skin.

Tapaswini did not preach nor give any instructions on meditation to Yogini, who was totally free left to herself. She read some books on alchemy, tantra and meditation. Many of the books were in Sanskrit. When she was alone, she meditated. At times when she woke up at night, she would spend time meditating on the bed.

The luminous apparition appeared every time after midnight and invariably she woke up to witness the phenomenon. She was getting used to it. The initial fear was no longer bothering her now. She determined to question Tapaswini. She did not go to sleep. She took out a book from the cupboard and sat on the bed reading. It was a book on tantra. She had read many books at home. Sanath had collected every book on philosophy and occultism. After 11 p.m., Tapaswini entered the bedroom. "Surprise, any problem?" She asked.

Tapaswini smiled and went and sat on the bed. Yogini hesitated. Then she made up her mind and told, " I want to ask you about something."

"Shoot," Tapaswini told in a jovial mood.

"Daily I wake up frightened and find a luminous apparition hovering near your cot."

"Oh that, that is why I wanted you to sleep for a few days in my room."

"What's it?"

"An Ally"

"What's an Ally?"

"It's my protector. When you enter into the other dimension and continuously inhabit it, you become very vulnerable, sensitive. You become the centre of attraction. A time comes, when a benevolent force comes to assist you, protect you from evil. It comes and stays with your consent."

"Is it harmful to others?"

"Not to you certainly. You are also entitled to the protection afforded to me. You will come to know about it gradually. Nothing should be attained before it is due. It becomes risky."

Tapaswini got up, went to the mirror and unwound her hairs which fell on her shoulders covering her back. She slowly undressed unmindful of Yogini who hesitated to look at her. She could not avoid it. She stroked the small breast and also her whole body. She came slowly, stood facing Yogini who was embarrassed, shy and diffident. Her skin was fair and luminous; she was slim and shapely; still she retained her youthful demeanour. The muscles were not sagging. She was all smiles. The abdomen was not bulging. She had probably not borne any children Yogini thought.

"Will you come for pranayam and meditation with me?"

Yogini was hesitating, not knowing what to do next. Undress'? Staring in her eyes which held a mischievous glint, she fumbled for words.

"Come on, get up."

Yogini quietly stood up. Shy like a bride. Tapaswini came near, took her in her arms, embraced her. "I will help you my dear," she told.

She started removing her saree feeling her firm body. Yogini felt aroused sexually. Her nipples hardened. She was thrilled. 'What is happening to me? Is she a homo? Tapaswini was staring at her nakedness. "You are beautiful," she told smiling at her awkwardness.

Yogini wanted to express her apprehension. "I am sexually

aroused by your touch. Is it your intention?" Innocently Yogini asked as if imprisoned by a Queen Bee.

Tapaswini smiled and mentioned, "There are inhibitions in every; segment of body as a heritage of self. I will talk to you some other times. There is nothing wrong in sex. You are not merely a female nor male."

"I do not understand,"

"That is a good beginning. Come on."

She led her to the centre of the room and both sat cross-legged. Closing their eyes they started listening between their eyebrow. Yogini prayed for giving her strength, purity and wisdom. She felt energy engulfing her. After some interval, both opened their eyes simultaneously. Tapaswini gave lesson on pranayam. Awareness of abdomen and breathing in and out; of chest breathing in and out; of chest and abdomen, breathing in and out. Breathing exercises for purification.

Yogini for the first time slept without any distraction. When she woke up in the morning, she was alive energetic.

Yogini woke up crying, calling, "Kumud, my baby Kumud."

Time 4 a.m. Tapaswini was also awakened by her cries and asked her, "Did you see any dream?"

"My daughter Kumudini was choked with sobs and grovelling on the floor in tears and a young woman stood on her. The young woman was an embodiment of light and beauty."

Tapaswini closed her eyes for sometime then told, "Your daughter has given birth to a female baby who will be an enlightened soul."

Yogini was pleased. She counted on her fingers and exclaimed, "Yes, this is the time."

There was everything provided in the house except telephone. Perhaps there was no need for it. Communicating with the past meant corrupting one's soul. Past was losing its ardour, strength and grip on her. Yet there was pain because the wound was still raw. Not yet healed even after the passage of one year.

Tapaswini took her one day on the outskirts of the farm. There was a small temple belonging to the past, a thousand years ago. No one visited it. No pujas were offered. Tapaswini had maintained it with care so that the ancient monument was not destroyed. Light came from two holes inside the temple once in the morning and then in the evening. Yogini went inside accompanied by Tapaswini. The stone idol of Shiva was flooded with light from the rising sun. White stone with green tinge here and there. About three feet in height. Half of the body was man, the other half woman. Yogini could not take away her eyes. It was beauty. The qualities of male and female flowed imperceptibly into one another. It was difficult to identify the absolute male from the absolute female. The idol spoke eloquently and held a cryptic message which was difficult to define with precision. It was extremely erotic. Is it another version of Linga? In Linga male and female genitals are so intimately held together making it difficult to separate the identity of the participants. It was a symbol of unity in diversity. The fountain of creativity exploded from the confluence of the two forces, the male and the female. Thus Yogini brooded over the idol unable to grasp the meaning. Yogini was lost in deep contemplation.

After some interval Yogini slowly moved outside. Tapaswini did not attempt to explain. Definition gave a distorted view according to her.

Yogini sat on the cot waiting. The idol of Shiva, ardhanarinateshwara lingered 'in her mind. She remembered some months ago Tapaswini mentioning that no one is totally male nor female. Tapaswini had left the rest unsaid.

Yogini was aware that she was left to herself; never she was being led by Tapaswini. If Tapaswini wanted to convey any message, it was done indirectly.

Tapaswini and Yogini sat for meditation. Tapaswini had closed her eyes and plunged into intense meditation. A bewitching smile pervaded her face. Yogini became thoughtful. But within only a short time she was being pulled away by an alien force. As if Tapaswini was in a mood never letting her off. Yogini involuntarily gave herself freely. The female in her seemed to respond to the male force as if of Tapaswini. Both of them remained in communion; in a state of confluence. They were not seperate entities but united beyond the bounds of fragile bodies unconditionally. She was surrounded by a flood of dark vibrant melody which was sensuality of a superior order, where every cell of her body was involved. When she woke up, she saw that Tapaswini was in a trance like samachi. Her eyes were half closed bereft of sight. Face was flooded by a charm, an unearthly light. She was engrossed in the other dimension. Yogini felt sleepy, kept her head on her laps and closed her eyes. She was engulfed in the depths of an eerie silence, sound and stream. Eternity!

It was the first initiation she received in the cult of Tantra. It was never repeated. Yogini felt a deep sense of change with this initiation. She was not only freed from depression but was uprooted from her old habits and conventional life. She thought: 'Sexuality is only a mechanism to invoke love, open the door to unlimited energy. Even though the primary function is to lodge the sperm in the womb, it has a higher role in that it is instrumental in breaking the limitations of mind. There is also another facet to sexuality. It is immaterial whether it appears between man and woman or woman and woman, the stress is on dissolution of self. Sex conditioning is a powerful barrier with the weight of time and it is not easy to transcend it, with learning or academic knowledge.' When Yogini voiced her opinion, Tapaswini kept a discreet silence.

She told, "We do not preach. We do not guide. We live. Our destiny is Truth, nothing less than Truth. Every attempt on this path is sacred. Nothing is unholy."

The memories of earlier life with her father, mother, Sanath, Deepak, Kumudini and Chandra gradually receded from the horizon of her mind like a forgotten dream. She busied more and more in the present. Living was a joy. Her body was invigorated. She breathed deeply, evenly and happily. This was her new home, permanent home. She had evinced interest in the farm. She economised expenditure and showed that the income could be doubled. Tapaswini was pleased with the work. Pointing to the farm and the house, she remarked, "Yours forever."

The school bus arrived at 2 p.m. The laughter and gossip of children subsided as soon as they descended from the bus. Tapaswini always went near the bus to receive the children. Before resuming the class, she introduced Yogini to Gopal, a Sanskrit teacher.

"Yogini, you may spend an hour with Gopal who will teach you Sanskrit. He will be here with you twice in a week. On other days, Sumangala will be with you. Both are proficient in Sanskrit."

Yogini asked doubting . "At this age, you want me to learn?"

Tapaswini became serious. A faint smile lingered on her face. "Never late, many years are there for you to live. A full hundred years. Learn thoroughly."

Yogini reverentially told, "I shall start right now."

Yagini started doubting whether they were living with a purpose. They were superior entities with a vision. Whether they belonged to that dimension which had no beginning and end, no time with its shadow there? Her complexion had changed; She looked younger than her age. Worry was totally eliminated. The gossip and bustle of urban life and warring segments rarely reached the remote hermitage.

Yogini had come nearer and nearer to Tapaswini but she had not known much about her antecedents. Whether she was married? How she happened to be on the farm? Who was her Guru? What was her mission in life? It was not mere curiosity. She had to know because she was becoming part and parcel of that habitat. Tapaswini wanted her to be the inheritor of everything. Slowly the secrets of the other dimension were being revealed to her. She was certainly on probation. Life with Tapaswini meant unassumed austerity. There was never a moment of indiscretion, eroticism, indulgence. Yet nothing was prohibited. Every experience became a holy ritual. Naturalness was the hallmark of living with her. Her name strangely symbolised it.

Sunday. It was raining. There were no yoga classes. It was a day meant for relaxation. Tapaswini liked to roam freely in the farm and the garden, play badminton and spend time with Yogini. She called on the workers, talked to them about their problems. She had studied homeopathy and Ayurveda. Little ailments were diagnosed and treated by her.

She was in a relaxed mood. Yogini sat with her on the verandah. She made up her mind to question. Tapaswini sensed her inquisitiveness and asked, "Your have a question?"

"Yes, about you."

"Oh come out, let me hear."

"We are like dropouts completely withdrawn from society; Living in a world of personal consciousness pursuing philosophy, apolitical based perhaps on universal love. It's rather vague. Is there a purpose? What is your mission?"

Tapaswini listened attentively. She told quietly "I do not know Yogini."

"It appears our life will be ultimately pointless. Do you agree with me?"

Again Tapaswini smiled and soberly told, "Probably. But I do not agree with you. Even though in essence living in this world is meaningless, it is pointless if you have not come upon the 'Other!'

"So I presume our mission is to make ourselves fit to be consumed by Truth?"

" Perhaps you are not wrong."

"I wanted to know more about you. Who are you? Where were you born? Were you married? Have you any children? How did you happen to stay here? Why have you taken sanyasa? Who is your Guru?"

Tapaswini looked at her in amusement. "Okay I shall tell you a little later. The mystery shall not be revealed until the ultimate chapter of my life. The day I disclose, you shall lose me!"

Yogini was frightened. "No, do not tell me." She pleaded.

"Your have to know a little later. Therefore you are here."

5

The morning sun shone through the green tops of trees spreading rays of dazzling light on earth. The birds chirped and flew at random to try their wings against the breeze. Children danced at the street comers playing marbles. There was a new beginning on earth. New hopes sprouted in the hearts of men. There were moments in life when you were carried away by the mood of nature.

However Shailaja sat in her chamber on the third floor of the Nursing Home and looked out of the window with a heavy heart. There was a lone tree bare of leaves and flowers in the middle of the garden. The melancholy sound of the wind pounded on her heart. Like the tree she was lone and blue, she thought. Pathi was expected to come over by 10 a.m. During a decade of married life, they had no children. He was either busy or confessed that he was not very particular about children. He was but concerned about the mental health of Shailaja who had of late become moody. She evinced little interest in social activities. The relatives of Pathi commented on her state of health. They questioned among themselves whether she was barren. What would happen to the wealth? Sensing her plight, Pathi had given consent, to get examined.

He came an hour late. Shailaja was over joyed. He was received by the principal Doctor who was waiting for him at the gate. Pathi went straight to the chamber of Shailaja.

She whispered, "Thank you Pathi."

He came near his wife, wiped her tears and said humorously, "Okay, take me to your Specialists."

She did not speak. They had discussed at length about this matter. They wanted to try whatever possible. If they failed, they would accept it as their fate. The Specialists held the view that there was nothing wrong with them.

During the might when Pathi came, he asked, "What do they say, your Specialists?"

She was sad, sat with downcast eyes, "Nothing wrong with both of us", she declared.

He humorously remarked, "Then you should be glad." Shailaja looked at him. He appeared to be unconcerned. She told, "You have always refused to pray. For my sake, let us visit Varanasi."

Pathi was cynical about his wife's vow to visit Varanasi. He had not entered temple in his life time. He believed in hard work and if possible wiping the tears of those who were deserving. God did not exist for him. Shailaja was also like him relied on moving on her legs to reach the desired end. But of late, she was keenly becoming aware of an unknown factor working in life that prevented her from getting what she desired most, inspite of all the best efforts. Therefore she wanted to experiment with prayer.

"If I have got to be like you, my confidence will collapse and it would be the end of the business." Pathi mentioned seriously.

"Money is not everything, Pathi." Shailaja suggested.

"I know, that's why I pursued you to the end of the world and married you."

"Like me don't you need a son from me?"

"Very much. But will praying give me a son?"

"I do not know. Why not ask?"

"Give me some time to think."

"Thought is the Devil. It prevents...."

"God!" Pathi laughed.

Inspite of everything, unlimited wealth, a loving husband, she had not become greedy. She lived like a lotus untouched by the lure of wealth and position. 'Why should I be singled out for being barren? What sins have I committed? From the very beginning, I have led a very austere life. Why cannot I bear the seed of Pathi, feed it, writhe in pain and give birth? I am prepared to do anything. Anything. Oh God, if you exist, help me.'

Whenever she was alone, she prayed.

Pathi's mother craved for a grandson. There was another problem. Due to an ancient family feud, his cousins happened to be his mortal enemies. If there was no progeny for Pathi, they would come to usurp the property. She was aware of the whole problem. An year ago, she suggested to her husband to get married to some other woman. At this suggestion, Pathi was wild with fury. He categorically informed, "I do not want any children, if it's not from you."

Her thoughts raced ahead anticipating a solution. But there could only be desolation. Her life was becoming meaningless. Once her mother suggested, "Pathi may not get children. If you do not, an empire will be lost. Why not try secretly another man?"

She felt a feeling of disgust at her suggestion. Sensations whorled through her mind too rapidly for her to assimilated. She cursed her mother. If she was not old and struck with arthritis and asthma, she would have hit her with her fist. "Do not bother Ma. You are counting your days. Be contented that I am alive."

Once Shailaja suggested an orphan. Pathi did not agree. "Why are you so despondent?"

"I am getting old."

"You are only thirty-six. There is still time."

After only a couple of years of marriage, Shailaja realised that she was not freed from a sense of appalling desolation and emptiness. Year after year, she discovered that the vast emptiness in her was not transitory phenomenon; it was not to be filled with wealth, a devoted husband, position and name. At times, in her biggest moments of joy, there lingered a feeling of desperate need for something which she could not decipher. A keen sense of want and desperation persisted. From her tender age, she was endowed with the gift of indifference to personal joys and sorrow. When Pathi entered her life, she became aware of unlimited wealth but she did not change her attitude which had become her second nature. She had inherent faculty of culture. The thrill of initial sex with Pathi had opened a new dimension in her life, but soon she realised that it also weaned away losing it's ardour and appeal. Pathi had also become aware of her illness which affected her psycho spiritual being. He was helpless. He wanted her to plunge in business and assist him. As a diversion, she shared his chamber in his office and looked into the complicated devices meant for bringing in more and more wealth but there also, she expressed soon that she was incapable of spending her whole of being concerned with money alone. Her views were so unacceptable that Pathi wondered what on earth could possibly meet her approval. Shailaja was despondent because her condition would not improve.

Pathi had become suspicious and collected intelligence to find out whether Shailaja had any extra marital affairs which were not fulfilled. He took this extreme step because Shailaja was unaware she was failing in her duty as a wife; she was not responsive in bed. His investigation resolved that she was devoted to him and to no other man.

She told once Pathi, "I feel I am an alien in this world. My pulse beats reveal that I want to go to a remote place, a hermitage and spend the rest of life." "Is it your wishful thinking?" Pathi asked.

"It is not superficial, bear with me Pathi. You have given me everything, love, wealth, name, education and the whole world on the spread of my palm. Still I am left an orphan. You cannot heal me. I am afraid even if I get a son I might remain the same. I don't know my destiny. If I die, marry again and live happily." Pathi closed her mouth. "In this life, no other woman could fill your place." he told.

The condition of her mother deteriorated day by day. Inspite of best medical care, she could not be saved. According to her wish, the last rites were to be performed at Varanasi. Pathi was agreeable to accompany Shailaja. This was also an occasion to fulfill her vow.

After performing the last rites, Pathi and Shailaja prayed at the Viswanath temple for blessing them with a son. It was a novel experience for both of them. As they were descending the steps from the temple they met two women sanyasinis. Tapaswini stopped on seeing Shailaja. A perpetual smile lingered on her lips. Yogini looked on with amusement. Shailaja moved closer to Tapaswini and touched her feet.

"Be blessed with a son soon!" Tapaswini placed her palm on her head. Shailaja looked at the shining face of Tapaswini. Tears rushed down her cheeks.

"Even after ten years, I haven't got any children."

Pathi was crestfallen seeing the pathetic condition of Shailaja. Tapaswini became serious. "What will you give me if you get a son soon?"

Pathi and Shailaja took this question lightly. Shailaja once again touched her feet and promised "Anything!"

Tapaswini looked at Pathi demanding his reaction. "Yes, I agree with her," he assured.

Tapaswini turned to Yogini and told, "You are the witness."

She then turned to Shailaja, "I shall ask you later. Not now."

The prediction came true within only an year!

6

Kumudini sat on the terrace where her father and mother used to spend time meditating. It was a beautiful place opening on all the sides to the distant mountains, green fields and the swaying trees of the farm. She spent sometime whenever she felt bored or moody at this place. On such occasions Kumudini would feel enveloped by a sense of warm sleepy contentment. She was aware that she was not engaged in any meaningful activity. With her sad eyes she looked at an eagle gyrating majestically up into the sky for a thousand feet before plunging down on his prey. She was not aware that Chandra stood behind tenderly watching her.

Suddenly she whorled round and asked, "When did you come here?"

"Kumud, it's time for you to do some work on the farm so that I have some leisure."

She did not as usual take his words seriously. She told, "Why don't you sit some time and talk?"

"I cannot afford that luxury."

He was affected. For the first time in many days, Kumudini saw him. Worry was writ large on his otherwise innocent face. She clutched his hand and dragged him. "Come on tell me what should I do to relieve you. You know I had to look after Suma. Now that she is three and there is an Aya, I can do something."

Chandra wanted Kumudini to be responsible and active. Otherwise, he thought that she might become a victim of psychotic delusion. "Kumud, you are intelligent, capable and educated. Mother used to take so much interest in the farm especially accounts. I learnt from her certain very essential points of management."

Kumudini told soberly, "She was M.Com. I am not even a graduate."

"Never mind. You have immense capabilities. Manage the farm. I shall take you round and show you what to do."

She was thirty five, slim and agile. She had grown her hairs and combed neatly into a single blade. Having remained at home most of the time she had improved her complexion which tended to be creamy. She was still a beauty. Chandra often wondered at her beauty and felt that he was not her equal. He introduced her to all the workers and to the key man, Kumar. Sarangapani was sober, honest and sympathetic to the workers. Kumar was just the opposite. He treated the workers high handedly and rarely complaints reached Chandra. Kumar was paid well, nearly twice of what his father earned, because under his supervision the income had doubled. Chandra had not bestowed any attention after the death of Sanath and disappearance of Yogini.

Kumudini had an aversion for the family members of Yogini. They rarely visited them. Kumar came only on family business. Kumudini would not even tell him to sit. He would wait till Chandra came. Chandra gave him the respect due to a family member. Sometime he would get annoyed by her behaviour and tell her, "Your blood is not different, your mother his sister."

"My father's lover. I have no concern."

"What makes you detest them?" Chandra asked deploring her boorish manners.

"My blood revolts. I do not want to go back to that muddy waters."

Chandra was angry. "If Ma was there she would have taken you to task for that statement," he told. "How are you so sure?" Kumudini asked him pointedly.

Chandra remembered Yogini hitting Sanath on the cheek only a week after his arrival to the house. It was fresh in his memory. Sanath had kept quiet like an erring child. He thought that it was not proper to disclose. He kept quiet. Kumudini was still young and inexperienced. She would mature, he thought.

After one month, Kumudini was left to herself, to mind the business of the farm. The staff at home sought her approval for the accounts and before making purchases. Unlike Chandra, she asked for all the details, when and where it would be purchased, the prevailing prices and also the need. She accompanied them while making major purchases. She did not attempt such supervision only once but made it a routine. The staff realised that there was no scope for mischief.

She was now more busy than Chandra, rarely had time to attend to Suma who was looked after by a special Aya.

Kumar was entrusted with the supervision of the labourers and payment of salary. It was a shock for him when he found Kumudini reaching him in time for the disbursal of salary. She took the payroll and asked Kumar to make payment. Kumar was nervous. It was the first time the workers received full salary. Inwardly they sensed a keen desire to thank her for her presence. On one or two occasions, Kumar told Kumudini that the worker did not deserve full salary as he had not put in full hours. Kumudini enquired with the concerned and when it was revealed that the reasons were justified, she ordered full payment. Before leaving the place, she declared, "Kumar, in future, do not disburse salary unless I am present."

Kumar was annoyed. He used to collect atleast Rs. 1000/- p.m., on pay day. The presence of Kumudini would mean that he would be a loser. Kumudini instinctively felt that there was something wrong in the management of farm. She looked at him in her pitiless eyes before leaving him perspired.

The next day she drove to the worker's quarters. It was Sunday and she expected to meet them in their homes. Chandra preferred to stay at home and play, with the children. He was apprehensive of her activities. He did not question her because he was confident that she would approach him in case of necessity. Kumudini had not revealed anything so far. She met briefly in bed and that too most of the time she slept away thinking about the problems of the farm. Chandra wanted to see how far she would go to improve the farm.

At 4 p.m., she stopped the car near the first house on the south block. There were two children playing outside. Kumudini asked the boy. "Where is your father?"

"Sleeping, not well."

She went inside. An old man was on the floor. By his side sat an elderly woman who got up seeing Kumudini.

"Since when he is like this?"

"Seven days!"

"Who works on his behalf?"

"None."

"Why? Can you not do some work?"

"We are ready but Madam, Kumar has not agreed."

"Why?"

"He wants Rs. 200. We can afford only Rs. 100."

Kumudini took down the names of the members and assured them that she would be provided with work.

She visited the second, third and fourth. They were newcomers and were not prepared to complain. In the next house, a young woman who was cleaning rice got up when Kumudini entered the house. She was a tall girl in wheat complexion and appeared to be pregnant. She offered her a chair and by then her father came from inside. He introduced his daughter as 'Laxmi'.

"What is her husband doing?"

The man fumbled for words and kept silent. Kumudini talked in a low tone to gain his confidence. "She appears to be pregnant. What has happened?"

Her father in tears explained. "Madam, Kumar has ruined my family. He has molested my daughter."

"Is she not working?"

"How can I send her? Other women make fun of her."

Kumudini came outside and looked at the other houses. It was enough for the day, she thought. The facts were however suppressed.

Kumar had lost his wife during the first delivery. The male baby was also short-lived. Laxmi who was seventeen continued to work in the house, cooking, cleaning, washing. Kumar was thirty five. He had started taking drinks in the company of a few friends. One day Sabi, one of his friends taunted him. "Kumar, you need not go out for street girls. Laxmi is a sumptuous woman."

Kumar was enraged. "She is working in my house since the days of my wife. Do not talk about her," he warned.

"If so, some others will take care of her. She can't be left alone. Such a beauty;" Kumar was drunk. Feeling dizzy. Sabi continued, "I won't talk to her nor take her consent. A young woman should be talked through the body language."

Sabi laughed derisively and also others. They were playing cards in the house of Kumar.

"What would you do? Speak clearly. I am your boss." Kumar told pompously.

"Boss!" Sabi mocked contemptuously. "I would see her under me every day till she bears my seed."

Kumar did not get sleep. He used to be busy during the day and by the time, he returned, Laxmi would have left the place keeping the food ready. During the time when his wife was there, he had no occasion to look at other women. She took care of him and he had no inclination to go for drinks. After the death of both baby and wife, he became melancholy, depressed and lonely. Sabi and a few others took this opportunity to give him company. Laxmi was aware of the activities of Kumar and secretly suffered because she wanted him to be good. Even though she did not crave for his company, she desired that he should be saved from the evil company.

Sunday. Kumar remained at home. After bath, he sat leisurely on the verandah waiting for the meals. He wanted an opportunity to talk with Laxmi. It would be his first talk. Stealthily gathering courage, he went near the kitchen and looked at her. She was standing her back to the door. She was a woman, graceful and sensuous, untouched by any so far. Sabi was right. She would not be left alone for a long time. She was very sensitive. She turned suddenly with a jerk as if sensing a danger.

"Anything wrong?" She asked with intensity.

He was nervous. "Let me have a cup of tea Laxmi."

"Please wait outside." It was an order.

He unceremoniously came out without word. With tea, she came to his room. He stared at her from head to toe; for the first time, she felt that he was looking at her. 'What an idiot I was? Going for those street urchins.' He forgot to take tea. Laxmi was afraid. "Tea" she almost shouted.

He woke up from his stupor. "Yes, give it."

She kept the tea cup on the table and when she was rushing out, he asked. "Why are you afraid of me?"

She stood with her back to him and told, "No, I am not."

"I want to talk to you"

"Talk with my father."

He was amused. "It has nothing to do with him. You are not so young."

She did not speak. It was even embarrassing for her to listen to him. Every time she met him in the past, she shied away from looking into his eyes. He remained a stranger. "I have brought a saree. After so many days, I am thinking about you," he told her nervously.

He came near her. He offered the best silk saree of his wife. Laxmi had seen the saree on his wife who was an attractive woman. She looked beautiful in it. On several occasions, she had imagined that she would never in her life wear such a saree. It was heavy and while ironing, she would touch it, tenderly fondle it, smell it, wrap it around her unseen by the house lady. Instinctively she touched the saree which was still in his hand and suddenly recoiled.

"No, I do not want."

"You have worked for nearly five years. My wife would have given you many things. I have forgotten you. Please Laxmi."

She did not move.

"I am not going to marry again. No woman in my life."

She was angry. "Because you have those strumpets!" she almost shouted.

He was humbled. "I want to change" he touched her bare shoulder. "I want to be good. Give me sometime, Laxmi."

His palm slid down on her shoulder, down on her bottom. He had embraced her. How it happened? When it happened? Both wondered later. She became pregnant. To her repeated pleadings to marry her he started evading. He promised to look after her and the baby. He started drinking again, keeping company with Sabi; eventually neglecting Laxmi, her need. She stopped going to his house when her pregnancy became known by her friends.

On her way back home Kumudini stopped the car near Kumar's house. The house was quite large. It had an independent compound. Before construction of the house, Sanath used to live there with his mother. Thereafter it was allowed to Sarangapani. She went slowly inside the compound. Suddenly there was laughter and clapping of hands: a commotion. From the sounds she realised, there were nearly half a dozen men. She retraced her steps. When she was outside the gate, she looked back. Kumar was standing on the door step. He was drunk, balancing himself. "Hello, what do you want?" he shouted.

He was rude. Kumudini was enraged. She looked from the car and shouted, "Come at 11 a.m. to the office."

He waved his hand as if to brush her aside murmuring under his breath, "Strumpet!"

Kumudini became furious. She challenged him by her look, determined to teach him a lesson.

She analysed the factors that led to the present predicament. First of all, it was Sanath who must have shown some laxity because he had married Yogini who was niece of Sarangapani. Sarangapani was indirectly responsible, because he was honest to the core and accounted for every paise. Naturally there was no necessity to supervise. Sanath became increasingly withdrawn and spent time meditating. Yogini who was M.Com., managed the farm for sometime and trained Chandra. Then struck tragedy one after another. With the passing away of Sarangapani, Kumar who was working in the Telephone Department was asked to come and take over. This was done at the 'instance of Yogini who was of the view that her family had lived on the farm since many years; should not severe connection. The tradition was continued. Chandra was busy with the hospital work. Kumar was shrewd. He fawned over Yogini and sneered when she was gone. Sanath and Yogini seemed to be more concerned with the other dimension. This was the time when the family forgot about the farm. With the new management under Kumar, the income had doubled. He had also devised ways to swindle money. This was the time when he lost his wife and baby. The untimely death of Sanath, disappearance of Yogini, suffering and shock of Chandra and Kumudini left Kumar totally free to manipulate. He slowly turned his house into a gambling den and spent time drinking with his friends. Kumudini blamed herself for this state of affairs. Kumar had grown into Kumar sab or Kumar Swami. He was held with great fear; the workers recognised him as the real boss. A tyrant had grown and stood his ground. Kumudini wondered how fortunes swayed when they slept.

She did not mention anything to Chandra. She wanted to handle the case independently Chandra went away to the dispensary at 10 a.m. Kumar came at 11 a.m. accompanied by Sabi. Kumudini informed them to wait outside in the office. She instructed the senior Accountant who was aware of the farm dealings for nearly a decade to be present at the meeting.

Kumar was called inside but was not allowed a seat. His henchman Sabi was not called inside. Kumar was nervous. He stood fidgeting and rubbing his palms. He felt her to be haughty and capricious. She slowly unleashed her attack with her contemptible rudeness.

"Kumar, I am not satisfied by the way you handle the affairs of the farm."

She waited for his reaction. Kumar gave a curt rejoinder, "The income has doubled under my supervision."

His tone roused her up. A surly insubordinate servant, she thought. "I have investigated into the affairs of the farm and I find that there are serious allegations against you, irregularities deserving condemnation."

Kumar looked at her with disdain. 'My so called sister through Yogini!' He did not talk.

Kumudini opened her diary. "You demanded Rs. 200 from Somu and Raju for giving them work?"

"Lie, I will tackle these liars."

"I shall mange. It's not for you," she told curtly.

Kumar moved on his feet. "Why do you deny full salary to the staff?"

"It's not true."

"Why did you stop Laxmi from work?"

Kumar became alert. He was surprised. He stuttered, "She was not well."

"What do you mean?"

"I do not know. I did not stop her from work."

'How did she manage to get at the facts. Did that fink, her father ventured to tell? Or did Laxmi disclose? I must teach that slut.' Kumar thought nervously.

"Do you know she is pregnant?"

He was wary. His breath quickened. "Why should I know?"

"You raped her?"

He perspired. He made an ugly beastly face. He would have lynched her, hoped she dissolved before his eyes. He wiped his perspiration swearing under his breath, murmuring, 'I will teach you strumpet.' The accusations resulted in his public humiliation. 'Laxmi, how dare she disclosed this affair? I give her sustenance every month, and sarees even though she does not care to come and cook.' His reason failed him.

Kumudini decided to round up all his friends. She wanted to start a mopping up operation.

During the next week, Chandra noticed that Kumudini was not in her proper mood. She did not disclose any of the episodes to him. She was capable of keeping secrets. It kept her restless and on her feet. She had totally neglected her duties at home. The servants managed the work without giving room for complaints. Chandra was amused by her indifference. He wanted to question her, find out what kept her so busy, so worried. She was like a detective handling some colossal affair single-handed. He was worried whether she would come upon some disaster.

Chandra did not go to sleep. He wanted to talk to her about the role played by her in the farm. She came at 11.30 p.m. She appeared to be worried. She was surprised to find Chandra still awake sitting without doing anything.

"Chandra, how are you?"

He was surprised seeing the way she was making enquiries about him, as if he was a stranger; she was not in contact with him for nearly a month right from the day she took charge of the farm.

"Kumud, I am contacted today." The voice revealed that he was hurt.

She looked at his innocent face for the first time in many day. She came near him in her customary style, sure of him, keeping her hand on his shoulder affectionately whispered, I am so sorry, I am obsessed by the farm."

Chandra became serious. "Are you so much involved?"

She was restless, moved away from him and sat opposite on the sofa.

"I wanted to have a frank talk with you Chandra. We have, I think neglected the farm."

Chandra was not convinced by her statement. He told cautiously, "The income seems to have doubled."

"Do you know it could be four times more?" She asserted vehemently.

"What is wrong then?" Chandra asked doubting.

"Not today, I shall tell you later with all the data. Why should we spoil the sleep?"

Chandra reminded her gently, "Do not exert much. Remember one thing, we are dealing with human beings who are liable for errors. We have to be considerate."

Suddenly as if attacked by an enemy, she exploded, "Do you tell me to favour vipers and snakes?"

Chandra was stunned by her sudden outburst. "Kumud, what is wrong? Be as blunt as you like but tell the truth."

She evaded the answer, "Let us sleep, not today," she told.

Chandra wondered at her mood. He was sure now that something was not well with the farm. 'Whether I have done the right thing in entrusting the work of the farm to her? It's late to withdraw since she is seized of the problem.' He kept thinking and woke up late.

It was 8 a.m. Kumudini was heatedly arguing with the workers. A young woman in her teens was crying sitting on the floor. "What happened?" he asked reaching Kumudini in a hurry. She explained. How she had come to know about the plight of Laxmi, questioning of Kumar and the various irregularities. In retaliation, Sabi and few friends of Kumar had forcibly taken Laxmi and raped her. Her condition appeared to be pathetic.

Chandra was dumbstruck. Should he believe that Kumar was capable of such things? He became alert. He felt that it was dangerous for Kumudini to handle the case alone. She should be careful.

"Do you want to pursue the case?" he asked hesitantly.

"Do you want this to go unpunished?" she asked and without waiting for further comments, she took Laxmi, her father and a few workers in her car and drove to the Police Station. Kumar and Sabi were arrested the same day.

Within a month however, they managed to return, because the Police on enquiry came to know that Laxmi was voluntarily working in the house of Kumar and she was pregnant without marriage. Because of her doubtful character and the bribe offered, Laxmi's father was advised to withdraw the case.

On coming to know of the news, Kumudini was angry. She decided to oust Kumar and his henchman from the farm. When Chandra came to know of her resolve, he pleaded to exercise restraint. "Kumar is your maternal uncle. They have lived on the farm for fifty years. He may not own the house but they were there all the time. Your mother was born there. She visited them often. We cannot break the bond so easily."

"He is a viper, arrogant, a drunkard. He swindles. I do not want him as Supervisor."

"I will talk to him, please give me some time. Thereafter we may decide."

Kumudini was satisfied. But she made a suggestion, "All his henchmen, four of them, I have identified, should be removed forthwith. They are all new entrants on the farm. Their records reveal that they are rowdies of the neighborhood."

Chandra agreed seeing her intolerant mood and her determination and hard work all these days. She had managed the farm single-handed. She was definitely treading on a dangerous path.

Kumar was sufficiently subdued when he received a call from Chandra. His henchmen were dismissed and it was ensured that they would not return to the Farm. It was revealed that they were wanted criminals. When they moved away with their families, the houses were allotted to the new workers.

Chandra received Kumar with due respect unlike Kumudini. He offered him a seat and after tea, when he recovered from initial embarrassment told, "Do you know you are one of us? You have tarnished our good name."

Kumar unexpectedly broke down and started crying. Kumudini who watched the drama from inside was baffled at the human behaviour. So unpredictable! Is he the same criminal the one who raped an innocent woman who became pregnant and offered her to his friends? She stood there unseen watching the further drama.

"If I am removed, I shall die," he was moaning in a low tone.

Chandra waited till he became calm.

"Save me, I am ruined Sir." Kumar pleaded.

"Why do you address me as 'Sir? You belong to us.

Listen, will you be truthful today?"

"Yes, whatever you say?"

"Did you keep Laxmi in your house before her pregnancy?"

He became alert. He flinched from thinking about her.

"Do not be afraid. I want to help you. I want truth, nothing less than truth."

He was humbled looking back with shame on his past amorous episodes with Laxmi. "Yes," he told timidly.

"I have seen her. She is a good looking girl, tall, healthy, innocent, pregnant from you!"

He blurted out as if Chandra was making a false accusation against him, "Sabi and others have raped her."

"Only under your direction. And that too recently, a pregnant girl. She is having your child. You are a father, a responsible father."

He was choked with sobs.

"Kumar, Laxmi is a good girl. And also faithful to you. Save her honour."

He asked nonplussed and looked up with tearful eyes, "How?"

"Marry her. I will perform the marriage here in this house."

Kumar lifted his face which had an admirable character cursed by the tragic flaw of pride. Kumudini watched the coup de main the way Chandra was proceeding. She thought that he was tactful, considerate of others and at the same time careful.

"Yes, I will but she will never excuse me."

"Leave that to me."

Under the sobering influence of Chandra and affectionate persuasion, Laxmi married Kumar. The marriage was performed in the presence of Chandra and Kumudini in the spacious lawns of his house. It turned out to be a holiday for all workers.

Kumar became an altered man. He worked hard and the income of the farm increased ten times. Kumudini continued to supervise. But Kumar was no longer a servant. He got a female baby and the couple led a good life.

3

1

It was midnight. Tapaswini and Yogini slept side by side. Both were naked. They were within an arms distance but remained separated. They had securely locked the doors. Only the ventilators were open. The light in the room was dim. Tapaswini and Yogini were listening to the sound, the silence of the night, the whispers of the trees, the breeze, the barking of the street dogs, the heart beat, the breathing, the thoughts, the beliefs, the outpourings of words in different known and unknown languages and the past which had no limit. Listening encompassing seeing, feeling, the totality which not only constituted 'self' but even beyond the confines of 'self'; not space which was still limited. Listening to time with the fluttering wings of desires and the unfulfilled imagination. Gradually the attention bestowed by listening created a feeling of pressure between the eyebrows, a pulsating movement. Unexpectedly they reached a saturation point simultaneously. They were hitting within the confines of the skull as if to emerge; the body was a prison. Yogini felt that her form was unreal. What was real was a formless form which was floating beyond the body. She became aware of another form beside her and instantly recognised as that of Tapaswini, Both started moving in space which was not bound by gravitation. The formless apparitions were linked to their bodies by luminous threads.

Both were aware of their mission. Yogini was almost involuntarily following the luminous replica of Tapaswini. Then they stopped; Yogini was aware of a body lying on the floor.

They moved round the body for some time and then started moving again.

Tapaswini woke up and found Yogini entering the body. She expected that she would wake up and talk to her about her experiences. Instead Yogini entered into deep sleep. Tapaswini felt that she was still a novice. She did not disturb her. She also slept by her side. This was necessary because Yogini was exposed to the other dimension inhabited by dangerous forces. A time was nearing when she would be provided with an ally who would take care of her. Till then she was under her protection.

In the morning, Yogini woke up enveloped by the movement of a vibrant media. She turned and looked at Tapaswini who was looking at her lovingly. They had a rapport and instant communication where language was inadequate to quantify their expression. They had reached a point where the need for gross bodies to invoke sex or any state was found to be superfluous. By a mere look, they reached the sensuous orgasm of the fusion of two souls. Like the linga, not the gross, in essence they embedded the ecstasy of fusion.

Tapaswini asked, "What do you feel?"

"Fine. But on return to the body I felt sleepy. It was not a voluntary act.

"What are your views about the young woman?"

"I am yet to learn the language of signs, symbols, colours."

"What did you dream?"

"The young woman wanted to accompany us. She was pleading. She was fed up with her life, with money, with position and her family. Something really unique at her age. She is a very advanced soul."

Tapaswini was pleased. "True, you have dreamt well. But learn to grasp without the intervention of dreams. Those who walk in that dimension renounce their bodies and naturally, words are unnecessary for interpretation. If you were awake on return, you would have told the same thing. At times dreams may be misleading."

"When are we meeting again?"

"I do not know Yogini. There is an Intelligence working which is beyond our comprehension. You will come to know. Do not be anxious. Anxiety can be a distraction."

Yogini had totally lost interest in the past. So much so, it was like past life. She was reborn. The body remained the same Even the body had materially altered. She appeared younger by two decades. She had not asked Tapaswini her age. Perhaps she was very old she thought because of the lines below her eyes and chin. Time had lost meaning. She had studied Sanskrit thoroughly and read all the books. Mostly they were on Tantra.

Once Yogini asked, "Tapaswini Ma, why do you seek only women? Are you an unrelenting crusader for women's rights?"

Tapaswini kept a discreet silence. She approached her question from a different angle. "There is no difference between man and woman. Both aspiring to be wedded to Truth. In actuality, even the man has to reach the quality of woman to be eligible to be fructified by the Other. Man and woman enjoy the same status as far as the search of Truth is concerned."

"Still my question remains unanswered?" Yogini mentioned seriously.

Tapaswini looked at the distant horizon and explained. "If you take a global view, this is a macho world. Women are suppressed since the beginning of time. Our literature, epics and philosophies reveal male supremacy. Characters are created in order to assert male chauvinism. Our marriage customs, conventions are parochial favouring the male species. Women have become a commodity for sale. They are exploited for man's comforts. Even in this country, where we talk high of motherhood and womenhood, in every home, women are treated as second hand human beings. There are Sapta Rishis, three God Heads. Truth of course is the only thing which is beyond sex. These Gods are not real, creations of the male hegemony! The Great Initiator, the

Hierophant is neither male nor female. The true representation of Shiva is Ardhanarenateswara neither male nor female. That is our true state of being."

Yogini felt that Tapaswini was voicing her pent up feelings. The human race was speaking through her. "So we will create an order with female dominance?" Yogini asked.

"Not dominate. This is a niche where we would assemble and work to get right the imbalance. Not by pleading nor by political stirrings but by coming upon the Essence which basically constitutes creation. It's a formidable task."

Yogini wondered whether it denoted a veneration or a kind of worship that was not theistic in principle and was perhaps faddish in practice. Noticing her doubting mind, Tapaswini concluded, "We have dedicated ourselves for a noble cause."

"Has it the approval of the Higher Intelligence."

Tapaswini smiled. "What do you mean by Higher?"

Yogini was puzzled and told, "At times you have used that word."

"Intelligence has no division. You will know about it only when you come upon it. It's not a function of the brain. It uses the brain. Your question indicates that you have no self-confidence, in undertaking the work. Do you feel what we are attempting here has relevance?"

"Yes, it has tremendous relevance."

"Will you devote yourself for the cause?"

"Yes."

"Remember the door is always open. Your stay here is not out of compulsion. You are free. For your information it has the approval of Intelligence. We are blessed."

Tapaswini herself never even once gave any advice. She waited till Yogini, out of curiosity asked. This meant that she was not prepared to impose herself on Yogini. She was free to accept whatever she wanted, absorb and grow taking her own time. That was the law in the hermitage.

Once Yogini asked, "I have read the books in the library. They reveal only the superficial aspects of the mystery. The underlying principles continue to elude the grasp of human intellect."

Tapaswini waited her to speak out her mind.

Yogini continued. "Human beings are a complex lot with centuries of evolution behind their seeming facade. I wonder whether this journey through cycles of birth and death was necessary. No answers are available."

Tapaswini asked. "Yogini, are you aware that there is an impulse in every human being to continue in separation even though Truth is whole, indivisible?"

"Yes vaguely. Particularly I feel restless when I remember the stream of life which at times comes and engulfs me. Is there need to continue and struggle?"

"It's important to put an end to that impulse which perpetuates separation. The books should reveal a mechanism leading to the summit."

"But what about descent?"

"The path of descent is unpredictable. It's not our concern. Not under our control. Here comes the role of compassion, grace!"

"What should one do?" Yogini asked like a child.

"It's beyond comprehension. Only one thing for me is important, to be pure, innocent, whole. Without worry. Let go of everything."

At another time Yogini asked her, "When I move out of the body and float in that dimension, time appears to have ceased. Because hardly within a minute, we contacted that woman."

Tapaswini smiled tenderly and told, "Even without movement, you can reach some day."

"How?"

"Everything is within you on the stretch of your palm."

"Is it academic?"

"No, you have to do it actually."

Yogini missed the point and asked incredulously, "Shall I learn this mechanism?"

"By and by, eternity is before you. There is no end to learning. Till perhaps you bestride the Great Bird of life. Till perhaps you encompass the sea of delusion within the space of a wink."

Listening to Tapaswini, Yogini felt for the first time that she had to learn a lot and that she had not even reached the noble path.

At times Tapswini talked to her in sanskrit and got her reply in sanskrit.

Yogini asked her, "You have great fascination to indulge in sanskrit, Why?"

"Sanskrit is nearer to the source of energy. It invokes sounds that make up for eternity."

The face of Tapaswini appeared to be a very ancient face; Thousand aeons bore their insignia on her liquid features.

Sunday. Tapaswini and Yogini leisurely sat on the lawn enjoying the evening breeze. This was the time when Yogini asked questions about doubts pestering her mind.

"Is God concerned about the destiny of human beings on earth?"

Tapaswini expressed surprise at the question. "Yogini there is no mystery. See around these small plants. If the gardener fails to water, they would die. God is not bothered."

Yogini was puzzled. She continued.

"You are hungry you should do something about it. God will not bring food."

"Does it mean that there is no God looking after us?"

Tapaswini kept discreet silence.

"What is God?" Yogini asked wondering.

"A big question. Answer should come Yogini."

Yogini stared dumb founded. "You have blasted my beliefs," she told.

Tapaswini did not respond.

"Is there no God?"

"If he is there, he is beyond comprehension. Beyond space, time and causation. He cannot be understood. His role is not subject to analysis. When it is there, everything ceases. In his withdrawal, the phenomenal existence breathes relieved of his spell. Yogini I am prepared to take any number of births if I am assured of a glimpse of Truth once."

"Are we toiling to have a glimpse?"

"We live, toil and toil to be fit and eligible for it to come and pick us up. Normally it should not involve any efforts. Doing anything with motivation moves you away from it. Self-consciousness is alive only at the periphery. It's breath, anxiety, hope, frustration, desire. Moving round and round the centre. It's very fragile. It can be stopped by a minor shock or a medicine."

"What do you mean by a medicine?"

"We are going to the forbidden parlour today. You have not yet taken up the study. Now I think is the time. Come on."

Tapaswini started walking towards the centre of the farm. It was protected around by barbed wire fence. The gate was locked. The area comprised about an acre. The shrubs, herbs and trees were well protected. Looked after with care. There were signs painted on steel plates. Left 1 : Tapaswini showed Yogini the sign and told her to walk always keeping to the left. We will come back from the next lane after reaching that end. Do not cross in the middle."

"Is it necessary to observe these rules?"

"Yes at present. Because you are a novice. You may mistake one for the other. On the left we have seven primordial shrubs and on the return path, there are seven variants which resemble the original but with divergent qualities."

"What are these shrubs?"

"They are lethal species. We have grown them since decades but not used them even once. They are just sacred relic from the past."

Yogini was puzzled. "What is the purpose?" she asked.

"Nothing. I will by and by tell you about the nature of these shrubs. They can wipe away consciousness in a fraction of a second and open up hazardous avenues of the other dimension where evil forces inhabit. At times if you are not ready, your brain will be permanently damaged as these hungry forces will envelope the space provided in the brain. The grey matter acts like receptors."

"Am I expected to experiment on these shrubs some time?"

"Never. Without the aid of these plants, we will walk into that dimension well protected by our Allies."

Tapaswini showed the seven primordial shrubs and told her, "Today is Sunday, the full moon day. It's not yet sunset. On any other day, do not visit these shrubs."

Yogini stood aghast. "Why?" she asked.

"These shrubs have the potential to invoke the brain to look into that dimension. Naturally it's surrounded by evil forces. So we are following this custom."

Tapaswini showed the seven primordial shrubs which contained various degrees of potentiality in subduing consciousness. On return journey she showed the seven variants. "These are the intoxicants."

Yogini examined them minutely. "They resemble the original but the flowers show a slight variance but recognizable."

"Right you are."

"Are they also harmful?"

"Like liquor or any other intoxicant corrupt the brain."

"If so why do you feed them?"

"For the sake of recognition. Moreover we do not destroy anything. For us everything has its place. Take care of them.

Then they walked to the right. Tapaswini showed the herbs. "They are life giving medical herbs. Each one has a value. There is an almanac. You will study these plants, their properties, how they are administered and so on. You will become an adept."

"How much time I might require?"

"About two years. We get acquainted with them as you get acquainted with living persons. The herbs have been given names resembling human beings but all females."

Tapaswini chortled in her joy.

"Do they cover all the deceases?"

"Most of them. If there are any difficult cases, we have to send them to the city. Soon we are going to have a foreign trained doctor, an expert." Yogini was curious. "Who? Will she come and stay with us?" she asked.

"Naturally."

"When will she come?"

"Very shortly we have made our rounds."

"How do you know she is a doctor?"

"You will also learn to know in due course."

"Are you so sure of her."

"As I was sure of you, she will not escape her fate."

Yogini became aware of the relentless Tapaswini pursuing her victims.

Just then on the left, the shrubs started shaking caught up in the imaginary wind.

"What is it? There is no wind yet these plants move?"

"Do not be frightened, their forces cannot go beyond that movement."

"The gate is locked. Who waters them?"

"They are looked after by a family. We have provided them shelter. You will visit them some day."

"You are always talking on behalf of us. Who are we?"

"There are others. Now I and you of course."

Tapaswini looked at the western horizon and hurriedly walked towards the gate. Yogini followed her briskly.

"Before sunset we should move out."

"May I ask why" Yogini asked with apprehension.

"We allow them freedom."

Yogini could not understand. Tapaswini locked the gate and moved towards the house. The full moon was displayed brilliantly in the Eastern sky behind the tall coconut trees. The birds were chirping from a thousand throats on the peepul tree. The house was lit by a golden beam from the setting sun.

Tapaswini stopped for a while for Yogini to catch up with her. She held her hand and walked.

"It's so lovely!" Yogini exclaimed.

"Without words treasure it."

2

Pathi woke up with a start and searched for Shailaja. She was not by his side. He sat up. He was shocked to see her on the floor sleeping naked. Like a dead body. Her eyes were open but there was no recognition. It was a corpse. He was terrified. His heart pounded in his chest. 'What does it mean? Is she out of mind?' She had unwound her dark hairs which covered the floor upto her buttocks. The lower part of the body was thus protected. The other part was on the floor. Her face was peaceful.

He did not move. She was in a trance. After some half hour, she got up suddenly, searched for her nightie and put it on. Then she saw Pathi.

"I am sorry Pathi."

Shailaja came and sat near him. "Are you afraid?" she asked. Pathi nodded. "I am not insane Pathi. Believe me please. At times when I feel totally empty, I feel like dying. I throw away my clothes in recognition of having given up everything that cling to 'self' and sleep naked on the floor. I feel refreshed, when I wake up."

Pathi remembered having read somewhere that it was Shavasana.

"Are you practicing Yoga?"

"I have been doing it for the last four years."

"Your eyes were open having a fixed stare on the roof. What were you doing?"

"Nothing. I remember, I had closed my eyes. Only few minutes ago, I woke up." "Any dream?"

She smiled and told. "Not a dream. I saw the faces of two sanyasinis, women. They appeared to be the same two who we met at Varanasi!"

Pathi was unnerved and asked, "What did they want?"

"They were looking at me lovingly for a long time."

"Then what happened?"

"I wanted to go with them. I pleaded. They smiled and went away without telling anything."

Pathi looked at her. He was baffled, whether the woman by his side was his wife Shailaja. Without giving further room for any suspicion, she took him in her embrace and posed for sleeping. She made him warm and comfortable. He felt aroused. He kissed her cheeks and slowly caressed her naked buttocks. She opened her eyes wide and moved away indicating an abrupt refusal. "Not today Pathi. I feel polluted. Today I am in no mood. I have met the holy, excuse me. "He felt subdued by her pleading. Shailaja came near him, "Come, let us sleep," she told.

They slept in each other's arms without further skirmishes.

Daily Shailaja and Pathi went together by 10 a.m. Pathi would drop Shailaja at her Nursing Home and go away to office.

When they were approaching the Nursing Home, a scooter came in the opposite direction on the wrong side and sprayed bullets on the wind shield by the side of Pathi. The driver sped away turning into a bylane. The window panes were closed as usual. Shailaja was frightened. There was however no damage to the car anywhere. Pathi disclosed that it was bulletproof. She did not allow him to proceed to office. "Let us go home. Will they harm my son?"

"He is taken care of in our absence. No worry."

"By whom?" Shailaja asked wondering.

"Security. The family feud has taken a different turn with the birth of Harsha. It's survival contest."

"Am I also covered?"

"Of course. Let me introduce."

Pathi on reaching the Nursing Home called a number. Four persons stepped in before him. All the four were appointed in the Nursing Home at the instance of Pathi. Their place of duty happened to be near the office of Shailaja. Everyone carried underneath their dress loaded revolvers.

"How long this would continue?" She asked worried.

"Till the trouble maker is eliminated. The time is nearing, Shailaja. I do not trouble others. But if they cross my way like today, I must eliminate them for my survival."

Shailaja was terrified. "You remain with me today," She told him.

"No, I am going. Do not worry."

The trouble maker, his uncle was killed in his chamber by his own watchman after hardly four hours. The watchman was killed by an unidentified man who escaped undetected. Shailaja was not happy. Pathi felt relieved and informed her about the elimination of the trouble maker.

"Did you plan to kill him?" she asked.

Pathi looked at the innocent sensitive face of Shailaja and asked; "Why are you worried?"

"Is not killing a crime?"

"Crime refers to an act that attracts Criminal Procedure Code. I am not interested in the code. An animal charges at you and your family. What should you do? Appeal to police or plunge into action to save yourself and your family. You are certain to be killed; also your family."

"I do not know. Did you commit two murders?"

Pathi was speechless. After some time he told,

"I saved you, my son, myself."

"Will there be revenge?"

"Not so soon. The two children are in the schools. Others are scared to death. None would dare because apart from jealousy, there isn't cause for action." "But with these two killings, will there be no sufficient cause for reprisals?"

Pathi became silent. It struck him as possible. "It will be taken care of," he declared.

Shailaja became aware of a new hard core of Pathi. He was invincible. Fearless. She felt that he had spread a spider's web and sat in the centre. If there was any feeling, he could bestow only on the family, his wife, son, himself. Business for him meant money which should multiply, means were not important. Money value was the sole justification for living. She had instant dejection for the kind of life in which she was found. She loved him. Yet her survival was at stake. She felt suffocated by the quality of life around. She wanted to be lifted on her wings free from all compulsions. Instead of having greater rapport with Pathi, Shailaja started looking at him with averted eyes. She had no explanation to offer. Her nature revolted. There was no other way of escaping from the calamity, because the dragon had come out in the open to put an end to Pathi, herself and her son. Yet she felt that murder was murder, unacceptable.

Once she told Pathi when he was in a relaxed mood, "If I am to die or go away permanently, do not grieve. Live freely, marrying once again without ruining your life."

Pathi was exasperated. "Why do you anticipate such a crisis? I live in the present," he told.

"The present has lost meaning to me."

He could not grasp the depth of her statement. He told, "Shailaja, everything is there. Why should present be meaningless to you?"

"Is life we lead meaningful?" Shailaja asked pathetically.

Harsha was five. He was a lovely boy. Shailaja had prayed that she would bring him to Varanasi and offer pooja at the Vishwanath Temple. Pathi also thought that if the vow was fulfilled, Shailaja might regain her mental poise. He also very badly needed a holiday.

It was a radiant spring day. They drove in their car. After reaching Varanasi and taking rest, they set out to complete their vow. Shailaja prayed and found that she could not ask anything; not for her son, Pathi or herself. Her heart ached for the final meaning of life on earth. Coming out and walking away, she remembered that she had not prayed at all. The next day while departing to their place, she pleaded, "Let us go to the temple once again. I want to pray."

Pathi turned the car and reached the temple. He looked at Shailaja-morose, lonely, heartbroken; waiting as if for some miracle to happen. Shailaja wanted God Viswanath to engulf her and make her part of his being. Pathi followed like a defeated man. He held the tender palm of Harsha who would walk by his side till death and perform his last rites; he would grow, come to possess his unlimited wealth and live happily. Why am I thinking of those last days, he wondered.

Just then they saw two sanyasinis coming before them. One was in ochre robe and another in a white silk saree. They were the sanyasinis whom they had met five years ago. As they approached nearer, Shailaja remembered the dream; she had seen them atleast half a dozen times. Looking at their effulgent faces, she stood with utter humility and devotion. An unearthly light was around them. She prostrated at the feet of Tapaswini involuntarily.

Tapaswini lifted her. "Stupid, we do not accept the weak. You are our equal."

A smile flickered on her lips. Slowly she came to Harsha, patted his cheeks and asked Shailaja; "You got a son atlast!"

She nodded, grateful for her blessings. She coaxed Harsha to touch the feet of Tapaswini. When he was about to comply, Tapaswini took the boy in her embrace and announced, "He would be a good man."

Looking towards Pathi, she then asked Shailaja, "Your promise to me?"

Pathi became alert. Tapaswini was not joking. Her pitiless eyes were focused on Shailaja. "You are to offer me, not him," she told.

Pathi felt humiliated, humbled.

"Yes, whatever you demand?" Shailaja told emphatically.

Pathi was waiting. Tapaswini commanded, "Shailaja, come with us. It's time for you to live with us. Come!"

Pathi was aghast and asked "Where do you take her?"

Tapaswini did not answer. She kept discreet silence. She would not be explicit about the destination.

Shailaja touched the feet of Pathi, stroked the hairs of Harsha and told Tapaswini, "I am ready."

The three women started moving. Pathi stared helplessly; his mind boggled reacting to the strange happening. It's only when they disappeared, he realised that she had not taken her suitcase nor had he taken her address. He drove in the direction of the three women but he could not trace them. He dashed to the station to verify the departing train but to his utter shock, the three had disappeared. He wanted to aquaint the police about the mysterious disappearance of Shailaja but he restrained remembering the words of his wife, 'if I die or go away permanently...'. She was perhaps preparing for this day since ages, he thought.

Shailaja sat opposite Yogini and Tapaswini, the hounds who had brought the prodigal daughter home. She was undergoing pangs of death, dying to her whole past. The process had begun years ago, perhaps since the day she was born. Circumstances were such that she was subjected to all kinds of hardships. She had only love in her in abundance to offer others. Pathi convinced her for the first time in her life that there was hope in the world, men with angelic hearts inhabited, men who would go far to seek only the good to others. She was however disillusioned when she realised the unbelievable predicament in which Pathi was capable of double murder. An ultimate good is only an ideal, a Cross which rarely appeared on earth. Man essentially is hominoid liable to errors. When she was lost in this thought, she woke up startled at the slight touch of Yogini. "Lunch."

After food she closed her eyes only to be again carried away by an army of thoughts. Harsha played on her heart, the tender boy who was her darling. Yet she came away at the slightest hint of Tapaswini, because she knew she was being prepared for this occasion since many years. She opened her eyes, they were smiling at her, not talking. So clear it was, she had seen them atleast half a dozen times in the dream particularly when she was sleeping naked. At times she saw only their faces.

Tapaswini asked tenderly, "Any problem?"

"I have seen you, both of you, half a dozen times in my dream."

"Not dream. We came to meet you. You will know about it later."

Shailaja was confounded. It was not a dream!

She was pursued relentlessly by Tapaswini. Purpose? Why should they hunt me down? Where I am being led? She had let go everything : First the will to survive. Therefore it was not important what happened next moment.

After the train journey, the taxi took them outside the suburb for quite some time and atlast it entered a well maintained farm. It was evening. The sun in the western horizon had cooled down to form a ball of red gold. Rays of brilliant yellow created a landscape that was enchanting. Shailaja had not dreamt that she would be in such a place. The spacious house with modern furniture, the badminton court and the absolute stillness as if stillness lived and moved. She sat on the chair enthralled by the sight. She could not help but close her eyes and fall asleep in deep meditation. The beginning of initiation!

Yogini and Tapaswini left her and went inside smiling. The prey had succumbed to the place. No need to tame.

3

Seven years were over. Tapaswini, Yogini and Bhairavi (Shailaja) were sitting below the peepul tree after playing badminton. Tapaswini turned unexpectedly toward Yogini and told, "you are completing twelve years after four days. Before you complete you should visit your home, stay there for some time, as long as you please and then decide whether you should take sanyasa or remain with your family."

Yogini was stunned, it was like bombshell. "Is it compulsory? If I do not want to, what would happen?" she asked.

Tapaswini became serious. "We do not want regimentation. Suppression is not the way. Do not fear that you might feel drawn towards your family, you may not return. No, test yourself, whether you have that wisdom and strength to face your past. You must go. It's by all means mandatory."

Bhairavi was fascinated by the decision. She would also after five years visit Pathi. Meet Harsha; the whole past started flowing into her perceptibly; images accompanied by sensual contents. She realised what it meant to Yogini who was reluctant to undertake the task set before her. She had made rapid progress in the company of Yogini and Tapaswini. She had opened a clinic with all the modern equipments for the benefit of workers and also public mostly poor villagers. She had also studied Sanskrit and attained proficiency. At times all the three talked in Sanskrit and enjoyed the melody of that ancient language.

Yogini was undergoing a trauma. She sat like a statue on the cot. Bhairavi came and closed the door. During the seven years of the stay, she had grown slim, energetic, her eyes were pools of innocence. She went, sat watching Yogini who came out of the trance and smiled. There was not much life in it.

"Are you ready?" Bhairavi asked pleasantly.

"For what?" Yogini was not in the present.

"Home."

"I shall go and meet them."

Bhairavi got up and started undressing. Yogini kept to her seat. She had forgotten that it was time for meditation. Bhairavi bereft of all the clothes looked extremely sensual. She was smiling at Yogini and beckoning her to rouse up out of the present predicament of uncertainty.

"Come."

Yogini was struck up in the past, Sanath. Chandra, Kumudini, Deepak, the baby girl. Bhairavi was like a river, moving and never stagnant. She came near her, lifted her face, dragged her up, took her in her arms, embraced her. Her hairs were tied in a knot on the top of her head. She unwound the hairs and left them to fall in abundance. She caressed her hairs slowly and looking into her eyes questioned like a lover. "Come to the present." Bhairavi beckoned her.

Yogini woke up from her reverie and undressed. They spread the mattresses and started meditation. The past, the present and the future were wiped out.

On the day of departure, Tapaswini called Yogini to her room and told lovingly. "We thank you for your stay with us these twelve years. If you propose to stay at home continue meditating, helping others whenever there is an opportunity. If you decide to come back, there is some work."

"What's it?"

"I saw yesterday, you will come in contact with a young girl, about eleven years. Bring her to me."

Yogini approached the house taking her suitcase. A tall young man came out and watched her with curious eyes. She recognised him. Deepak. She climbed the steps and came inside.

"Who are you?" the young man asked.

"You are Deepak no?" Yogini smiled.

"Yes, but who are you?

She came inside and saw the young girl sitting on the sofa. "Who is she?" she asked.

"Suma."

"Oh, lovely like Kumud, same eyes, hairs!"

"But who are you?" Deepak persisted.

"I am Your Grand Ma,"

They were puzzled. Yogini looked young, younger than their mother. Not a single hair grey. Sparkling innocent eyes of a teenager. Slim, perfect body. She wore a fine silk saree. Long dark hairs. A striking woman, thought Deepak.

Yogini looked around. Elegant furniture had replaced the old. The floor was carpeted. Walls finely painted. Alluring sensual figures here and there revealed the era of the younger generation. She was pleased. On the opposite wall, the photo of Deepak and Suma. Higher up she saw the photos of Sanath and herself. They had already garlanded the pair. She was taken as dead.

She looked around and asked, "Where is Kumud?" Deepak told, "She has gone out, expected by about five in the evening."

Still two hours. She went inside followed by the prying eyes. The kitchen had undergone complete change. Modern with a large freezer and panelled walls. A dining table big enough to accommodate a dozen guests. Everything was fine.

"Where is your father?"

"Hospital."

"Where is it?"

"Near the city."

"When will he come?"

"About 8 P.M."

She saw the phone and rang up the number. It was Chandra, his unmistakable voice.

"Chandra, how are you?"

He had an inkling; the voice had a recognition but he could not place it.

"Who is speaking?"

"Can you not recognise your mother? I did it."

"Impossible to believe. Ma wait."

She waited with telephone in her hand but there was no response. So she disconnected the phone and wandered to her room accompanied by Deepak and Suma who did not believe her. The bed inside was left with clean bed sheet. Not a speck of dust. A photo of Sanath on the table. The same chairs. Nothing was replaced nor changed. They remembered them.

"Who sleeps here?" she asked Deepak.

"No one. Mother wants this room to be left unused."

She sat on the chair, her usual chair. After some time she went up and outside on the terrace. The chair where Sanath meditated! Everything was as before. Quiet, alive! She decided to spend her days in the same room and on the terrace.

She came down. The new ambassador car arrived. Chandra came galloping. His hairs were grey. She looked stupefied. She held him in her arms and looked into him for a long time closely. Tears welled up in her eyes. He tried to touch her feet. She stopped him.

"You look so young, you have not aged at all." Chandra told perplexed.

Chandra went to the kitchen, prepared tea and brought. "Ma, the cook is on leave. Kumud has gone to the farm. She manages the farm these days."

Yogini casually looked at a young girl, hardly eleven standing at the kitchen door. An innocent face, clear complexion and long hairs combed neatly. There was a charm around her, an irresistible charm even though she was wearing a cheap skirt. Yogini asked, "Who is that girl?"

"Kumari', daughter of Kumar. He is no more, died last year" Kumudini was talking. Chandra watching silently.

"What happened to him?"

"After death of his wife, he started drinking, got liver complications, he married a local girl, one of the workers and has two children Kumari and a boy of three."

Yogini called the girl to come near her; she came hesitantly; she stood at a distance, nervous, shy, expecting.

Kumudini continued, "Her mother doesn't want her to go to school. So I have kept her with me. She assists me in the kitchen."

Yogini got up from the seat, went near her, lifted her face and uttered, "Lovely!"

She embraced her, made her sit on her lap. Kumudini was discomfited. Chandra felt nervous.

"Kumud, she is the same age as Suma. Why did you not send her to school?"

Kumudini was unnerved. She could not answer. She had never thought on those lines.

"I will take her with me, send her to school. Let me talk to her mother." Yogini declared.

Chandra got up to leave, "Ma, I have not yet closed the hospital."

"You may go Chandra. But tell Kumari's mother to come and see me."

Yogini was sensitive and did not like the way Kumari was treated in her home. She remembered her childhood days when she had to fight all along to take education and suffer great hardship. How much Sarangapani had stood by her side and protected. He saved and gave money for her education and it was the greatest thing when he brought her to Sanath for introduction. Her life had changed from that moment. In return, his grand daughter was turned into a servant in her house. What a world! She was visibly annoyed. In fact Chandra had suggested to send her to school but Kumudini rejected the idea telling that her mother wanted to earn making her work in the farm. We are proposing a better deal for her, paying double the money.

After dinner, Yogini told both Chandra and Kumudini, "Chandra, the entire property is in my name. I do not want any share but I want an assurance that Kumar's wife and son should be looked after like our family, not servants. The boy should receive the best education like your own son. Will you assure me?"

"Yes Ma. I shall attend to it from this day."

"The widow will receive Rs. 1000/- per month whether she works or not. Do not give her any menial work. Leave it to her to decide her fate."

Kumudini was taken aback. Chandra meekly told, "Yes Ma, I shall give it to her today."

Yogini was enchanted to meet the young woman. Kumari sat by the side of Yogini. The young woman was Kumar's wife Laxmi who appeared to be determined to lead a good life by hard work. Yogini had to force her to sit on the sofa.

Yogini asked Chandra, "Where do they live?"

"In the same house Ma, her old father is with her."

"Very well. Let them continue to stay there."

On hearing the decision about her son, tears filled her eyes. "Thank you very much grand Ma. We would remember you forever," she told meekly.

"You need not do menial work. From today you will receive for your maintenance Rs. 1000/- per month. Your son's education will be looked after by Chandra.

It was providential fortune. The young woman received the news with wide open eyes.

Yogini took her hand in her hand and told lovingly, "The house will be written in your name."

She was simply listening disbelieving her ears. "I want to take Kumari with me. I will educate her. Will you give your consent?"

Kumudini thought that all the major concessions were shown only to snatch away Kumari.

"Yes," Kumar's wife told and stepped down and touched her feet.

It was settled. Yogini wanted Chandra to call an advocate so that she would transfer the property in the name of Chandra. Chandra however showed disinclination.

"Let it remain in your name Ma."

"No. Chandra I am not coming back again."

"In that case, let it be in the name of Kumudini."

"No, it shall be yours. The farmhouse will be transferred to Kumar's family. The rest you shall do as I have told."

After finishing the work, Yogini spent the rest of the time on the terrace. The past played a havoc. The memories were not dead. They came back with renewed strength, the sensual, the spiritual, the emotional moments; the day when she met Sanath to the day he breathed his last; scene by scene, the talks, the whispers, the groans, the orgasm, the ecstasy, the worry, the pangs of child birth and the Joy in the growing up of Kumudini. The whole of the past was alive in her, the meaningless cosmos; the seeds ready to be sown which would sprout and continue to grow and inhabit the earth through eternity! She became aware of the contents of 'self', a bundle of memories and reactions; a battlefield raging with fury. She had suppressed, not looked at the contents, carried away perhaps in spiritual exercises. Here there was the crux of the matter; the 'self' where her real work had to begin. She had returned home to discover her 'self'.

She closed her eyes and quietly watched the whole army of thoughts. Her mind was exceptionally quiet. Dark melodious vibrations enveloped from horizon to horizon, like a moving river. The life giving sounds, the 'kleem, hreem, sreem' exploded and moved in great joy. It moved with an unpredictable rhythm, moved backward, forward, sideways and suddenly rushing forth, and dancing all the way to an unknown destiny. The river touched her, started moving in her, awakening every cell of her body, silencing the mind. Something touched between her legs and a force, 'herself', recoiled, started onward movement with enchanting sounds, bursting forth in ecstasy, stopping at the seven centres and finally coming to the skull, exploding breaking the barrier of body. She lost consciousness only to be merged in the eternal. When she came back searching her body, she found her brain cells luminous. In between her eyebrows she could look and comprehend a translucent thread in which she had to lodge herself, which was not a bondage, yet it was not that freedom!

After considerable time she came down. Chandra and Kumudini were eagerly waiting for her, for breakfast. Looking at her quiet face, they wondered whether she was the same person they had met the day before. They felt she belonged to another dimension.

"I am leaving after breakfast accompanied by Kumari."

Chandra and Kumudini did not feel it right to tell anything.

Tapaswini was enraptured on seeing Yogini coming back to her. "So it happened as expected?" She remarked.

"Thank you. I have discarded the old self I am no more."

Bhairavi looked at them in innocence unable to grasp the inner meaning of those words.

Yogini introduced Kumari to Tapaswini who held her face in her palm, looked at it for a long time and then murmured, "Splendid!"

Kumari was entrusted to the care of Yogini. She was admitted in one of the best schools in the city. At the hermitage, she was taught yoga exercises, pranayam and meditation.

Yogini was offered the ochre robe in the Shiva temple in a simple ceremony. Bhairavi was the only witness. Yogini accepted the robe with utmost devotion.

The next day, Tapaswini wanted Yogini and Bhairavi to take bath in the evening, fruits and milk for dinner and assemble in the meditation hall. She apprised them seriously, "Today we are going to investigate into the nether regions of the other dimension which is inhabited by the departed souls."

They were sleeping naked on the floor; Bhairavi in the middle, Tapaswini in the left and Yogini to the right. Before beginning the exercise, Tapaswini told, "Yogini, we have to take care of Bhairavi."

They fixed attention on the middle of the eyebrows and listened calmly. They were not in a hurry, not determined to do any miracle, just leisurely listening everything, every nuance of time that was night. Simultaneously without the least effort the essences of their being filled with the orifices of their skulls, struck the brain matrix, the last impediment. Slowly they oozed out of their bodies like luminous sheaths of space. Bhairavi and Yogini followed Tapaswini. If she stopped, automatically, they also stopped. Eventually, they entered a dark door, hazy in outline and melancholy. On the other side, they comprehended a world, a vast area with crevices large enough to inhabit. Unexpectedly out of a crevice, a dark compact powerful vapour like apparition came hurtling towards Bhairavi and struck with tremendous force. Tapaswini intervened and tried to drag her away from the evil influence but it was rather difficult. The attacking apparition was a blind force; the most gruesome phenomena! Inspite of the intervention of Tapaswini the blind force continued to attack Bhairavi. Yogini did not know how to intervene. She was however observing Tapaswini and learning. Why there was this attack particularly on Bhairavi, it was not clear.

Tapaswini discontinued further investigation and rushed back to the house. Yogini and Tapaswini woke up. Bhairavi was still moaning. Then Tapaswini uttered the Mahakali Mantra repeatedly and sprinkled water on her face. She woke up and took about half-hour to attain normality.

Tapaswini asked Bhairavi, "Who was that apparition?"

"My mother," She told relieved of her burden and sorrow. "That's the danger, I spoke to you Yogini. Nevertheless we have to explore. Next time she would be safe."

"Are you still attached to your mother?" Yogini asked Bhairavi.

"I do not know."

"You are. Otherwise why should it come to you?"

"Yogini is right. Bhairavi, go into the hidden memories of childhood, youth till your mother died; feel everything and take stock of the contents. Unless the 'self' is burnt, you are not safe on that dimension. A seeker should stalk the 'self' as if it's the enemy. Stalking and killing is accomplished remaining passive, eliminating motive, remaining in the "Mean" between seeing and not seeing, hearing and not hearing, the left and the right eyebrows."

Bhairavi looked like an innocent child. Yogini took her in her embrace and told, "You sleep in my arms."

Tapaswini had another plan. "Bhairavi shall sleep in my room till she is freed from any intimidation from the other dimension."

The three were like children; innocence their armour. They were fearless, indomitable and stood fast in gaining mastery over the slippery path. They had made useful contacts. Yogini had found her Ally who would be with her for many days to come till she was strong enough to discard and stand alone. It was necessary to map the vast Unknown, identify the benevolent forces, the Evil and the forbidden. Utmost care was necessary; a careless step in any eventuality might lead one near the forbidden, the elusive boundary of the unknowable! Before returning near the boundary one should divest oneself of all the extraneous qualities like the gross animality, the subtle causal coverage and the palpitating urge to continue.

Tapaswini was talking leisurely below the peepul tree to Yogini and Bhairavi. "Our culture is essentially a sensual culture. We still name our progeny after Gopal, Rama, Krishna, Keshava, Radha, Seetha, Draupadi etc. Our Sahasranama, the Devi stotṛas are essentially expression of sensuality. Our ancient temples eulogize sensual congress as the epitome of holiness. The whole phenomenal existence is the expression of sex and sensuality, the other name being creativity."

Bhairavi asked, "What is beauty?"

"It's not eternal as supposed to be. Beauty the epitome of energy is annihilated in Truth, the Unknowable! Truth is not beauty. Not Bliss. Satyam is not sundaram. It's neither this nor that, day nor night, man nor woman, time nor timelessness, right nor wrong; It's not awareness! Not perhaps life! I do not know what it is!"

"What is the use of sensuality and beauty?"

"None if it's not for reaching Truth."

"Is it the path?"

"Yes and no. Sensuality is not just sex. It's the totality of oneself, creation, the void of the heart through which one reaches Truth. The sun, the earth, the desire, the arrogant masculinity and the subdued femininity are parts of a whole separated momentarily only to be thrown together. Is it a sport? The self-seeking sanyasi who seeks idealistic sex-restraint and austerity remains deluded. We do not reject sensuality which is essential for the seeker to reach his destiny. It's the power to extinguish 'self' and lead one beyond."

"Does it mean the worship of the gross, the body?"

"Yes, till you have learnt to dwell on the essence when you can grasp and feel the living principles which constitute the two headed sensuality."

"What is meant by two headed?"

"Masculinity versus femininity. In its unity it forms the inseparable Linga, the Ardhanarenateswara!"

4

Pathi felt that Shailaja had betrayed him. During the period of ten years, when she lived with him, she was struggiing to understand herself. She had an insatiable urge to become a mendicant. Nothing brought her close to happiness. She would stare blankly during the happiest moments of Pathi as if life had given her a step motherly treatment. Pathi took her stance as a demand for greater love; she was in need of change. He took her out constantly on pleasure trips but his efforts were in vain. During this period they had no children. They felt deeply that if they were blessed with a child, life would change.

Pathi was defeated when even Harsha, a lovely boy failed to delight her. There was no change. He wanted to seek the assistance of a psychiatrist but Shailaja pleaded that it was not a case for them to investigate, she was not helpless being caught up in any urge or tension but she was not fit to lead the routine life.

While returning from Varanasi, Pathi who never winced at the loss of anything in his life felt totally crushed. He shed tears and wondered whether he could cry. He was unable to give any explanation to Harsha who started troubling him. "Why have you sent Mummy away? Get her back before we go home."

"She has gone out with her friends. She will come home directly. Let us go soon and meet her."

On reaching home, Pathi had to face another ordeal with his grieving son. He knew in the inner core of his heart that she would thereafter never return; it was the case of a person who preferred to get lost. It never occurred to him that out of the horde of females who were ready to win over him, he could get a companion to fill the void. Shailaja had made him insensitive to other women. He disliked drinks. Drugs and cigarettes were not appealing. He took work as the greatest elixir and it brought him money in abundance. He was disciplined and dealt with an iron hand the subordinate staff but paid them well, 10% more than other companies.

At home, he employed an elderly lady to look after Harsha. When he was eight, he sent him to Valley school in Andhra Pradesh. He believed that the Institution would create opportunities for his son to grow into an integrated human being.

In the absence of his son, he felt terribly lonely. He wondered whether Shailaja felt like him. Whether she had become a wandering sanyasi? What fascination she had for a monastic life? A foreign educated Doctor with plenty of money, a Nursing Home, a lovable husband and a charming son! Why did she give up everything? It was a koan!

His cousins had come of age. They were properly tutored by their relatives about their father's death. Their young blood revolted. They were stung by the virus of revenge. They made two vain attempts on Pathi's life in quick succession. Pathi had to get ready for another ordeal. Should he manoeuver and eliminate both the cousins? He remembered Shailaja who had started detesting him particularly after the murder of his uncle and the watchman. Should he merely defend himself? On his behalf, his friends negotiated relating the circumstances leading to the death of their father. Pathi was not at fault; he was acting in self-defence. They were not convinced. It was an open war by wit and man hunting. Pathi was always accompanied by a band of four security men. The expenditure continued to be heavy.

Pathi as a last resort threatened to liquidate them and sent an advance intimation. The response was not good. They had determined to fight irrespective of the consequences. Even Harsha was not safe. He had arranged for his studies in utmost secrecy; praying God Viswanath to spare his life. At this critical juncture, he thought of shifting his business premises to a neighboring State. He appointed a 'Think tank' to work out concrete proposals. He desired deeply that Shailaja should have been there with him to guide with her intuition because he was scared to think about Harsha. "If he becomes a victim, what would be his fate?' He did not rely on a handful of relatives who were not in his measure, above the level of suspicion.

Pathi spent sleepless nights. The two murders were not casual affairs. They breeded worries, enmity and reprisals. The wheel of life was determinate and most cruel. Action had reaction. There was no deviation. As you sow, you reap.

The report prepared by the 'Think tank' was most encouraging. They preferred Bangalore to be the venue where Pathi had studied for M.B.B.S. They proposed disposal of some share from the losing companies and running of the other companies by remote control with the help of reliable efficient staff and setting up of new Industries on the outskirts of the city. They had proposed to sell away the large house and the landed property and suggested the names of the parties who would be interested to accept at market rates. They had also approached the State Government for assistance and got positive results.

Pathi okayed the proposal and dispatched an advance party to find out a suitable house from the point of view of security.

Harsha was twelve years. There were no news from Shailaja during these seven years. Pathi knew that she was dead for the family. He led a restrained life. His decision to shift from Orissa to Bangalore was a moral decision. He could have eliminated the cousins but he was restrained by his conscience. How can he kill human beings like animals simply because they were a threat to his life? Two were enough. He thought that it was very unlikely that the cousins would dare come to Bangalore. They would on the contrary greatly benefit by his disappearance from Orissa, as they would be having few competitors.

Pathi had to start everything from a scratch. He was ready for it because he took delight in working hard devising innovations and taking risks.

Ram was not contented learning about the proposed departure of Pathi. Laxman his brother wavered whether they should continue the feud or should it be ended? Ram however was adamant. "We shouldn't give up like cowards. Our life is also at stake. There are reasons. Your response is not adequate because you do not know the facts."

"I am given to understand that father had arranged to kill Pathi. I do not know the facts." Laxman conceded.

The facts :

Dhanaraj, a city businessman had two sons, Raghuveer and Gyani. Gyani was the eldest, twenty two and Raghuveer, ten. He entrusted the property to the care of Gyani who happened to be very much devoted to his father and also his younger brother. Gyani managed the property with the greatest care and during the period of ten years, created a number of companies which started yielding excellent results. He became avaricious and when Raghuveer came of age, refused to share the property. Raghuveer was given half of the property without taking into account the growth rate. Raghuveer pleaded for equal share through his well wishers and when it did not pay, fought in the court. Before the supreme money power of Gyani, he failed. Gyani had only one son Pathi. When Raghuveer became a disgruntled element, Gyani sent Pathi away so that he was not harmed by Raghuveer who wanted to take revenge. He did not succeed as long as Gyani was alive. Pathi after the death of his father learnt about the affairs of the business and excelled his father. Pathi was apprised by Gyani, a grief striken man when he was bedridden, that his life was not safe, there was growing animosity between him and Raghuveer, he had to maintain a proper security to remain alive. Raghuveer tried to put an end to Pathi; he planned two attacks and failed. When the dragon was in the open field, Pathi mustered courage to eliminate

Raghuveer. At the time of death, Raghuveer had two minor children, Ram thirteen and Laxman nine.

The children had grown up now. They were aware of the gross injustice meted out to them by Gyani, the immense wealth of Pathi, the massacre of their father.

Ram after narration of the facts asked his brother, "Laxman, what do you feel? Should we forget Pathi because he is running away from this place?"

Laxman was horrified to learn about the facts. Ram took out the photo of his father sitting on the chair with two bullet holes in the chest. Laxman covered his face.

"Why do you want to penalise me?"

"Should we forget Pathi?"

"No, I will go to the end of the world to eliminate him."

Ram cautioned Laxman. "It's dangerous. Our fate may also be like that of father.

"But let us not give up. Let us plan. We must eliminate Pathi. His wife has run away. Only one son Harsha. He has hidden him."

Ram gave his verdict. "Let us concentrate on Pathi. Not on his son. Later that boy. The cause justifies action. Not only share of our rightful property but revenge against the murder of our father. It's a sacred deed."

Laxman had completed the computer course. Ram decided to send away Laxman to Bangalore where he would be provided with a job. His main purpose was to find out everything about Pathi; track down his habits; whether he was alone, his friends and the whereabouts of his son; where he could be confronted. It was a huge task not possible for a single person to accomplish. Ram had proposed to take the assistance of a trustworthy Detective Agency and collect all the particulars.

Ram gave him a parting advice. "Be careful. Do not meet the foe seen by him. Ram killed Wali hiding behind a tree. Strive for success. Time is not important. We shall plan after getting all particulars."

2

Kumudini was unable to reconcile with the fact that the widow of Kumar should be given away every month Rs. 1000/- for doing nothing. She told Chandra, "Perhaps my mother wants to repay the debt to her past. She was born there, brought up there and educated there. Should we really lose that much?"

Chandra did not feel that it was unreasonable. He explained to her, "Kumud, that has no relevance. Sarangapani worked on the farm ceaselessly for three decades. Your father did not bother to manage. He took things rather leisurely. He was interested on subjects which were not relevant for the upkeep of the farm. Kumar toiled for ten years and under him, though there were certain irregularities the income increased two fold and for the last few years, he brought the farm to its prime condition. For forty years service, what did they get? I would say Rs. 1000/- per month is a meagre sum by way of pension. They richly deserve it. We are getting enough from the farm and the hospital, more than enough."

Kumudini was not satisfied. "Her son, you have to look after his education. It should mean a lot. How are you going to justify?" she asked.

"Perhaps your mother wants this one done because we are related to Kumar through her."

"Would you adhere to her words?"

Chandra was visibly shaken. "Yes Kumud, even if it meant suffering for want of funds. Fortunately that's not the case. It will not mean a strain," he told.

"I detest the whole affair."

"It's not so Kumud. Your mother could have transferred her share to them. She has written everything in our name."

"What would happen to the house?" She asked.

"It has already been transferred to Laxmi."

She was shocked. “You did not disclose or take my consent?”

“Your mother has written down as an injunction. No use wavering now.”

“Does Laxmi deserve?” she asked contemptuously.

“Very much Kumud. She appears to be disciplined, young. Naturally she would need a house and money. Let us keep cordial relationship with her. We will better start treating them as family members. Not servants.”

Kumudini was angry. Chandra had objected when Kumudini brought home Kumari to do menial work instead of school.

“I cannot reconcile.”

“Perhaps that’s one of the reasons why your mother transferred the property in my name,” he told smiling knowingly.

“And father trusted mother. Love is blind.”

“Kumud, it’s complicated. I cannot deceive your mother.”

“Does she think you will never do anything wrong?”

“Your mother accepts me as I am. She trusts the best in me. No doubt, it’s a gamble of love. I do not wish to fail in her trust.”

“I wonder, she didn’t trust me even though she is my mother!”

“I am afraid, you have certain prejudices about them. You should trust man and treat him with respect. He won’t fall you. The outcome is worth the experiment. I am taking Promod to Queeny’s Convent for admission. They have a vehicle which comes to the door step.”

“Have you got time for all this work? A busy man you are!”

“Yesterday, I went from hospital to Kumar’s house and apprised Laxmi.”

“What happened there?” she asked pointedly.

“I did my duty Kumud. She was grateful. Promod is a lovely

boy. I am thrilled to bring him up and make him one day an educated man."

She grumbled. "What was the hurry? It could wait."

"No, it's not like that. Suppose Promod is our baby, what would you do? I have invited Laxmi to come for food with her father on Sunday. I hope you won't mind. Suma and Deepak are going out on a picnic."

Kumudini became silent with a disdainful nod. She got up and went inside. Yogini weighed heavily on her mind. Even though she went away renouncing everything, she had left a legacy which would occupy her mind for another two decades. "A trustworthy son-in-law!" she told coming with a tray of tea.

Chandra took the tea smiling. "Kumud, we must treat Laxmi with respect. She should feel we are her family members so that she would not fall a prey to others who might try to step in."

"Are you jealous? So fond of her already!"

Chandra took it lightly "You can't be replaced by any woman," he told her.

"Is it? So you give respect and consult me often?"

Laxmi came well dressed on Sunday with Promod. "Why did you not bring your father?" Chandra asked.

"He doesn't like to come. I have given him food."

Kumudini did not lift her eyes. Laxmi took out a sweater made out of fine quality wool and gave it to Kumudini.

"I have prepared for you."

Kumudini looked up almost challenging. It was a fine sweater. Lot of labour went into its making. She was hesitant. But her reserve was shattered.

"Do you prepare at home?" she asked.

"Yes, I have learnt about it when I was in the convent."

"Have you attended Convent?" Chandra asked pleased with her simplicity.

"For some years, upto S.S.C."

"How do you know it's my size?" Kumudini asked.

"You had sent a sweater to me with Kumari last year."

It was an old torn out sweater. Kumudini felt subdued by the gesture of Kumudini.

"What's the cost?" she asked pompously.

"Not for sale Madam. Please accept it. It's a labour of love. You have done so much to us!"

Chandra intervened, "Let me see."

He took it, fondled the material and realised that it was worth the presentation.

"Will you do for me, Deepak and Suma?

She displayed a winsome smile. "By all means I will take measurements today."

"One condition, on payment basis..." Chandra insisted. Her smile turned into an embarrassed blush. She appeared like a school girl. "No payment Sir. You get me wool. My labour is free."

Chandra agreed. "Do you do it for sale?"

"Yes, I have got some offers. I am engaged all the day. I have employed four girls."

Kumudini became alert. 'So she would make money out of sweater business!' She went inside, tried the sweater. Perfect match! She looked lovely. Hesitant she came out. Chandra clapped his hands and told, "Gorgeous Kumud! You look great. It fits you so well!"

Laxmi was glad. Her eyes sparkled. Sensing the warm feeling around, she felt at home. Promod ran out on the verandah to play. Chandra was overwhelmed by the change in Kumud. He prayed that her mood would last till evening.

Laxmi asked Kumudini, "Is there any letters from Grand Ma?"

Kumudini told her, "We do not receive any letters."

"Do you have the address?"

"No Laxmi. But Kumari is safe."

"What do they do?"

Chandra intervened, "They work for the welfare of the people. Teach Yoga to school children, spend time in meditation. Do not worry."

"I want to send them sweaters, Madam."

"Not a chance Laxmi. We do not know where they live." "Why do you call her madam?" Chandra asked, humorously. "You belong to us. Call her Kumud."

Kumudini stared accusingly at Chandra.

Laxmi nervously told, "It suits me to call her 'madam'."

In the evening, Chandra got ready to go out. Kumudini was curious to know where he proposed to go. Generally on Sunday, Chandra preferred to spend time with children and Kumudini.

"I am taking Promod out for bringing his uniform."

"What is the hurry?" she asked sternly.

"Tomorrow the school opens."

They were talking upstairs. Kumudini was arguing, "'Laxmi can manage the uniforms. Why should you bother?"

"Kumud, I have assured your mother that I would bear the cost of his education, as if Promod is my son."

"Oh! You are Harischandra! Not merely Chandra. Take Laxmi also with you, she is the mother, young, attractive, slim and tall. Convent educated."

"Why? Are you jealous?" he asked tactfully.

"Jealous? Of what? Get lost."

She went near the mirror. Chandra came down. Laxmi was getting ready to leave. He told her. "I am taking Promod out. I have to get his uniform."

Laxmi tried to conceal her discomposure. "I can get him," she told.

"No, I want to bear the entire expenditure. We have decided Laxmi."

Laxmi was uneasy to remain alone with Kumudini who did not feel comfortable in her presence.

"Let me go, my father might need me. Will you please leave Promod on way back at home?" she asked Chandra with hesitancy.

"Certainly."

Laxmi went inside to inform Kumudini who was rushing outside. "I am going home Madam."

Chandra was already in the car. Kumudini came near him and whispered, "Do not spend much."

"Okay." He did not like her attitude.

Kumudini saw Laxmi walking out of the gate. She called her back. "You drop her on the way."

Chandra was thrilled. "Great! When did you become so generous?" he asked her amusingly.

Laxmi declined. "No, Madam, let me walk."

Chandra opened the door and called her, "Come on Laxmi."

Promod also shouted joyously, "Ma please come."

She was forced into the car. Alone Kumudini watched them leaving.

Two years. Laxmi prospered in business. She opened a showroom near Chandra's hospital, where an empty outhouse was available. She turned her house into a mini-factory employing twenty-five young women who were the surplus staff of the farm. The new supervisor complained to Chandra telling that he would be deprived of workers if somebody were on leave. It was also objectionable to use the workers without permission. Laxmi was paying higher remuneration to them. Kumudini wanted to ask Laxmi to disband her workers but Chandra did not agree. In employing the surplus staff, Laxmi was actually helping the farm because there would be no discontent. When the supervisor came to know that Laxmi was related to Chandra, he kept silent.

Laxmi was now earning nearly Rs. 10,000/- per month after meeting expenditure on staff. The show room was known by the name 'Yogini knitwear'. Chandra was proud of Laxmi who kept implicit faith in him. Without the knowledge of Kumudini, Chandra had helped Laxmi in advertising the sweaters in the News papers. Laxmi was grateful. She was now busy. She had purchased a scooter as she had to manage not only the showroom but constantly go to the city to make purchases. Chandra stood by her side like a guardian. Once she suggested to Chandra, "Sir, I do not need Rs. 1000/- you give me every month. I can manage very well without it."

Chandra did not agree. "You get it Laxmi, not because you are helpless but because Sarangapani, Kumar and before them, the father of Sarangapani worked on the farm for the last sixty years or so. They were also part of the farm like us. Moreover Yogini, my mother was your aunt. So you get it as long as you live. You belong to us."

She smiled and said plaintively, "Thank you."

"I am proud of you, Laxmi."

Laxmi invited Chandra and his family for the anniversary of Kumar. Kumudini was reluctant. She told, "The children are not agreeable. You go. I will remain with them."

"The cook will prepare food. We need not be there to give them. You should come."

"I would also feel out of place there."

He felt it difficult to cope with the unexpressed prejudice of Kumudini. He accused her of narrow mindedness.

"If you do not come with me, anyway I am going. I shall hereafter never accompany you anywhere. Mother used to attend every function.

"Okay, no further lecture Boss."

It was the first time. Laxmi made elaborate arrangements. The house stood amid worker's tenements. It was a big house with a large compound. She got painted the bleak house that seemed almost uninhabitable with subdued colours and unexpectedly, it took a modern look. The spacious inner hall was converted into a dining hall with a dining table.

It was a cloudless sunny day with plenty of breeze from the swaying trees that was quite soothing to the spirits. Chandra accompanied by Kumudini arrived at her place at noon in his ambassador car. Promod received them at the gate. Laxmi came running down the steps and took them inside thanking them in all humility.

"Where are the children?" she asked anxiously.

"They are having friends." Kumudini bluffed casually. She was aware that Laxmi had turned over a new leaf, her appearance had undergone a change. She appeared refined; she wore clothes with taste. A new scooter stood inside the compound.

Chandra and Kumudini were pleased by the arrangement in the dining hall. Two rooms were used as bedrooms. The other rooms were used by the workers to get ready the sweaters. Already large stacks of them were kept for dispatch. Kumudini was surprised by the volume of business transacted by Laxmi. "How much do you earn per month?" She asked.

Laxmi hesitated. "After deducting expenses about Rs. 10 thousand per month," she told.

"That much within such a short time! Do you propose to expand?"

"I am forced to Madam. 'Yogini knitwears' are becoming popular."

Chandra told her proudly, "Kumud, Yogini knitwears are used by fashionable people. My friends and patients prefer them only. She has labelled the sweaters as 'Yogini knitwear'. You have not seen the advertisement in the newspapers!"

Kumudini became serious. 'Why should we lose Rs. 1000/- per month? I will tackle Chandra to stop payment.' She thought that it was good having come to the house!

They went behind the house. Fresh vegetables like cabbage, cauliflower, ladyfingers, brinjal were grown in abundance. There were a number of rose plants with beautiful flowers swaying in the breeze. Chandra was delighted and told, "Beautiful Laxmi, this place you have completely changed."

She coloured under his glance.

"Who looks after the garden?" Kumudini asked. "My father is fond of gardening, particularly vegetables and flowers. He sells them and earns his pocket money."

"Will you tell him to set up a Kitchen garden for us? I want to learn."

"Surely Madam, I will send him tomorrow."

Chandra did not like the idea. "Is he fit to come to our place?" he asked Laxmi.

"Oh yes, he wants to do work. He needs exercise."

Kumudini repeated. "I want to learn it as a hobby."

Chandra laughed and asked, "Will you Kumud? Learning vegetable growing!"

"What is there to laugh?" She asked seriously.

"You are carried away by the results. You have to toil in the mud and spoil your hands."

"I know," she mocked at his idea.

They came to the dining hall. At the level of eyes the walls were lined by old photos. Chandra and Kumudini were curious about photos of Yogini when she was twelve, fourteen, sixteen and twenty. She looked most charming. Her forehead was unusually luminous. Eyes quiet like pools of deep waters. Side by side, along with the photos of Yogini, there were the photos of Sanath as a boy standing with a cricket bat, as a young man with his father and Sarangapani who had treasured these photos. Chandra had not seen them previously. It was now clear, with so much of archaic reminiscences decorating the walls, Yogini must have been naturally attracted to Sanath. Though she accompanied her uncle on that fateful day, she knew in her heart that she would win over him one day and marry him. That was why she had studied hard and completed her M.Com. She was in love with him even before meeting him. With her looks she subdued him.

Laxmi brought an old album and gave it to them. The album contained photos of Sarangapani as a boy standing near his father and Keshav who was the father of Sanath. On the next page, they came across a strange photo of a young woman who resembled Kumudini.

"Who is this woman?" Kumudini asked.

"Mother of Yogini," Laxmi told. Kumudini was astonished. She had inherited her unique features from her grand mother. Chandra and Kumudini felt that they were exploring an archive where they found long forgotten memories reminding them of their roots.

Chandra whispered. "Do you atleast feel related? You are carrying some genes of the family!"

Kumudini expressed desire to have some of the photos. Chandra cautioned her, "It appears there are no spares. I do not think it proper."

"Why should she be interested?"

"I do not know. She is a sensitive girl."

"Girl!" Kumudini questioned haughtily.

"Sorry woman," he conceded jovially.

The food was served in stainless steel plates. Both started eating slowly. Chandra raised his eyebrows and lifted his hand in praise.

"Splendid!"

Kumudini asked, "Who prepares the food?"

"I cook Madam. These days, I have very little time."

"Do you feel like learning Kumud?"

Kumudini was annoyed. "You want me to be a cook?"

"It's an art Kumud. Our cook is incompetent Laxmi."

Kumudini felt depressed. It was true.

Laxmi was happy Chandra felt that she was an extremely genial host. She served them lovingly coaxing them to try various dishes. She was wearing the white silk saree given by Yogini. She looked beautiful and simple. Her face was naked without the red dot; her humility enhanced her beauty.

After food, Laxmi gave them some rare photos including that of Mother of Yogini.

"Why do you give them?" Chandra asked.

"They are duplicates." Kumudini was pleased.

Then she brought a carton of mangoes grown in the backyard. She had also packed food for the children in big tiffin carriers and insisted that it should be taken. Her affection forced Chandra to persuade Kumudini to accept.

Chandra woke up with a song in his heart. He was feeling weightless, whistled his way to the terrace. The sun was coming up in the eastern sky which was coloured in a lovely hue. The cool breeze, the melody of the birds from the distant threes had transformed the place into a world untouched by the past. It was an exquisite day breathtaking in its beauty.

Kumudini woke up late. Chandra laid the breakfast on the table and waited for his wife and children.

"Surprise!" Kumudini remarked.

"I woke up early today."

After breakfast, he drove to the hospital. There was already a long que. He did not show any preference to the rich or the influential. A worker woman rushed inside. There were protests, and general commotion in the que. Chandra came out and met the intruder at the half door.

"Why are you breaking the que?"

"Sir Laxmi has high fever. She has fainted."

Chandra took his medical chest and rushed to the showroom on the opposite lane, Laxmi sat on the chair with her head on the table. Chandra tenderly touched her on the shoulder, "Laxmi, how are you?"

She woke up. Her eyes were red. She had difficulty in breathing. Chandra touched her forehead. It was burning. He slowly lifted her in his embrace and made her lie down on the bench.

"Why did you come to showroom?"

"Since yesterday I had fever. Morning I felt better and came."

"You should have informed me at once."

"I thought it will pass away."

He gave her an injection. "You need rest. I will take you home."

"I can go on my scooter Doctor. Do not take trouble."

"No, listen to the doctor when you are not well."

He helped her to get up supporting her with an arm around her. She felt like a child. "Doctor, I can walk myself, I believe."

"No, Laxmi you are in delirium."

It was an experience for her. She considered him with reverence. She would never think of touching him. Instead she was being taken by him held in an affectionate embrace. He drove her to the house. In the car he made her lie on his shoulder because her head was unsteady. Her long hairs flew in the breeze covering his face. And she was unaware, absorbed in a sweet reverie by the side of her beloved doctor, warm by the touch of his body. When she reached the house, he stroked the hairs covering her face and patted her cheeks.

"Come on," he supported her and took her inside. After putting her to bed, he searched for her father. He was not there.

"Doctor, you will be late. I shall manage."

"No, I cannot leave you alone."

He brought ice cubes from the freezer and placed a clean cloth on her forehead. He gave her ice touch so that the fever would settle down. Tears filled her eyes, "You are very generous doctor."

"Do not talk, sleep."

He caressed her hairs from her eyes and wiped the tears of gratefulness. He covered her with woollen blanket, prepared coffee and brought.

She tried to get up. He supported her head on his shoulder and gave her coffee. She was shy; her cheeks had turned crimson. After coffee, he made her sleep.

Her father arrived. He was bewildered to see doctor and Laxmi.

"What happened? I had told her not to go."

Chandra gave detailed instructions and promised that he would come in the evening.

3

On every Sunday evening, they met under the peepul tree. It was an occasion when they would discuss subjects in which they evinced interest during the weekend or listen to Tapaswini. The tree was in the middle of the farm. With the setting sun, in the background, they would leisurely talk listening to the breeze rustling among leaves, the birds, and to the sounds of children playing on the outskirts of the farm. It was extremely peaceful.

"More than half of humanity constitute women. The private sorrows of women are manifold. In every home, they are being suppressed. There is implicit cultural assumption that men are superior to women. The boys are provided with good nourishing food whereas in many homes women are made to live on half the quota. The boys get pocket money whereas the girls are not allowed the freedom of the outside world. These private sorrows amount to public crimes," Yogini mentioned.

Bhairavi recollected from her past experience in California and told, "Rapes, prostitution, pornography, wife battering, wife swapping etc. are common occurrence not only in the foreign countries but in this country also. Dowry burning, Devadasi system continue even though on paper we oppose and call for action. These cases are not incidences of domestic problems or personal violence. When these instances are treated as private, there is scope to give explanations. They are essentially public crimes and society is responsible. They are crimes against half of humanity."

Tapaswini was serious. She told, "In the suppression of women who constitute half of humanity, the mankind is deprived of the wisdom and sagacity which could be got if the women were allowed the freedom to grow on par with men and encouraged."

Yogini mentioned, "There is a general impression that women lack in political consciousness, that they are irrational, emotional, and are threat to public life. Many of the women are not allowed to see the sunlight."

"When I was studying in California, an interesting thing came to my notice." Mentioned Bhairavi. "Medical research on women is neglected. Women are often treated according to protocol that have been done only on men. Scientific studies have not been designed and conducted to verify whether there are differences in the treatment of women as against men. I feel at times, we should come out in the open and fight for our rights."

Tapaswini told, "We are seized with the inner, harnessing the dormant power in women; creating a forum of women who would master the forces shaping humanity."

Yogini was not sure. She said, "I feel at times, we are creating a parochial order with deep hatred towards man. Will this not be anathema in a world which is essentially a man and woman world?"

Tapaswini defended in her own quiet way. "Yogini, you are mistaken. I am glad you are very frank. We are not creating any dissension. In a world with male domination and systematic suppression of women, in this corner of the world we are experimenting, having created an order exclusively for women. We are not detesting man. We are only considering the facts. Not that all men folk are brutes. There are those who feel like us. They are helpless like any of us. We have taken up the inner dimension which is sparsely inhabited. We want to establish our supremacy not in the sense to suppress man but attain excellence."

They sat silently looking at the western sky ablaze with the setting sun. Silently, they looked at the face of Tapaswini who sat closing her eyes as if lost in a trance. Slowly she opened her eyes.

"Tonight we are going on a scientific expedition exploring the space, precisely to feel the contents of the earth environment. Not quantitatively but qualitatively. The methodology is different. The acid test is feeling. Making the outer strata part of your consciousness. It is fraught with dangerous consequences. I want you to become aware of the pitfalls. Bhairavi may have to be protected. Be passive. Do not take motivated interest. That is the way we would proceed today. We would be on this journey linked together not independent voyagers as before."

They locked the doors and started on the preliminaries to free themselves from the gross bodies. They emerged like translucent apparitions. Holding their hands, they moved in space afloat vertically. Tapaswini remained higher, followed by Yogini. Bhairavi remained lower. They were aware of a dimension, vast and absolutely calm. They were not affected by gravitation. They were floating in a dimension of nascent energy. Bhairavi was ecstatic; felt like freeing herself from the link and moving, dancing all the way.

Tapaswini moved still higher. She pointed to distant horizons and showed luminous clusters of stars, the twelve zodiac encircling the sun. And still beyond, she pointed out another whorl of luminous manifestations. At this point, they became aware of a personage who had white flowing beard clothed in white light who stood at a distance higher up in space observing them. Then he blessed them and vanished.

Tapaswini moved further. Suddenly unexpectedly, they became aware of the lethal cosmic vibrations, thick, metallic, and vibrant. These vibrations struck the brain cells so hard that

Bhairavi felt that her brain would be blown away, even though they had left their bodies on earth. This showed that they were linked to their bodies by a luminous invisible cord. The dazzling waves of energy moved at tremendous speed from one end of the horizon to the other end. Tapaswini looked down and understood the discomfiture of Bhairavi and came down on terrafirma and back to their bodies. They had spent nearly four hours on worldly counts. It was midnight.

Bhairavi sat holding her head. "I feel as if my brain has been electrified. It was unbearable. At one point, I wanted to dislink and float away in space. I was so ecstatic."

Tapaswini cautioned. "It's not a joke. If you had done that, Bhairavi, you would have been swept away. Probably to another distant constellation. The lethal vibrations which you felt thrashing your brain cells would have reduced you to shambles."

"How can I break the barrier?"

"I think it's possible. We have already been blessed by the seer. He is the Guard of that plane of existence."

"Shall we pray to him?" Bhairavi asked.

"No, prayer doesn't help. Not easy plunge Bhairavi. Unless you divest yourself of the Causal body, you cannot transcend this barrier.

"What should be done?"

"Be aware of the contents of the 'self'. Just as the body should be left behind to nullify gravitation, you should divest of the luminous sheath which constitute your invisible body. Look into the 'self', the substances forming it. You belong to a particular religion, race and nationality; you belong to a caste, a sect or cult. You have certain beliefs, fears. Unless you understand these impediments and dissolve them, you cannot get very far."

"Am I fit to undertake this experiment?"

"Otherwise you would not be here. You have already emerged out of the gross body because you have divested yourself of the gross; the greed, acquisitiveness and cupidity but the subtle barriers still remain."

"What are these barriers?

"The barriers are manifold. Egoism, conceit, solipsism, narcissism, altruism, are all different shades of the barrier because 'self' is sustained by these attitudes."

Yogini, was not sure whether she had become aware of these barriers. She told, "I did not feel the harmful vibrations felt by Bhairavi. It was soothing life giving medium."

"Right you are. The barriers are shattered instantaneously if you are blessed with the awakenment of Energy. Thereafter such an individual has a third eye for which there is no veil in Nature. But to come upon, it's dangerous if you are not ready, not mature, if your nature belongs to earth. This power can destroy the body and also mind ruthlessly. Unless one attains complete elimination of 'self', any attempt towards it is fraught with dire consequences. Therefore we do not encourage efforts to awaken Kundalini. We fight with the trivialities and narrowness of self. In this exploration of self, you come upon Kundalini (Serpent power) in its primal glory."

Yogini asked doubtfully, "Still I feel, I am not independent in that dimension. For instance, what is the state of the sage who appeared in full form and blessed us?"

"He came well prepared, Yogini, you look very far. That sage has created a new body which requires great insight and meditation. Grace plays a prominent role in this dimension. Be aware of the barriers of space, you as separate from the other. As long as the 'self' is afflicted with the virus of separatism, the subject and object, you cannot dissolve, the subtle structure of 'self'. In becoming aware of this duality, there is a possibility to transcend the barrier of 'me' and 'not me'. Also be aware of the difference of sex that you are woman separated from man. Then perhaps you will emerge as the Master of creation and wander in space untouched by any manifestation of matter."

"Are there such immortal souls? How do they live? What is their nature?" Bhairavi asked wondering.

"I can only assure they are very much around us. But I cannot describe how they live nor their nature. Be like them and then you know."

4

Tapaswini woke up with a start hearing the shrieks of Bhairavi. She was crying uttering, "Pathi, where are you? Where is Harsha?"

Tapaswini was near her, shook her up, brought her to senses. "Are you dreaming?" Bhairavi took some time to come to the present, understand her situation. She got confused, sat cross-legged, rubbed her eyes, stroked her hairs back from her face.

"Ma, I saw a terrible dream!"

"Tell me."

She looked far into the night and started talking. "I am returning to Orissa. It's getting dark already. Strangely the roads are deserted as if there is curfew, no one around. I walk swiftly towards my home. None. There is deathly silence. Dried leaves have collected in the compound where once there was a beautiful garden. I run on the road to the Nursing Home. None there whom I could recognise; I am a stranger, I run to Pathi's office. It's locked. I run back towards home hoping he might come back. Just then I hear a scooter approaching, the same which once tried to finish us off. I hide myself behind a lamp post. There is no protection there. Two young men are on the scooter. I am convinced that they are ruthless, determined to kill me, kill Pathi and also Harsha. I am under a great panic. They are threatening as if to thrash us within inch of our lives. When they go towards the house, I started screaming. What would happen?"

Tapaswini recollected the killings narrated by Bhairavi, coolly told: "Action has reaction, Bhairavi."

"Can I do anything?"

Tapaswini came and sat before her. "Bhairavi understand.

We are not opposing fate, nature. The earth moves round the sun, rotates on its own axis. There are nights and days and seasons. You cannot do anything. When you sow seeds, the harvest is due. We are not here to change destiny. You are at liberty to go away Bhairavi. You are not a prisoner. But we have studied you for a long time before bringing you here. Your worry is only on the periphery. Do not grieve. If you try to intervene, you may also be eliminated. You have been saved because we think you can be of greater service to mankind."

She was not satisfied. "Are they alive or dead?" she asked.

Tapaswini sat for some time closing her eyes. "They are safe. They are not in the city. Your husband Pathi cannot remain safe for long."

"Will you tell me when he will be in danger?"

Tapaswini moved her head telling emphatically, "No Bhairavi, we do not waste our energy in probing into future nor trying to change destiny. Our mission is totally different. It's not imposition on the will of nature. We strive to understand. I am a heretic Bhairavi, a follower of Light."

5

Rama read the report prepared by Laxman after two years stay at Bangalore. The data collected comprised two hundred pages. They had prepared a report only when the movements of Pathi had crystallised into habits.

According to the report, even though Pathi had a heavy security staff, he appeared to have got into a state of complacency. His house was located near the police station. It was surrounded by houses on three sides, the main door faced the main road. It was well guarded by two watchmen. There were two Alsatian dogs who remained roaming in the compound.

The office was on the third floor in the centre of the city. The main door was double-locked. Visitors were screened before interview. Very rarely strangers were allowed to meet Pathi. There was absolutely no scope to confront him in office. Pathi was always surrounded by four friends. The Detective Agency who were entrusted with the work were of the view that these four never left his side.

In the morning, he regularly went for jogging. The four accompanied him. He was very meticulous about time. Six a.m. jogging, nine a.m. office, eight p.m. back home. He went to his office in an ambassador car which had bullet proof panes. He sat in the middle of two friends and the other two sat in the front seat. The eyes of these men revealed that they were undoubtedly connected with security. They were armed. On Sundays, he rarely moved out.

His son was not with him. The food was prepared by an old man who happened to be with him since decades. He didn't drink, smoke; it was established that he didn't take any drugs. He had not taken interest in any woman. He was thoroughly disciplined. He was very popular in political circles. But rarely attended parties. Perhaps he didn't want his security to become conspicuous.

A few days ago he visited Madras. The agency could not follow him outside the limits of the city in the absence of specific terms. It was presumed, he had business interest at Madras. He had a Postbox.

The only time he was exposed, when he went for jogging.

Pathi had established a sound business. The market response was commendable. Many of his trusted staff members had moved to Bangalore with their families. Pathi had proposed to construct houses for them. He was a man of protean imagination.

After completion of the academic year, Pathi had taken his son on an All India Tour. He did not like his son to visit Bangalore and become conspicuous. Pathi was instinctively aware that his life was not safe. Of late the security had advised him to exercise greater caution as they were definitely aware that his movements were being watched by a few persons. They could not ascribe any motives to these incidents because two years had passed without any instances pointing to attempts on his life.

Pathi had become suspicious when he learnt that Laxman lived at Bangalore for the last two years. Whether he was being followed by the two cousins? He had a premonition that something was being hatched. At times he woke up perspiring, sat on the bed alone recollecting the dream.

'He comes near a desolate place voluntarily. He is thirsty. Looks around. No one. He walks further and looks back. He finds he has lost his way. He then becomes aware of a house on a hillock nearby and walks up the hill. When the ground is level, he starts jogging. He reaches effortlessly the door which is broken. He enters. He moves in darkness stealthily. Something hits his head. He turns around terrified, a human skeleton afloat vertically in space; he rushes out but near the door stands a young man pointing a loaded revolver to his chest. The faceless person begins to acquire the semblance of his cousin. He seeks to escape. He looks backward, the skeleton is close by. He looks ahead, the man is masked with two slits for eyes. He starts screaming and strangely, Shailaja is there, alluring, and younger than before, holding him in her embrace but crying like a widow!"

Harsha was coming out of Valley school shortly. Pathi was aware that twelve years were over since the disappearance of his wife, twelve long years, stretched behind him like an aeon. His heart ached for reunion. Remote that possibility, he knew. Still he hoped by some miracle, she should atleast come once and meet him.

The place where he went for jogging was a secluded place, with a road encircling a suburb. On the left side, there was an empty space for some furlongs with large trees and shrubs. Some college boys came for jogging but they were early birds. By the time Pathi was jogging, they would have finished. During the past two days, Pathi and his friends saw a young woman coming running from the other direction. She was also an early bird because she was returning towards the city. She had well formed pointed breast which moved alluringly when she was jogging. She had long hairs tied neatly behind her head. Pathi as usual maintained discreet indifference. His four friends two in the front and two in the back ignored her as she was a novice.

The young woman became a regular feature for the last one month. Every morning by the time Pathi and his friends neared the spot where on the left side there were trees, she was found coming from the opposite direction. She did not pay any attention to Pathi nor to his friends. She appeared to be coming from a wealthy family.

One day, three young men were seen coming following the young woman, from a distance of about twenty meters. They appeared to be college athletes. They were laughing and talking to themselves. The young woman appeared to be embarrassed. She however went away without paying any heed to them. She was perhaps not scared because of Pathi and the four friends. They also started coming everyday. The young woman got adjusted to the young men who had proved that they were not much interested in teasing the girl.

Shailaja reached Orissa and took taxi to her house doubting because of the dream. It was inhabited by new people. She went to her relatives who disclosed that Pathi had left the place and shifted to Bangalore. She had no address. However she was sure of getting assistance from Surendra.

Surendra was surprised to see her after several years and found there was not much change in her except long hairs. She had not aged. There was greater freshness in her surprising agility. Not so Surendra who had become respectable, fat and unresponsive; taking things more leisurely. After a brief chat, he gave her Pathi's address and sent her in his car.

The house keeper had grown old but he recognised her. "Madam, you are most welcome. Let me ring up."

"Whom?"

"Boss."

"No, I will do it."

She rang the number, a female friendly voice took the line.

"Hello, what can I do for you?"

"I want Pathi."

"Who is speaking?"

"Shailaja?"

"Business?"

"None."

"Sorry."

The link was snapped. She called the housekeeper. Pathi came on the line instantly. On hearing the news, he jumped into the car and raced to the house. The friends had to take another car. They were panicked. At the house Pathi disclosed the news and went inside.

Pathi had aged visibly. But he was extremely alert, appeared disciplined and determined. He was not a mediocre type. He stood like a statue staring at her.

"You have grown younger than before and more beautiful!"

She was facing a man, she a woman. She had taken bath and was rubbing her wet hairs. He came near and whispered, "Are you my Shaila?"

She took him in her arms and whispered, "Now I am yours, only yours."

He did not bother about tomorrow. He lifted her face, looked at her a long time to measure her intentions, sound the depths of her heart but he failed to understand. Then he kissed her, took her to the bedroom, locked the door.

Shailaja was electrified. He took her on his laps and kissed her breast hungrily.

"I love you Shailaja, I love you, I love you." He murmured like a mad man. She caressed his hairs. "You have not taken any other...."

He kissed her again. "Never. No woman can fill your place. No man who has known you think of another."

His breath was hot. "Is it so urgent?" she asked him thinking of postponing any action after dinner. He fumbled for her blouse.

They lay exhausted side by side.

"Shall we take bath?"

"No, let me remain with this. This moment is precious. "How is Harsha?"

"He is in the valley School."

"He must have grown big. When is he completing?"

"In another few days. We shall go tomorrow."

"Are you safe here? Once I had a very bad dream."

Shaking his head, he said, 'No I am not. But for the last two years nothing has happened. What did you dream?"

"It's a dream. I went to our house at Orissa. It was getting dark, no one at home; I rush to the Nursing Home, no one recognised me; I rush to your office; its locked. Then I see the cousins coming on the scooter shooting all over the place." she gave a ready laugh.

He was serious. Shailaja asked curiously, "Will they still take revenge?"

"Shaila, there is something which I have not yet disclosed. I have written in a letter and locked it in a safe. If anything happens to me, only two people can have access to a few documents, yourself and Harsha."

She was cautious; she did not disclose her stay was only for a few days. She did not want him to worry and spoil the day."

"How do you spend your time Shaila? Are you in an Ashram?"

Shailaja closed his mouth and told "Not today. Let us be with the present. Come, let us move into the house."

They took shower bath together. She walked to the ward robe and to her astonishment found all her clothes as before; washed, scented, ironed. Someone loving and faithful had taken care. She turned and looked around. Pathi looked like a groom in a clean night gown. It was already dark outside. The aroma of the kitchen reached their palate and evoked sensual memories.

She was moved to tears; she chose her favourite silk, went behind the wooden curtain. In the full length mirror she looked at herself Pathi stepped inside. "Not for you this mirror. Today, I am the mirror."

Her nipples hardened at his touch and she slowly yielded, after some time told, "Wait till food." She dragged him to the balcony.

The sky was covered with darkening clouds. There was a depression at Madras. Bangalore was affected, cold breeze made Pathi and Shailaja expectant. There were four persons in the compound looking around suspiciously.

"Who are they?" she asked.

"The security. I am taking care."

She took him inside and closed the balcony door. Even while eating dinner, they rarely talked. They were eager to get back to the bedroom. They stared at each other hungrily.

"We have not talked at all much," Pathi told smiling cryptically.

"I have heard enough which you have not spoken."

Morning. She had a splitting headache. Pathi was not by her side. She looked outside the windows, the sky was still overcast with dark clouds. It threatened to rain, 'Where is Pathi?' She came down searching. He was not there. She went inside the bathroom. Then to the verandah. He was in his track suit.

"Where are you going?" she asked anxiously.

"Jogging."

"In this weather."

"It will clear Shaila. Will you also come?"

"I am having a splitting headache. From tomorrow. Are you going alone?"

"Never. My friends are already there."

"Excuse me Pathi, take care."

She went to the bedroom to sleep. Sleep eluded her. She

started thinking, recollecting. Since yesterday 4 p.m. thoughts had ceased. She had not remembered Tapaswini, Yogini, Kumari and the farm. Even Harsha, her beloved son had not crossed her mind. Time had ceased. She was considering whether she had done the right thing, in renouncing family life. The headache had subsided. Suddenly she remembered the morning dream. She was performing the last rites of Pathi in Varanasi. Harsha sat below the Peepul tree with a shaven head!

She rushed outside. One of the security members was guarding the door.

"Why, have you not gone with Pathi?"

"No, three have already gone. Today I have been told to guard the house."

"Do you know where Pathi is going for Jogging?"

"Yes"

"Come with me at once."

She took the car and under the watchful eye of the security man drove fast as per his direction. Cold melancholy wind was blowing. The sun was coming out of the dark clouds in the western horizon. The birds had not yet started flying, they sensed the weather perhaps. At the spot where they met invariably the young woman, no one was there. The three young men were also not there. Then they heard a low moaning sound of a woman coming from the left side of the road where tall trees and shrubs had created a wall. "Help, help!" A woman's voice became clear. Pathi and his friends looked in the direction of the sound. Suddenly out of the trees, emerged the young woman chased by three athletes. One of them dragged her by the hair and she fell down screaming.

Pathi involuntarily rushed to the scene. So also the three security men who cautioned Pathi not to go further but wait; they would take care of the athletes. They pounced upon the three men and started manhandling them.

Driving fast she saw on the left side of the secluded spot, the three security men struggling, a young woman running away out of the shrubs, a man emerging, with a mask on his head holding a revolver and approaching Pathi, who was engrossed observing the fight. Everything happened in the split of a second. Shailaja shouted, "Pathi, Pathi look out;" She and the security man ran down. Pathi on hearing the voice of Shailaja whirled around missing the masked man who fired three shots aiming at his chest. Pathi was falling down, Shailaja held him in her embrace keeping his head on her laps. He looked into her eyes momentarily in recognition of a deep bond and closed his eyes in peace. The security men chased the masked man and when it was not possible, shot him dead.

Pathi was rushed to the Nursing Home of Surendra. Shailaja pleaded him to do everything and save Pathi. She knew it was over before bringing him to hospital. She recollected the words of Tapaswini, "Today you must leave for your home. It's urgent."

Bhairavi wanted to go after a week. "No, it's an order, run," Tapaswini adamantly had told.

"If I had not succumbed to sex the whole night, I would have perhaps stopped Pathi; I would have remembered the dream in time. If I had run faster, both of us would have been killed. She remembered the words of Tapaswini, "Fate cannot be altered, it's irrevocable."

Harsha, tall, slim with wide eyes came near the dead body of his father who was the last loving person in his life. He saw a young woman with tearful eyes sitting near the head of his father fanning away the flies. He could not place her in his mind. He fell at the feet of his father, started sobbing uncontrollably. Shailaja moved slowly closer to him and took him in her arms. He tried to free himself.

"Harsha, you don't remember your mother?"

He was stunned. He started anxiously looking at her and wondering, "Is she my mother?" About whom he waited from the age of five, right from the day of Varanasi. He cried in her embrace like an infant.

The police unmasked the assassin. There were no

identification marks on him. No papers, no ring, no labels on the shirt. He was a young man about twenty-five or twenty-six. On discreet enquiries with Shailaja who had turned up in the life of Pathi after twelve years and who was also a suspect according to police, it was revealed that Pathi was a victim of a long standing family feud. The masked man was Rama, the cousin of Pathi who had come to the city a fortnight ago. They could not establish Laxman as an accomplice as he had left the city nearly two months ago. Ram in Bangalore had also received upto date information about the arrival of Shailaja and was determined to eliminate her also, if both were available at the spot meant for assassination. His plan failed as he had never expected her to come with a security man.

Varanasi. It was at this place Harsha knew that he had lost his mother. He sat brooding over the Ganges which had swallowed the last remains of his father. Shailaja looked closely at Harsha. Square jaw with a delicate long nose like Pathi; eyes half-closed meditative like herself, fair in complexion. Harsha asked his mother, "Where were you staying for the last several years?"

"Twelve years to be exact. In an Ashram near the Himalayas. We spend time meditating. We are also running a hospital and manage a farm which keeps us alive. We are conducting yoga classes for school children."

"Ma, at Valley School we are encouraged to meditate, think and find out the answers by ourselves without relying on books or any authority. They encourage us to be independent; free of all conditioning. Our valley school is a beautiful place. I am not interested in money making. Why is Daddy murdered?"

He was not ready to believe that his father was capable of murder. He looked at the woman who sat before him, his mother. Her eyes shone with a sparkle, face serene unaffected by circumstances. After some hesitation, she told slowly, "Harsha, your father wanted to save his life, your life, my life. He was a Godly man, compassionate, as a student he educated me in a Medical College and then at California without expecting any return. When my heart ached for renunciation, when I showed least interest in family life, he was hurt. He took me round the world, gave me everything, atlast a son but I was not to be. Normality meant mediocrity to me. At last when I was removed from my life by two sanyasinis, Pathi was heartbroken."

Harsha was moved emotionally listening to his mother. She was a stranger to him. He told "Ma, it has resulted in four deaths. I do not want money. Let me lead a quiet life like you meditating."

Shailaja turned and looked for the first time at her son. He was different, not like Pathi.

"What will you do after examination?"

"I want to study further."

She remembered the letter of Pathi addressed to her. He had concluded on a helpless note: 'I do not know what to do. I leave it to your discretion to manage the property. There is one job I entrust you which you would never ignore. Promise me Shaila that you would ensure that my son would not be killed.'

She sat meditating. After considerable time she opened her eyes. She told firmly in a convincing tone, "I propose to call Laxman for a talk. I want to put an end to the family enmity once for all. We will divide the entire property, his and ours equally. The first choice shall be Laxmans. Will you agree, Harsha?"

"Ma, I do not want money," he told.

Shailaja wondered at his apathetic attitude. "Harsha, money is needed. Don't you like what money brings? Even in the ashram, we earn money out of our farm. You have to live. Your parents have earned with hard work. There is a letter addressed to you by your father. I leave it to you to decide. It's your life. Even your father has not thought of influencing your career. Be free and decide."

Valley School. Shailaja was provided with a room in the guest house. Silence was a living force in the valley. Her life unfolded before her gaze: college, poverty, suffering, Pathi — a giant of a man who was in control of her destiny, extremely good but he was held in a whirlpool of action and reaction; causes set afoot by his father the sinner who was born to a sanyasini. It took four lives in succession. Around midnight thoughts slowed down. Only silence seemed to prevail. Silence was alive and listening. Her life seemed like a fragment a point without dimension. She felt like waking up from the slumber of eternities. She comprehended a point of light gliding in space; at its approach, her body became illuminated and turned into a shadow and started on a hazardous course about to be dissolved. Just then it retreated as if out of habit perhaps or it was the act of Intelligence; Shailaja was once again alive; not of yesteryears; a Bhairavi was born.

She came and stood outside. The Valley was waking up, the trees swayed in the cool breeze, birds floated in the air and swooped down on earth in search of food; there was gaiety in the flowers, music in the air not audible to the ears; felt only in hearts of a few listeners. Light and sound mingled, flowing, filling the universe. Time for her had really ceased and she was not responsible for anyone. She was non-existent.

An Englishman, a teacher came to see her. He wanted to talk to her about Harsha. "I am sorry to learn about the sad death of Pathi. He had contributed a lot for the development of the Valley School. Harsha is deeply interested in studies, very well behaved, intelligent. A deep respect for truth had been ingrained in him. We propose to educate him abroad. We want your advice."

She was mystified at the turn of events. Shailaja looked at the speaker who was a man of depth, open hearted and frank. She told, "I am living in an Ashram spending my time in meditation for the last twelve years. If Harsha is willing, and if it's his decision, no other person would be more glad than me. Money is no problem. It suits me."

Shailaja sent an emissary with a detailed proposal to Laxman in Orissa. 'Beginning with Dhanaraj, a sanyasi to the massacre of four persons, her recent knowledge about the facts; her life in the Ashram and her future as sanyasini; aim of Harsha to lead a good life without greed for money and the solution; division of all the property and equal distribution between Laxman and Harsha, first choice being left to Laxman.

Laxman conveyed his willingness to consider the proposal but he was not ready to visit Bangalore. Shailaja volunteered to meet him in Orissa. Harsha was not allowed to be present by the security; it was told he had examination. The family feud ended on a happy note.

Shailaja told in all humility to Laxman's mothers, "I am going away to Ashram. I am leaving my son Harsha to your care."

The old woman told with tears in her eyes, "Let him prosper. Let God take care of him; no harm in future shall come from us."

"I apologise for all the unfortunate happenings," Shailaja told.

Laxman and his mother were baffled. What an amount of effort and courage it took for her to come back to the murderer's house to apologise! They thought with a reverential attitude towards Shailaja.

Shailaja arrived at the abode of Tapaswini after four months. Tapaswini and Yogini were expecting her to come on that day.

"You have grown in these four months." Tapaswini told looking at her. Shailaja touched her feet.

"We do not like to be treated with such devotion. You are a friend."

Yogini embraced her and told, "Remembered you every day."

In the evening, they sat on the verandah listening to Shailaja. She narrated everything including the sexual episode. She told, "Ma, I have developed a weakness for Harsha. I have given my address to contact me if there is any problem abroad." Tapaswini looking at her unostentatious life style, asked, "Anything wrong if you have given address?"

Yogini was taken aback and told, "I have not communicated with my family members for twelve years and thereafter."

After making this statement she wavered why she told at all. "Did you feel you should contact them?"

"No, I don't think so," she said demurely.

Tapaswini turned to Kumari and asked, "Do you feel you should contact your mother or brother?"

"No Ma, I do not think about them."

Shailaja was nervous. She hung her head down. Tapaswini lifted her face lovingly and told, "Why? You are always free to communicate. I do not want you to be prisoners indifferent to the needs of the innocent. Relationship is existence, experience. I am glad you have done the right thing Shailaja. As long as you do not worry, anything you do is good. Find out his progress now and then. I am also interested, no joke. He belongs to us, the mendicants."

Shailaja was emboldened listening to the statement. Hesitantly she mentioned, "I have not disclosed another omission."

"What is it?" she asked seriously.

"In the will of my husband he has made it obligatory for me to receive Rs. 10 lakhs if I am to spend my life in an Ashram. If I rejected it, he felt it was rejection on my part of his love. Ma excuse me, I have accepted it."

Tapaswini became alert. "Something wrong with you all. Money is not abhorring. I accepted my share of wealth and came here, purchased this farm and house. Without this money, our work would never have been accomplished."

Yogini was shocked by these words, "I have refused to take my share even though my husband willed for it. I felt that I should not touch any money for which my daughter was greedily staking her claim. I also felt that it would be immoral to take money and get away. Out of my share, I gave our ancestral home which was in my name to Laxmi, Kumari's mother and a subsistence allowance of Rs. 1000/- per month."

Tapaswini told, "You do not know today what would be the result of your action tomorrow."

Then turning to Shailaja, she suggested, "Keep it with you, spend it with the best of intentions and discretion." In a lighter vein she added, "We are prospering Yogini."

"Is there any other omission Shailaja?"

"I do not know if there is any?"

"You have entered the flame and not mentioned a word about it."

Shailaja was stupefied at the intuitive grasp of Tapaswini.

"Sorry Ma."

"For this omission, you shall receive the ochre robe tomorrow in the Shiva temple."

Tears filled her eyes hearing the news of her elevation.

"You are a great soul Bhairavi. I am confident to collect my herd!"

6

Laxmi took some time to get ready these days. She was aware of Chandra becoming involved with her. He appreciated her looks, she thought. Whether it was casual filial sympathetic response or whether he sought in her a sexual charm, she was not sure. She believed that she was attractive but knew that she was not a match to Kumudini. Laxmi was tall, her height made her navel region visible. She was moderately well built but her height made her look slim, a profile with slight suggestion of a shapely body. She had an animal grace, an indifference to the glances of men who she appeared to have measured long ago. She had abundant hairs which flowed freely on her face inspite of her efforts to tie them securely at the back. Her eyes were observant and loving.

She came out started her scooter to go to the show room when she found to her shock, a familiar face at the gate. Sabi stood staring at her moving his tongue on his lips. She did not know how to handle him. She had forgotten that he was alive; didn't know that he was released from Jail only a week ago. She remembered the night with horror when she was taken forcibly to Kumar who was sitting deadly drunk and looked at her in his pitiless eyes. She was carrying his baby (Kumari), completed only three months. Kumar spat at her, Sabi came from behind, lifted her, took her inside and closed the door. He threatened to kill her if she shouted, pulled her saree, tore down her blouse and skirt. And then with vengeance... She stood like a statue unable to think further. She hurriedly went inside and called her father and her staff consisting of twenty five members. Sabi was stunned, he was not ready to create a scene; sporting a crooked smile, he went away. He was not prepared to give up because he had once access to her.

Daily Chandra before returning home for lunch would casually walk into the show room, talk for some time. She was not there. The sales woman disclosed that Laxmi didn't turn up. Chandra was worried. 'Not well?' He drove fast and halted the car at the gate. She was waiting for him, knew he would come. She was standing with a sunken face. Her large sparkling eyes were tearful; a calamity she declared with her simple looks without speaking. "What happened Laxmi?" he asked anxiously.

She went inside. Her father was sleeping in the bedroom. The workers had gone for lunch. Trembling in choking voice, she told, "Sabi has come back!"

"What did he do?"

She told in a feeble voice, "Morning 10 a.m. he stood there licking his lips like a dog."

She closed her face, started crying. He was puzzled. "Why should you cry?" he asked her coming near her.

How could she tell him? The terrible night, in that very house, where her father slept, she was raped by that ruffian. Chandra remembered the words of Kumudini. "I understand Laxmi, do not worry. I shall report to the Police," he assured her.

She sobbed placing her head on his shoulder. She did not move away. The place was quiet, no one. Still there was time for workers to come. It was the first time they were coming so close. He embraced her and muttered, I love you Laxmi, I love you since the day I saw you."

Her eyes widened, sparkled with hidden desire. "Go now, she will be waiting," she told in a hushed tone.

A police complaint was lodged and Sabi was warned at the Police Station. His animosity increased. He wanted to teach her a lesson. "Chandra, how is he so much interested?" He wanted to find out. She had prospered. "If I can lay hands on her body once again and get control? Has she changed so much during the time I rotted in jail? He decided to find out. Keeping quiet for about a month, like an animal returning to its prey he sauntered near the house. The car of Chandra! No one around. He stalked like a cat and peeped through the window. Chandra was sitting on the chair: by his side very near, Laxmi stood blushing, listening to him. Slowly he moved away. 'The bitch has taken a mongrel! I will teach her a lesson. Blackmail. Will his wife rely on my words? Or chase me away? Before lunch time, they met in the house.' He kept watch on the movements of Chandra. He was disappointed. There was no set pattern. He lingered near their show room. Yes, she went to him atleast once in a day. Not at the same time. He remembered the night, when he had plunged into her, worked up till she cried. 'My bitch!'

Kumudini was sitting on the verandah. Suma was pacing from one end to the other end reading a book. Just then, they both saw a crude looking man inside the gate. Kumudini thought him to be a worker.

"Who are you?" she asked in an authoritative voice. He was nervous. He gathered courage and told foolishly smiling "Sabi, Madam Sabi, you have forgotten."

She became alert and asked, "What do you want?"

"Nothing," he was nervous. He didn't know how to begin.

"Get out, otherwise..." Kumudini stood up.

Sabi gave an ugly sneer, made an obscene sign with both hands unmindful of Suma and shouted "Your husband and Laxmi," and went away.

Kumudini became suspicious. She wanted to call him back, ask what he meant, why he had come but he was gone. 'Is Chandra capable of playing with Laxmi?' She had observed on a number of occasions the roving eyes of Chandra appreciating Laxmi. She had listened to his words praising her. Have they gone so far?

Chandra came; the same smile; he went to Suma, stroked her cheeks and asked, "How is baby?"

"I am no longer a baby Dad," she grumbled.

Kumudini served meals. She opened the topic. "Sabi has come."

Chandra was shocked. "That bastard! What does he want?" he asked abruptly.

"Why did he come to you?" Kumudini asked. "He tried to molest Laxmi. I have lodged a complaint with the Police."

Kumudini's doubts were cleared. So he wanted to blackmail my husband!

Kumudini noticing that Suma was not there, told, "Sabi came inside the compound and when I threatened him, he made an obscene gesture by hand like this," she displayed the symbolic movement and added, "He shouted you and Laxmi. He went away hurriedly." She started laughing.

"How dare he took this liberty?" he was angry.

"Be cautious, he is a rogue." Kumudini warned smiling mischievously.

"I will tackle him, Kumud."

She asked humorously. "Do you have anything in common with Laxmi?"

Chandra stared blankly and then told, "Kumud, I love her, poor girl!"

"Oh still poor and you in love!" she laughed.

The police took Sabi into custody on charges of trespass. obscene gesture and threatening to molest Laxmi and Kumudini. He was Jailed again and sent away.

Laxmi was ecstatic and treasured the love she had with Chandra. As days passed, she became obsessed with her dreams; at times she condemned herself for trespassing into the life of Chandra and his family. Yet she knew she could not survive without his unstinted support. She wanted to move cautiously so that their relationship remained above suspicion.

7

Bhairavi went to the study room where Tapaswini spent most of the time writing and reading. She was working on a book about the Ashram. Seeing Bhairavi, she smiled and told, "Come, I was thinking about you."

"Thank you Ma."

"How is Harsha? When is he completing the studies?"

"He has already completed Ma."

"Oh very good. He is away from you since the age of five. Invite him to our Ashram. We have a number of rooms now."

Bhairavi was overwhelmed. She touched her feet and exclaimed, "I came to ask the same thing!"

Kumari had completed her M.B.B.S and was assisting Bhairavi in the hospital. She had grown into an attractive woman. Tall, slim, fair in complexion; sleepy half closed eyes; a glow on the forehead; plenty of hairs like her mother. Her oval face had striking chiseled features. She was also teaching Yoga and Pranayam to the school boys and girls. She was balanced in her outlook and rarely exhibited the gaiety and waywardness of the young. There was a sense of maturity.

Tapaswini had not initiated her into Tantric cult which supposed to involve sex. Kumari was taken to be busy and that was one of the reasons why it was postponed. After completion of her studies, Tapaswini started telling, "Who knows why she is here?"

Yogini and Bhairavi were perplexed at her repeated statements. Kumari was preserved like a daughter ready for betrothal.

The day arrived. It was a pleasant spring day. The garden was dazzling with flowers. Everything around appeared new, moving; ecstasy was in the air. Tapaswini called Kumari to her chamber and told, "Today, Harsha is coming from abroad. Be in excellent dress, you would receive him, look after him. We are sanyasinis, we have some limitations. Will you come up to the occasion?"

"Yes Ma."

She wore pink silk saree with a matching blouse; lightly touched her lips with pink lipstick; a pink dot on the forehead; a pink purse.

Tapaswini, Yogini and Bhairavi sat on the Verandah waiting for the arrival of Harsha.

"Where is Kumari?" Bhairavi murmured.

"She must be dressing herself for the occasion," Tapaswini smiled.

Yogini became thoughtful. They were inmates of an Ashram, not the usual family. Kumari came out of the room. Bhairavi and Yogini were dumb struck. She was a perfect model. She came like a doll and stood before Tapaswini, bent down and touched her feet. Tapaswini embraced her and patted her cheek, "I know you are a good girl."

Just then the car arrived. Bhairavi and Yogini stood up. Kumari went to the car and waited. A handsome tall young man dressed in western suit came out. "You are welcome Harsha." Kumari told in her alluring voice. Bhairavi started laughing ecstatically. "A beautiful hostess. I never expected it!" she told Yogini.

Tapaswini told, "I have arranged it. Harsha is our first guest." Another person emerged from the back seat. A young English woman.

Kumari shook hands with her. "Welcome Madam. How are you?"

"My name is Eileen. Yours?"

"Kumari."

"Do you live in the Ashram?"

"Yes, I am a doctor."

Then they moved towards the house. Harsha came and stood staring at his mother. She had become a sanyasini. He touched her feet. Bhairavi introduced him to Tapaswini. Looking at his face minutely, she told, "Remarkable, you have great destiny, my son."

Harsha hesitantly, in a faltering voice introduced, "Ma, Eileen, my classmate. She is a tourist. She is very much interested in spirituality, mysticism and occultism." Tapaswini holding her hand seriously remarked, "I was waiting for you."

She succumbed to the shining steady stare of Tapaswini. Involuntarily, Eileen bent down and touched her feet.

Kumari came on the scene again. "Harsha, please come, I will take you to your room."

Then she remembered Eileen and went to Tapaswini and consulted. Kumari showed Eileen a room by the side of Tapaswini. Harsha was allotted a room by the side of Bhairavi.

Eileen was inquisitive and outspoken. Bhairavi wanted to find out from her what her intentions were in accompanying Harsha. After playing badminton, when they were sitting on chair enjoying the evening, she asked. "When did you meet Harsha?"

"We are classmates for the last two years. Good friends."

"How do you find him?"

"He is a reserved sort, always thoughtful. He wants to run the business of his ancestors I believe."

"Did he mention?"

"Of course. Always. There are crores worth, it appears."

Bhairavi smiled. She asked deliberately. "Have you tried sex?"

"I am an outgoing type, bursting forth on everything. I had sex. But not with your son," she said casually. "He is prudish, so aloof. I have gone through every sort of sex and now I am bored. There isn't any joy. I am drying up for the last one year. I am out to trace my beginnings, roots."

"Has Harsha not mixed with women?" she wanted to explore further.

"Harsha, never. He is a novice, a monk at heart or perhaps the sort of woman has not come his way."

Bhairavi was glad. He was not in love with Eileen.

She remarked cautiously, "This is not like an Ashram!"

"Why?" Bhairavi asked.

"So modern. There are two doctors, a farm, a modern house, a new car, telephone and good food."

"We do not want to worry over these trifling things. So we would have enough time to explore and find out Truth."

She was impressed. Just then they saw Harsha and Kumari coming from the end of the Farm. Both were laughing. Bhairavi had not seen her so happy any other time. She was ebullient, radiant, and innocent . She had carried her long hair in a single blade on the front; holding the end and moving in circles. Harsha was engrossed in looking at her movements. Both stopped abruptly and looked at the sunset.

"It's so marvelous!" Harsha exclaimed.

Kumari turned and looked at his face shining in the evening light.

"I love you Kumari." Words crossed his lips and fell on her heart.

Kumari was smitten with love. She suddenly left him and ran away. He turned to look where she went. He came hesitantly towards the house.

Bhairavi and Eileen sat without talking. Eileen asked nervously, "Who is Kumari?"

"She is an inmate. She was brought here at the age of eleven."

"Is she meant for sanyasa?"

Bhairavi was thoughtful. "I do not know Eileen."

Why did Tapaswini ask Kumari to look after Harsha? It appears under her guidance, she dressed. Why did she not initiate her into Tantra? Harsha is taking absorbing interest in her. She is also completing twelve years shortly. Will she return? Bhairavi was lost in thought when Eileen intervened.

"What are you thinking? You are not with me."

"Sorry."

Harsha became aware of them.

"Ma how are you?" he turned to Eileen. "Delighted to meet you."

"Thank you" Eileen got up and went to her room.

Harsha sat with his mother, "What have you decided?"

"Ma, I like Kumari."

Bhairavi was bewildered. Her son was so soon obsessed with her. She told calmly, "I am asking about business."

He was embarrassed. "I want to fulfil my father's wish. I will run the business."

"I bless you Harsha with a long fruitful life."

"Thank you Ma. You are in a beautiful place. I can come sometime whenever I am bored. Tapaswini told me to come often."

"When did you meet her?"

"She came yesterday after dinner with Kumari."

"What did she tell?"

"Nothing in particular. Kumari showed me some Yogic exercises. She taught me to do."

"Next?" Bhairavi became suspicious.

"Tapaswini taught me pranayam."

"How long they were with you?"

"Till midnight."

So much time without my knowledge! Bhairavi did not like

the way things were moving. She wanted her son to marry a woman who was not a sanyasini at heart. She was afraid that his life would be like that of her husband. Like her, Kumari was a doctor. Like her poor, brought up by others; like her capable and beautiful. Like her is she not a sanyasini at heart? She doubted, she was helpless.

Tapaswini came out of the study room. She walked towards them. Both of them got up.

"Be seated Bhairavi. Harsha, how long shall we have your company?"

"Ma another week perhaps."

"Where do you propose to move?"

"Bangalore is the main centre."

"Eileen wants to stay for some time. She is stuck up."

Harsha did not mention anything. Tapaswini looked at Bhairavi who was not in her proper mood. "Are you not well?"

"I am Okay Ma, nothing wrong with me."

"Do not worry over future. You are a typical person. When everything is there, you become morose. Future is not in our hands. Look at the present how it moves, the nuances, the beauty of relationship, the innocent hearts leaping with joy, everything is locked up in the present! Comprehending it, is Yoga Bhairavi!

Bhairavi stared as if she was in a trance.

"You cannot control the present."

Bhairavi realised that her worries were unfounded. Meaningless.

"Harsha, I want you to do a favour to me" Tapaswini told.

"Yes Ma, whatever it is?"

Looking at Bhairavi, she continued, "Kumari is completing twelve years. Please take her to Bangalore to her mother."

Harsha was obviously pleased. Bhairavi noticed.

"Yes Ma, I like her." He was blushing. So out-spoken. Perhaps he wanted his mother to understand.

Tapaswini did not comment. She got up and walked away. Bhairavi sat silently. She closed her eyes, meditated for a long time. Harsha did not disturb her. He took it as natural with her. It was becoming clear to her why Kumari was not initiated; why Tapaswini repeatedly hinted, 'Who knows why she is here?' Why should I worry, she thought.

Eileen stayed in the Ashram. She failed to understand why Kumari should go with Harsha. She was frustrated; the last hold on some thing desirable was also slipping away. She had nowhere to go. Riches did not appeal to her. She had enough in her accounts left by her father.

Kumari came and prostrated at the feet of Tapaswini. She asked, "Any problem?" She sat at her feet.

"No, get up, come here by my side."

She sat with her head hung in silence.

"What is it?" Tapaswini probed.

"Harsha loves me."

"So?"

"I am not sure whether it's right!"

Tapaswini was amused, "Good Kumari, if you doubt. But do you love him."

She sat looking at her fingers. Her face was coloured. Words ceased.

"You are completing twelve years. Harsha will take you to your mother,"

"Why should I go away?"

"It's not an issue to discuss. All should go after twelve years, whether you should return or not is left to you; your decision shall be final."

Kumari and Harsha left for Bangalore. Harsha asked her, "That day when I announced that I love you, you ran away. What is your decision?"

"I ran away because I also love you," she was ecstatic.

They both smiled. She placed her hand on his and looked out. Very far!

Harsha told in a trembling voice, “Let us marry.”

“How shall we live? Money?”

He giggled, “Plenty.”

They first reached Deepak’s house. When Harsha arrived with the young woman, Deepak noticed that she had a captivating figure. Kumudini and Deepak received them cordially. Kumudini did not recognize Kumari. When Harsha disclosed that the young woman was Dr. Kumari, her grand mother was Yogini, a sanyasini, they were surprised. “Kumari!” Kumudini gasped.

Suma had grown into a beautiful young woman. She had completed B.E., in Computer. She was tall, fair with soft fine hairs at the level of neck. She preferred to wear jeans. She was very talkative. She liked Harsha, his mannerism, and perhaps above all, his immense wealth. She did not like however Kumari with Harsha.

Kumari was a serious type of girl, who rarely smiled; calm, gracious, talked only when it was absolutely necessary. She was very intimate with Harsha who showed reverence while responding to her words. Chandra was very much impressed with the girl.

“How is Yogini?” he asked Kumari.

“Fine. She has taken sanyasa; not a single hair on her head has turned grey,” talking she looked at Kumudini.

“What do you do at the Ashram?”

“I am a Doctor. We run a Hospital. Harsha’s mother is also a doctor.”

Kumudini was jealous. She deliberately asked her, “Do you also propose to take sanyasa?”

“It’s not in our hands, Madam.

“How long you will be here?” Kumudini persisted.

“I have not thought over, Madam.” she told and smiled graciously.

Kumari turned to Harsha, "Harsha, shall we make a move?"

Kumudini was annoyed. 'Who is she to take Harsha?' She told Chandra, "Will you please leave her at her mother's place?"

"I must. I am bound by the words of Tapaswini and Yogini. Let me take her to her mother and then only, I am free. Moreover, I want to meet her mother."

Chandra drove them to Laxmi's house. Seeing the car, she came down the steps. Kumari stepped out of the car and ran to her. "Ma, how are you?"

Laxmi could not believe her eyes. She embraced her, started crying, not out of sorrow but unexpected sentimental joy. "Why so long you have remained aloof? Come, who is he?"

"Harsha Ma. His mother is also a sanyasini with Yogini Ma,"

Laxmi looked at him suspiciously and called him inside. Kumari whispered in the ears of Harsha, "You stay with us. I do not like you going there."

"But why?" Harsha asked.

"That girl Suma is after you."

"So what?"

She was angry. Harsha laughed and told, "This Harsha is after you. Be assured."

Their laughter, talking in whispers aroused further suspicion in the mind of Laxmi. She watched Harsha seriously, and questioned Chandra by gesture. He apprised her, "Harsha is a very rich man, the only son of a businessman with crores."

"Will he spoil my daughter and ruin her life?"

Chandra looked up towards stars & gestured because it was too early to form any opinion.

Deepak was not happy. Kumudini was visibly annoyed. Suma exasperated. "Why did you not bring him, Daddy?" Deepak asked.

"Kumari wanted him to stay."

“What arrangements they have for guests?” Suma questioned arrogantly.

Chandra told firmly, “Chandra seems to like the affection showered by Kumari.”

Harsha arrived the next day. He stayed only for about an hour with Deepak and Suma. Then he rang up his office. Within half hour, four cars rushed to the Farm house. From one of the imported cars, four young men walked towards Harsha and introduced themselves as security. From the other cars emerged the twelve members of the Committee of Advisers who came and stood in attention.

“I shall resume work from tomorrow. Thank you everyone.” They left except the security who remained. Chandra, Kumudini, Deepak and Suma were stunned seeing the way Harsha was treated. They could not speak.

Harsha told Deepak, “You are most welcome Deepak if you propose to join us. You will not repent.”

“Let me think,” Deepak told.

Suma asked, “Harsha, don’t neglect women. What about me? I am a computer Engineer. Will I be of any use in your establishment?”

He told humorously, “Very much Suma. I shall assign you a very important job. Ring me up tomorrow.”

Then he thanked Chandra and Kumudini and went away.

Kumudini was carried away by the glamour of wealth, the dignified bearing of Harsha. She told Chandra, “Why should we not propose Suma?”

“It’s not so easy Kumud. He is worth crores. Originally from Orissa. I do not know whether he is not already engaged.”

“He appears to be interested in Suma. They talk with each other lovingly. They appear made for each other. Same class and style.”

“I think I will be the happiest man if what you say comes true. But I am not sure,” he mentioned.

Kumudini was insisting, "Why are you not sure?"

"My intuition Kumud," he told.

She called Deepak and asked, "When did Harsha come to India?"

"Along with me Ma. About a month ago."

"How long he was in the Ashram?"

"Why?"

"I want to know whether he knows Kumari so well." Suma who was listening all the while retorted, "Kumari is a servant's daughter. Why do you bother Ma?" Kumudini added, "You are right Suma. A lion seeks a lion, a lamb a lamb."

Chandra did not like the way the conversation was proceeding. "Suma, do not talk like this. No one is a servant. Are they not related to us? The distinction based on caste or status is not proper, not relevant. What is essential is character, the worth of an individual. She has I feel character like her mother."

Kumudini laughed cryptically and exclaimed, "Like her mother who was raped by four men, pregnant before marriage! Character?"

Chandra answered harshly, "Kumud, we are at an age when we should learn to grasp the essential. Raped in the instant case is most honourable to me than flirting for the sake of fun. Kumari however is totally innocent."

Remembering her past, Kumudini felt nonplussed. Still she asked, "Do you consider that Suma has no character?"

Chandra smiled not without humor and told, "Your daughter is beautiful. A computer Engineer. But she is talkative, a bit frivolous and outspoken."

Suma was angry. She challenged her father, "What do you mean by frivolous?" she asked.

Chandra realised the gravity of the mistake. He laughed and explained, "Not calm, not dignified, not thinking before talking. Not exercising discretion."

"Who has these qualities?" Suma asked challenging.

"I think Kumari impressed me greatly. You can make out a person by a mere look, a class by herself. Her outward behavior testifies to an inward state of peace, Grace."

Kumudini looked at Chandra in her customary style and retorted, "You are I believe more influenced by Laxmi?"

Chandra understood the catch. "Kumud, Harsha was brought up at the Valley School where emphasis is laid on character building, where from the tender age, children are encouraged to think independently and meditate. By his looks, you can make out he is not superficial. His wealth is not the issue here. And take Kumari. From the tender age, she was brought up in an Ashram. She is a Doctor, a Yoga teacher. Her stature, her luminous face; she is so dignified! I am afraid they are made for each other."

Suma felt humiliated. Kumudini was angry. Suma asked accusingly, "Why did you not send us to Valley School?"

"Very late to ask my dear."

Kumudini asked, "How do you know for certain that he is interested in her?"

Chandra kept quiet, got up and went away.

Deepak was in a dilemma. 'What should be done?' Join the firm proposed by Harsha or struggle to get into I.A.S. He was not interested in the Farm which was being managed by his mother. Kumudini prevailed on him to take up the job offered by Harsha. "How much you would be getting by I.A.S?" She asked.

He answered his mother, "Beginning in I.A.S., about Rs. 8000 after a decade Rs. 14000 or so, at the time of retirement about Rs. 20,000."

"How much would Harsha offer?"

"Anything around Rs. 15000 initially. Within a couple of years almost double."

"Why do you hesitate then?"

"No, Ma, I wouldn't but in a private concern, change is imminent."

"Do you rely on Harsha?" Chandra asked.

"Very much. He has studied in the Valley School where they emphasize on character."

"Then I feel, you should join your friend."

So it was settled. Suma also joined Harsha.

Kumudini was listening to the talk of Suma and Deepak. Suma was telling, "The P.A., Miss Philomena. had no business to stop me. Whenever I propose to meet Harsha she questions."

Deepak told her seriously, "Office is not meant for friendly gossip. Miss Philomena is a very senior person. She was there with his father. Harsha depends on her for everything":

"Do you know what he told when I complained about her?"

"What?"

"Not to question me in future."

"Congrats Suma. Not because of you. You are my sister. What do you do daily going over to him?"

"He talks on several matters and tells me to note. He would revert on these matters some time later."

"Be sure of what you have heard and if he finds that you have missed, he might not spare you. Know one thing, for him time is money."

Suma was adamant and told, "When he is busy he politely tells me to come later, I feel like inviting him for a Video Show."

"Not a chance, forget. He doesn't like. He remains aloof from all clubs, entertainment. I have studied him for five years. Eileen, a classmate of him tried and failed. She came with him to India. I think she stayed back in the Ashram. She was a beauty."

"Then I am lucky. With me he is happy, talks freely."

"Best of luck Suma, hope you endure, but I am not sure."

Kumudini guessed that Suma and Harsha were getting close. She told Chandra, "We must invite Harsha for lunch. He is alone here."

Chandra nodded, continued reading the newspaper.

"I am calling him tomorrow."

"Do it by all means. I think I am busy, I may come late."

Harsha gladly accepted the invitation. He enjoyed the company of Suma and Deepak. Kumudini told Suma to wear Saree instead of the usual jeans. She appeared serene in her silk and decided to play the perfect hostess. When he arrived without entourage of security, Suma asked pointedly, "Where are your friends?"

"You have not invited them. Suma I do not need them. They are forced on me by my faithful staff."

Kumudini served them meals and sat with them to get an opportunity to win over Harsha who sat opposite Suma.

"Do you contact your mother at the Ashram?" Kumudini asked Harsha.

"My mother Yogini never remembers us."

"My mother does not contact me. I contact her on special occasions."

"Are they having good living conditions?"

"Fine, they are having a modern house with six or seven bedrooms, with attached bath, a car, a hospital, yoga class room, meditation hall, modern kitchen with dining table, badminton court etc. Kumari used to teach Yoga and I learnt from her. They speak fluently in sanskrit, even Kumari."

At the repeated mention of her name, Kumudini wanted to find out the mind of Harsha.

"Is she returning to Ashram?"

"I am not sure. She is a young girl with a future. Something must have forced her to go there."

Kumudini got the opportunity. She decided to disclose the

murky past. She wanted to align Harsha permanently on the side of Suma.

"Kumari was working in our Kitchen as a servant girl when my mother took her to the Ashram." It was a fact she thought. She was not concocting.

Harsha lifted his eyes and looked at Kumudini. "Is she not related you?" he asked remembering Kumaris version of her ancestry.

"No, her mother was a worker on our farm living in servant's quarters. Kumar, a supervisor of the farm and a widower employed her as a cook. I should not trouble you with other details Harsha."

Deepak was not happy to listen the way his mother was dragging Kumari. "Ma, we are not interested in the past."

Suma wished her mother continued but she could not openly mention. She desired that Kumari should not dare come near Harsha, who she had enthroned in her heart.

Harsha became curious. "I want to know more about Kumari's ancestry. Tell me," he insisted.

Kumudini hesitated wondering how to begin. Such an opportunity might not come on her way again. She narrated leaving nothing. 'Laxmi working as a cook in Kumar's house; her pregnancy, desertion by Kumar who was addicted to drinks and bad habits; efforts by her to punish him; vengeance and rape of Laxmi by his friends, four to be exact; her decision to complain to police; Chandra's mediation with Kumar and marriage with Laxmi; birth of Kumari who was born out of raping to be accurate; birth of Promod, death of Kumar, helping Kumari to earn out a living in the kitchen, arrival of Yogini and admission to the Ashram.'

Harsha asked quietly, confidently, "Is she not related to you in any way?"

"In a way, yes. My father had married Kumar's cousin sister. It was a love marriage."

Harsha smiled. "So Kumari has not bluffed. Kumari's mother was raped when she was pregnant, I believe."

Kumudini was speechless. She murmured "Yes, poor woman."

The story did not change Harsha. On the contrary he was more drawn towards her. He felt dejected by the way Kumudini was assassinating the character of Laxmi and indirectly of Kumari. He told, "It appears Laxmi was totally innocent, helpless and it's really great that she has survived the crisis and lived a virtuous life."

Kumudini was perplexed listening to him. Whether she had done the right thing in narrating the sordid details?

When he got up to leave after lunch, Suma wanted him to spend another hour to view the video. He politely rejected the idea telling that he had an important assignment in another half hour.

He went to Kumari. She was working in the garden with her grand father. She looked beautiful with her hairs flying all over her face in the breeze and her lightning smile at him.

"Hi, enjoying gardening?"

"How are you Harsha? Missing for about a fortnight at length."

"Busy Kumari. Work at the office is complicated. I am learning. Why don't you join me? Deepak and Suma are with us already."

"Ask my, mother. She suspects."

"What? I am not deceiving."

"I know. She suspects everyone except perhaps Chandra."

"Have you not told her about us? Our decision."

"How can I tell! She is so busy also."

She washed her hand with soap and water. "Shall I prepare tea?"

"No Kumari, I had lunch with Deepak at his place. When is your mother available?" "Now, she comes for lunch."

Just then Laxmi arrived on the scooter. She saw the new car and knew that Harsha was inside.

She smiled and then asked him, "Can I serve you food?"

"No Ma, I have taken lunch in Deepak's house."

She started taking food hurriedly. Without preliminaries, she told. "Harsha, I want Kumari to open a hospital."

He did not think on those lines. "Have you asked Kumari what she proposes to do?"

Laxmi looked at Kumari who was standing near the wall. "What have you decided?" she asked.

"I want to join Harsha in office."

"What work a Doctor will do?" Laxmi asked doubting.

"She will be a Director of our company."

"How much she will earn?" she asked casually.

"Rs. 30,000 and more."

She became suspicious. "Harsha, I wish to have a serious talk with you."

"I am ready Ma."

"What is your interest in Kumari? Be frank." She stopped taking food and looked up.

"I love her Ma. We want to marry. Tapaswini has initiated this proposal. Yogini and my mother have supported it."

It was partly true but nothing was decided openly. There was acceptance of facts. "Kumari did not tell me. But there is something you should know about us. The past is not so pleasant. Harsha, we have made a humble beginning."

"I know, Kumudini told everything."

Laxmi was exasperated. 'Why should she tell? She must have disclosed the sordid detail as she was having a long standing grudge against my family.'

She told, "Yogini lifted us out of poverty and shameful life. She gave us this house for doing nothing. Would you still accept Kumari?"

“Yes Ma, I love her more now.”

Tears welled up in Kumari’s eyes. She started crying closing her face with both the palms. Laxmi looked into his eyes and told, “Go inside and console her now. You are the cause.”

Harsha went inside. He embraced her for the first time and told, “Instead of laughing, you are crying. Fool, tomorrow, you will join me in office. Mind at 9.30 a.m., I am coming to pick you up.”

There was a struggle within her of emotions so intense, she could hardly speak.

The next day Suma arrived from office early. She had gone for the first time in a beautiful saree instead of the usual jeans. She appeared completely shattered. Kumudini was shocked. “What happened?” she asked.

“I do not wish to work with Harsha, Ma.”

“Why?”

“Kumari came today accompanied by Harsha. He has appointed her as Director. She is in charge of office. She supervises the work of even Deepak.”

She could not speak further. Words did not come out. She was crying as if she lost everything.

“Director? What is her salary?”

“Rs. 30,000 and plus!”

Kumudini felt her mouth drying up. She took a glass of water. Have I erred in disclosing the facts yesterday? Are they in love? Have they planned to marry? She wanted to contact Laxmi and find out.

Deepak was not discontented. He understood the day he arrived with Kumari.

“Do you propose to continue?” Kumudini asked.

“Of course. After two years, he has promised a Managing Director’s post.”

“But Kumari is already Director.”

“Ma, she becomes his family. After marriage, she might not come to office. Suma is a fool dreaming about things which are not within her grasp.”

Kumudini murmured, “What a luck!”

“Ma, atleast now you will treat Kumari as a family member.”

She sat thinking : ‘Laxmi! My children will be provided employment by her mercy. Kumari! A servant girl marrying a prince! Suma is no match to him. Chandra is right. He has intuition. Perhaps Laxmi will now be his favourite.’

As a last resort, she wanted to influence Laxmi and prevent Kumari from marrying Harsha. ‘Will I succeed? Why not try? She has taken the maximum benefit from us. If my mother had not taken Kumari to the Ashram and educated her, she would not have been a doctor. If I had not taken her to the Police station, Chandra mediated with Kumar, what would be her fate? She married Kumar, brought up a family because of us. Payment of Rs. 1000 per month for doing nothing and she has prospered. Promod got educated by us. Why should she not sacrifice a little for the sake of Suma.’ Laxmi was busy, she knew. So she sent a word through her clerk that she should come and meet her at 10 a.m. Chandra would not be there; Suma would be there because she had abstained from going to office.

At 10 a.m., Laxmi came on her scooter. She was not like before, a worker woman. She was in a simple white silk saree. A naked face. She had used cosmetic and looked attractive. Her income had increased many fold. She was getting around Rs. 30,000 per month, Kumudini knew and was jealous. Laxmi, over and above, was not behaving as before in a servile attitude; not submissive either.

Kumudini went and invited her at the door. “I am troubling you Laxmi, please come.”

Laxmi who hesitated in the past to sit before her, quietly resumed her seat on a sofa and looked around. She was visiting the house after nearly twelve years. A servant girl brought tea and placed it before her.

"How is work?" Kumudini asked.

"Usual, not bad. How are you Madam?"

Laxmi was speaking as an intellectual. Kumudini felt the change. She asked, "When is Kumari going back to Ashram?"

Her voice was a little rude even though she intended it to be polite. Laxmi, a sensitive woman grasped the background and wondered why her daughter should go back to the Ashram?

"Why should she go back?" she asked seriously.

Kumudini felt that she had taken a wrong step. Suma, standing behind the door, listened. With her heart beating in her ears.

"No, I mean whether she intends to continue with you?"

"I do not know. I am so busy. She is with me only for a couple of months. Perhaps too early to enquire for her departure."

Kumudini thought that she was again on the wrong side. Why should Kumari go away? She decided to approach it from a different angle.

"Laxmi, I want some help from you." Kumudini stopped. Rather her voice faltered. She wondered whether she had done the night thing in seeking help being a superior person.

Laxmi sat expectant, listening.

"Suma is in love with Harsha! She is heart broken for the last two days."

Laxmi smiled involuntarily. She understood the problem. She kept quiet. She had nothing to say. Suma watched her from behind the door and was angry.

"Will you tell Kumari not to stand in her way?"

Laxmi felt as if a cobra had stung her; she was startled. "I do not know. Kumari is independent. I wanted her to open a hospital. She has refused, joined Harsha. I cannot stop her from any of her decisions."

Kumudini was annoyed. Suma desperate.

Kumudini bursted out, spilling all over. "Laxmi, you have taken from us so much of help; we have lifted you out of poverty, gave you house, educated your daughter, paid Rs. 1000 per month, educated Promod; you aren't prepared to do a little for us?"

Laxmi got up form the seat. Kumudini shouted, "Take tea, why are you getting up?"

"I am already late. If I can do something, please tell me. I will help. I do not wish to interfere in Kumari's life. Harsha loves her. Suma would do better to keep aloof."

She started walking out. Kumudini snapped, "You mind your own business. Why should you advise Suma?"

"Look how arrogant she behaves! You tell Daddy."

"Your Daddy, he licks her arse."

Chandra came home whistling. Suma was sitting with a sunken face. "Kumud, how are you?"

"Why are you so happy? That girl is heartbroken. You enjoy."

"Heartbroken! Within only a fortnight of meeting a man. Tell her to mend her heart. Nonsense."

Kumudini followed him inside, "What is nonsense"

"How can she fall in love?" Chandra asked seriously.

"Like Kumari."

"Harsha loves her Kumud."

"Can you help your daughter?"

"How?"

"Talk to Laxmi. She will listen to you. You have done so much."

"What should I talk?"

"To tell Kumari to stay away from Harsha."

"That's all. You think they would stop loving. Even if Kumari stays away, your daughter cannot get near Harsha."

5

Shivaranjani (Eileen) was asked to publish a monthly magazine highlighting the activities of the Ashram. Tapaswini was of the view that a time had come when there was need to apprise the world of the potentiality of women; also about the existing inequality of opportunities and travails suffered by them. Shivaranjani laid special emphasis on the role of mass media in shaping public opinion and creating opportunities for women to come out of the traditional grooves. There was need to educate women to view themselves as better half not outdated outmoded specimen. Even though women had better opportunities for work and education as compared with those in the past, they were still habituated to respond in a more conventional manner. She had an ambitious role to counter the gender role stereotypes and to inspire public to become aware of the need of women.

Shivaranjani under the able guidance of Tapaswini, Yogini and Bhairavi made remarkable progress within only a short time. She attained a state of being which was most flexible, eagerness to learn that was challenging and exciting.

She had discarded the western dress and preferred to wear saree. In the beginning of her initiation into the modes of meditation, she was dismayed when Bhairavi stood naked before her without a stitch of cloth. An Indian woman naked! Shivaranjani stared with doubts. Her suppressed impulses which were held in abeyance for nearly two years unleashed their hoods. Her nostrils dilated, eyes widened, mouth watered. Above all when Bhairavi invited her with a smile, she doubted whether she had done the right thing 'in having remained behind Harsha in the Ashram? Homosexuality was not new to her. Is it prevalent in this Ashram? Are they deceiving themselves? Whether I am carried away by the glamour of this place'? She was influenced by books which prescribed strict discipline, avoidance of sex in any form and sadhana. What is this women provoking me to do? Bhairavi slowly walked towards her. "Come Shivaranjani, why do you hesitate'? What makes you shrink? Give up everything which you hold as right, moral. Come." she told her.

Shivaranjani did not move. Bhairavi came and put her arms around her and lifted her. She stood up reluctantly and was about to ask, "Why?" Bhairavi closed her mouth with her fingers and started unbuttoning her skirt. Bhairavi looked at her naked body, embraced her affectionately. Shivaranjani lost all restraint, discrimination of good and evil and felt that merging with Bhairavi was the only real, everything else was evil. When Shivaranjani was out of her groove still wondering expecting more episodes of sensual indulgence, Bhairavi took her to the centre of the room and made her sit cross-legged. She taught her pranayam and yogasanas. After half-hour they both closed their eyes and meditated. They were unconcerned about ideas, right or wrong. Innocence was the source from where they made their beginning, innocence was the middle and it was the end. What was important was not the methodology, what they had already done, what they intended to do hereafter but the unsatiable thirst for the unknowable, Truth, without knowing anything about it. Knowledge, they had realised would act as an impediment; no guide would take them to that abode. If there was anyone who undertook journey, the one who by chance came upon it, would have lost track of journey on the threshold of the unknowable because it was not perhaps awareness, which normally was part of consciousness. 'There is no path', they knew for certain.

Shivaranjani woke up from the trance-like meditation only when Bhairavi repeatedly uttered 'Om'.

When she woke up, she was a new individual who had lost peripheral phobias, parameters of moral and immoral, the good and the bad. She was out of duality.

Tapaswini these days often closetted with Yogini. There were several nights when they were together exploring secretly.

One day, Tapaswini called Yogini to join her in a unique experiment. Tapaswini closed her eyes and meditated : Yogini was instructed to watch. The face of Tapaswini was illumined by an unearthly light, her naked body was surrounded by a mist of vapour. Sometime she was there, and at other times she was not there! Yogini doubted, pinched herself to make sure that she was not being hypnotised nor sleeping. Then before her very eyes, Tapaswini vanished.

Yogini shook herself up. There was silence. The room was empty. For the first time, a chill fear seized her. She was in the presence of a strange person who was not the mediocre type, not a homo sapien. She looked around and suddenly turned back to see whether she was there making fun. No. She moved her hand slowly at the place where she sat. It was not an illusion, nothing solid was there.

One hour passed. She started praying, failing, she closed her eyes and meditated. Somebody was knocking at the door. She woke up with a start. 'Should she open?' She walked slowly, hesitantly, opened the door. Tapaswini came inside smiling. She was not naked. She was wearing a different saree. Tapaswini closed the door, came and sat down.

Yogini sat spell bound. Tapaswini tried to explain; "In listening, becoming aware of thought, you lose thought, if it is true listening. In becoming aware of feeling, you lose the barrier of sense organs. In becoming aware of form as separate from space, you lose form-barrier. In becoming aware of time, the object and subject, you lose the sense of both. Not only the sense, the Eye of the Spirit lifts the gross matter of body to the stature of its nature. This is not a magic but a distinct possibility for everyone who has vowed to tread on the path."

Yogini asked innocently. "Does it mean, no need for this body to age, suffer from diseases and disintegration?"

"What is there to disintegrate?"

Tapaswini asked, "I have not understood"

"A shadow has no substance, Yogini,"

"But still your body is there now, solid, it has weight, colour, form. Is it not subject to age, desease, and death like any other body?"

"Yes and no. I am complete without it and also with it. That is Truth!"

"Will you teach me? This knowledge appears to be strange!"

"Nothing is there to teach Yogini. When You become aware of subject and object, the duality, learning begins. What you take as awareness is held in the fist of sensations. It's not awareness. It's a dualistic response of the struggle for survival of self. True awareness is immeasurable! It should come. It's not yours nor anothers. When It's there duality leaves no residue. Then the door opens. As one grows in spirituality, one becomes less mortal, more aligned with eternal things. A time comes when death becomes an art of living and opens up vast possibilities."

Tapaswini was becoming a rarity. She was not available for discussion to Bhairavi and Shivaranjani. Only through Yogini, she contacted the outside world. However once in a month she appeared on the verandah, a little distance away from all of them. The only communication appeared to be her smile. All compassionate and glowing. She did not talk to them. It appeared she was involved in some major sadhana which was not becoming accessible for their knowledge.

Once Bhairavi and Shivaranjani ventured to go near her but were stopped by an invisible force which was like concentrated wind preventing them in their onward movement. On that day, she smiled and whispered, "Sit down."

They sat down on the floor. Yogini stood by the side of Tapaswini.

Bhairavi told anxiously, "Ma, we are worried about you. Are you not well?"

"I am alright Bhairavi. I need seclusion. Co-operate with me."

"We were prevented from approaching you by an invisible force."

"You were prevented by your own aura. Consciousness. When I am in this state, you cannot come near at times. Do not be anxious. Fruit takes time to appear. It should not be forced."

Shivaranjani elucidated the major events in the Ashram in the magazine 'Tapaswini'. It was becoming popular, not only among women but all over the country. A regular stream of visitors kept them busy. Tapaswini did not meet them. Majority of the visitors came seeking miracles influenced by the articles of Shivaranjani. Unlike other Ashrams where visitors were fed on superstitions, assurances and false hopes, here there were no incentives. Some of the serious individuals however were much impressed by the serenity of the place and the baffling silence that enveloped the Ashram. Those who sought fulfillment of their selfish needs became disappointed and generally, did not return. Some persons stayed in the Guest House and spent time discussing intricate problems of the spiritual dimension. These discussions were protests from some young men who were intent on joining the Ashram when they, learnt a blanket prohibition on males. Yogini did not give any specific reasons. "We are not yet ready to receive man. Moreover, this is a private Ashram not for public. It's not managed on public contribution."

"Does it not amount to discrimination?" Some of them argued.

"May be." Yogini would smile simply and tell, "We have been discriminated since ages and we have borne it with a smile. Permit us to live peacefully."

Some of them asked to be initiated by Tapaswini. She clarified through Yogini, "We do not initiate anyone. Not even the inmates here. We are followers of light. We are not practicing any method, any sadhana. There is no Path to Truth. It should come!"

Yogini was endowed by a rare insight. To be accurate, she had attained a Median View. She comprehended the solution to many of the problems by an insight between her eyebrows. A third Eye had opened which had become natural for her. She grasped not by analytical study of problems. She asked Shivaranjani, "You are here for the last four years. You have not corresponded with your families. Forgotten. What is on your mind?"

"Ma, I am allowing myself a grand exposure to your culture. There is no urge to get away."

"Shivaranjani, have you any compulsions, hidden or likely to materialize in the near future?

Shivaranjani thought over and then told, "If there are, it should be concerned with my own nature, about which I am still uncertain. Family? I have no father. An old mother is looked after by my two brothers. I am independent. No lovers." She smiled and continued, "I do not think any one has taken sexual interest in me. If there were some previous contact, the very fact that they have not bothered to trouble me for the last four years discredit my suitors. Ma, allow me some more time."

Yogini liked her, appreciated her grasp of human nature.

"What is your inner desire?"

"Is it Ashram? Devoting life for exploration of the Unknown, the Unknowable? I am still wondering. I am more inclined to continue."

"Good, tonight, we shall take you on a trip."

Returning to her body, Shivaranjani fully aware of the journey looked at Bhairavi and Yogini with a feeling of total elation. It was a rebirth in another dimension. The next day she came forward to donate the balance in her savings, Rs. 4 lakhs.

Yogini told her. "You have already paid us Rs. 1 lakh. We are not demanding money as long as we can manage with our own resources. If you are giving out of your free will, we accept it provided the offer is unconditional. After completion of twelve years, every member is free to go back to his place. Then you have to decide whether to come back or stay away. You may need money then."

The testing period was unduly long, thought Shivaranjani.

Tapaswini was fasting every night. She lived mostly on fruits, herbs and milk. She had grown slim. Her face had become luminous. On the New Moon day, she called Yogini to her room and closed the door. "Yogini, some time ago, you wanted to know about my past. I think the time has come for you to know," she averred.

Yogini became panicky. "Can it not wait?" she asked.

"No, Yogini, there are certain compulsions."

She kept quiet filling the presence of Tapaswini in her eyes. She was doubtful that she might be lost permanently to her."

"There is a higher dimension Yogini where liberated individuals have sought to walk back from the abode of Truth. They have proposed to remain tethered to the phenomenal existence. They are the compassionate luminous entities. They reincarnate on earth to create a new Order for the liberation of mankind. I have come from that Dimension, Yogini. You shall be my media till you are also ready to join us.

"Where is this place? Who guides?"

"You will come to know about it in due course of time. The one who guides is a most ancient soul. A supreme Yogi, perhaps the first one who returned. He remained on earth to get that light for the regeneration of the world."

"Is not Truth concerned with the upliftment and growth of phenomenal existence?" "I am not sure Yogini. Truth is a terrible thing; everything gets burnt out. The immeasurable existence becomes a mere shadow, Chaya Brahma! Vanishes. Nothing. If you want to assist mankind, you have to stake your life. It's a solemn task. Our past rishis were content with liberation. They waited for the dissolution of body. There were very few who took the body as media an important source of rich matter which could be transformed and made an essential part, unit of that

Light. Such individuals can work on this planet and save humanity."

"Why cannot one remain in gross body and help?"

"This body has certain limitations. In it's present form, it's subject to time, decease, deterioration and death. It's imperfect and cannot be a proper media. It cannot develop an attitude untainted by selfish thought. Service rendered with the help of body has to be limited. So realising that the body turns into a shadow in that Light, a new vehicle can be created keeping oneself open to Divine Grace. Such an individual has unique capacity; he can commune with the thought structure of the human race. He can influence to a great extent remaining in the background of mind. Such a body is also not perishable by our standards. It has a greater longevity, greater functionability, a greater purpose. It's new to you, strange; but I am becoming aware of a new hierarchy unknown to common man."

"What is the food of this body? Does it breathe?

Tapaswini looked at Yogini, her childlike innocence.

"Energy is the food. It doesn't breathe."

"Has it any sex?"

"Yes, it retains its identity but in essence, it's both male and female."

"Can it do more work?"

"That's the crux. It has greater potential, greater vulnerability. It functions in a new biosphere. It's more psycho than a Bio. Man has gradually, involuntarily tread on a path where he has realised that 'I am the world.' This means one mind. In such a world the transformed entities have a greater role to play with their new bodies."

"Is it not a Divine Plan?"

"It must be. There isn't anything which is not that. But the credit goes to him who returns after attaining Truth and takes up the formidable task of restructuring body and mind. Rather speeding up evolution and creating a mutant."

"Can you name the ancient one, the First who broke away from Truth, who took up this task? The one who held the Evil, drank the poison destroying the world?"

"When you name, it creates division, It gives room for prejudice. He is essentially the Unnamed! The Supreme, the Greatest in the art of yoga. The Initiator. Let us not name him."

"Is he male or female?"

"He is both in one, symbolically, the union of the two."

"Is he then Shiva, Neelakantha, the Ardhanarinateswara, the Linga?"

"Why do you want to recognise? Why do you give him a name? It's the highest sanctity. It's not a Hindu theme. No, never."

Yogini kept quiet, puzzled.

Tapaswini continued, "I am today leaving you. I am confident you are endowed with high potentiality I entrust to your care this Ashram. I will visit you again."

Yogini like an innocent child asked, "Ma, you have not disclosed much about you. Who are your parents? How do you happen to be on this farm? What is your name? Were you married? Any children?"

Tapaswini was fascinated by her questions. There were enough mysteries; it was not necessary to hide any further information.

(i)

Risi Datta was a devout soul. He and his wife Sulaxana lived a quiet life in a village in West Bengal. They had enough landed property but no children. They visited all the sacred places praying and performing pujas but their efforts proved to be unfruitful. Finally, they gave up hope and resolved to lead the rest of their lives in contemplation. They were humbled before the unpredictable forces of fate.

Within only a few days, a sanyasini came to their house

unexpectedly. Seeing the pathetic face of Sulaxana, she asked, "Why are you so sorrowful?"

"We don't have any children," she started crying. The sanyasini asked humorously, "Do you want a son or daughter?"

"Beggars have no choice," she told in all humility. After some thought the sanyasini asked, "Will you give me your first baby?" "Certainly!" Sulaxana blurted out joyously.

The prediction proved to be correct. The first one was a female baby followed by two sons. They called the female baby as Tapa in gratitude for the sanyasini.

When Tapa was thirteen years, the sanyasini returned to claim the child. Risi Datta and Sulaxana were shocked. They had looked after Tapa with great care and love. It was a problem for them to disclose to Tapa that she belonged to the sanyasini. Sulaxana pleaded before the sanyasini to reconsider her demand, telling even that she could take one of their sons. Strangely she wanted only Tapa. She boldly went to Tapa and asked, "What do you want in this life?"

Tapa became serious and without the least hesitation told, I wish to be like you."

"Will you come with me?" the sanyasini asked, looking into her eyes steadily.

"Yes"

Risi Datta and Sulaxana stood gazing helplessly. Tapa started walking with the Sanyasini without turning back, without wishing, without any second thought. They did not know from where the sanyasini came, where she was going, her address. On second thought, Datta ran in the direction the two had walked away but after a thorough search, he returned exhausted without finding them.

The sanyasini was Bhuvaneswari Ma who took Tapa to a hermitage near the Himalaya. The hermitage consisted of a farm, a building covering about ten squares and four outhouses comprising twenty rooms. The inmates were students studying in a City college. The hermitage offered them boarding and lodging facilities and supplemented their education with yoga and meditation.

Tapa was given a room in the building. There were two more girls studying in a college. They were Brahmcharinis who would eventually become sanyasis. Tapa was admitted in a convent. She was taught sanskrit in the Ashram.

Swami Shambhudanandaji was an old man, eighty two. He had long silvery beard and mustache. He lived on the first floor along with another monk Swami Devu Maharaj. He was a middle-aged man, tall, ramrod straight and with a black beard and mustache. He was fair in complexion. Long dark hairs flowed below his neck. He managed everything in the Ashram. He conducted yoga classes, supervised the activities of the students and gave lectures on eastern philosophy. Swami Shambhudanandaji engaged the students only on Sundays. It was essentially a question and answer session. The main topic was Tantra.

Tapa could not grasp her role in the Ashram. She studied hard in the school and always in the top echelons. She was appearing for S.S.C. and would enter college. She was under the care of Bhuvaneswari Ma. Tapa had a tight schedule. She woke up at 5 a.m., took bath, did her yogasanas and pranayam and spent in meditation for about an hour. Thereafter she collected flowers for the puja. Breakfast and studies followed. She would dress up by 10 a.m. and leave for school. Evening prayer in the Shiva Temple, attending discourses of Devu Maharaj; early dinner, homework and 11 p.m. to bed.

Tapa was sixteen. Her examination was over. Bhuvaneswari Ma called her one day after meditation and told, "Tapa tomorrow midnight, you will be initiated according to Tantra."

Tapa innocently asked. "What does Tantra initiation mean?"

"It's a simple ceremony Tapa. For some, it may appear to be difficult, even immoral, unethical and probably unessential. We attach the highest importance to this initiation because it is intended to reorientate your sensuality in the central core of your being. Elevation is aimed to the height of spirituality."

"Were you also initiated Ma?" Tapa asked innocently.

"Yes, by Swami Shambhudanandaji."

"Who will initiate me Ma."

"Swami Devu Maharaj."

The Tantra ritual was performed with utmost secrecy. Preparations were being made with the greatest care adhering to the ancient tantric codes which came down the line of heritage from Guru to his trusted disciple and the possibility of leakage was ruled out.

Swami Devu Maharaj was already sitting in the hall wearing a white dhoti with the upper part of the torso naked except for a white silk shawl. His forehead was decorated with sandal paste. His navel region was exposed. He looked like a bull, but a solemn one ready for a tantric ritual.

At the stroke of midnight, Bhuvaneswari Ma brought Tapa to the main hall. In the centre of the hall, a wooden seat was placed. Intricate mandals were drawn around the seat. Bhuvaneswari Ma told Tapa, "Before you are initiated, show your willingness prostrating before Guruji."

Tapa complied. Swami Shambhudanandaji lifted her tenderly and asked, "Are you ready Tapa?"

"Yes Sir."

He blessed her, gave her the sacred mantram and whispered, "Tapa from today you shall be known by the name Tapaswini. This body is a shrine and you are the Goddess; every movement in it is holy."

He got up and went away.

Bhuvaneswari Ma took her behind the curtain which was in a corner, told softly, "Tapa, tantric ritual begins with a naked body. Undress."

Tapa was rudely shaken. Involuntarily like a child knowing

too well her fate; she timidly pointed to the man behind the curtain.

"Tapaswini, you have been named. Halfway you cannot withdraw."

She brought the jasmine garland and placed it round her neck. She unwound her hairs, left them to cover her back. She slowly removed her saree much against her silent protests. Her breasts were small, not sagging. Nipples stood erect. She was completely naked.

"You are beautiful, a Goddess, the Consort of Shiva."

"What should I do?"

Words escaped, her voice trembling. "Go and stand on the wooden seat for fifteen minutes. He is the priest who worships you. Observe with divine compassion. He is your devotee. Whatever he asks, offer him wholeheartedly."

Tapaswini felt a new vigour when she woke up the next day. The morning breeze entered her chamber but it had a melody. Dark unfathomable music moved from horizon to horizon. She was not Tapa, Tapaswini, the consort of the Universal God. The sensuality was raging through her body like a storm in every cell of her body. But it had one result, annihilation of 'self'. The forces in her consciousness, the greed, the lust, the anger etc. had lost their specific characteristics and become a unitive force the Kundalini Shakti, Primordial Energy. She had attained the Godhead. When he separated from her and lay there exhausted, she kept her left foot on his chest and retired. He was shocked. When she sat for meditation, she forgot herself. Thoughts no longer continued as a source of turbulence; her face radiated a glow, unearthly and magical!

Swami Devu Maharaj, however was not liberated. He was bound by gravitation and time. Even though, he had initiated two girls in the past, this one seemed to destroy him. His vices took shape and dragged him down. He had sucked her nipples, kissed her sensual lips, licked her body from head to toe; enjoyed her repeatedly. Tapaswini like a dominant Goddess stood on the testing ground with grace and agility. He hankered after her. In the Class room when he was expected to talk on philosophy, his eyes strayed on the strategic points on her body. She sat unaware of her predicament. His spirit was sagging. The symbolic ochre robe which was expected to burn away sensuality was in danger of getting polluted. Tantra prescribed ending, dying as the only sure way which he ignored; he rejoiced in continuation, repetition. He was stinking of success!

One day when Tapaswini was busy doing her homework he strayed inside the room. At the sound of the wooden sandals, Tapaswini turned to look at him. She stood up.

"How are you Tapa?"

The voice was not authoritative; it came from an intruder.

"I am Tapaswini, Maharaj," she reminded him in her resonant voice.

He looked at her face-fearless, calm, radiant; not a thought of the initiation seemed to torture her. Strange, he thought. In respect of the other two girls, he had a chance to advise them to look into their minds, the sensual images on the waves of space. He stared at her for some time as if accusing her of insubordination.

Tapaswini asked in a clear voice. "Do you want anything?"

"No, how are you?"

"Fine."

He walked out, went away humiliated, rather hurriedly. Entering his room, he closed the door, held his chest pounding. "What has happened to me?" he murmured, 'Is it my downfall?'

There was no understanding that could sustain him and make him whole, not broken to pieces. Restraint was not the byword in the hermitage. "Understand sensuality," not suppression either. It was quite late now. It was assumed that he had crossed the barrier; he was an Arhat standing on the other shore; where he should have earned an ochre robe. Where did he slip? His ego came in his way. He wanted to go and put his doubts before

Shambhudanandaji but he was afraid. He was supposed to be the Priest of Initiation. Not a victim. He was not aware of the other dimension. The unknowable remained unattainable. Not so for Tapaswini; There was a noticable change in his posture. He stooped at times. His eyes which should have exuded nobility, austerity, flickered like a candle held in a storm. He was desperate about something. His lecture on religion lacked appeal; emotional content. The Priest had failed; he had lost the Goddess! Instead of dissolving the 'self' in the fusion with Tapaswini and raising beyond the bounds of body, he had remained imprisoned by it. He seemed to treasure duality which Tantra abhorred. It never perhaps occurred to him that Tantra strangely strives towards indivisible whole; its bedrock continues to remain austerity, impeccability and all consuming living energy.

Tapaswini passed in first class. Swami Shambhudanandaji decided to send her to Varanasi to study philosophy in sanskrit. Swami Devu Maharaj was heart broken.

Tapaswini was leaving in the evening. Swami Devu Maharaj once gain strayed into her room to make an abortive attempt. Tapaswini was busy packing her clothes. Seeing him cross the boundaries of her room, she looked up. He had already come inside and stood near her.

"What do you want?" she asked in a tense voice. She had forgotten to give pranam. Instead she had looked directly into his eyes.

This is the moment to touch her; she would be lost forever probably I would remain craving, sleepless, restless and suffering, he thought. He came and placed his hand on her shoulder.

"Tapa," a word leaped out of his throat.

"I am Tapaswini!" she stepped back. Her eyes widened, there was a glint of fire!

He shamelessly stooped ahead to clasp her waist. But she struck him on his face with all her might. He was stunned; his cheek reddened at the places where her fingers touched him.

"Get out" she shouted in her majestic voice. She was still a Goddess, taming her crew!

(ii)

Varanasi. The final years of Tapaswini. She had avoided visiting the hermitage under the excuse that special classes were being conducted during the vacation. Swami Devu Maharaj was unhappy. His protests were ignored by Swamiji. Two months were left for final examination. A heartening news awaited her; Swami Shambhudanandaji was no more. He succumbed to a massive heart attack. His foremost disciple Swami Devu Maharaj had taken over. She was shocked.

She did not return even for paying, her last respects as her examination was due. But the real reason for not returning was the new Swamiji. She knew her fate. The financial assistance was discontinued. She was asked to come back and she refused. After the final examination, she wrote a letter to Bhuvaneswari Ma.

"Mother,

I have done very well in the examination. I do not propose to return to the hermitage as long as Devu Maharaj continues to be the head. I am aware that I should devote my life to Truth, I should become a sanyasini and live in the Ashram."

Bhuvaneswari Ma showed the letter to Swami Devu Maharaj. He was furious. "Tapaswini, a rebel!" 'I would have given her a death penalty for this offence if I had the power over her life,' he murmured. At the bottom of his heart, he pined for the body of Tapaswini. It was strange how such an undeserving soul was brought up to the stature of a monk.

At this juncture, she was appointed as superintendent of hostels. She had passed in First Class and was appointed a Lecturer. She was also permitted to undertake post-graduate studies.

She came in contact with Tribhuvan, a post-graduate student during this time. His father was an Industrialist of considerable reputation in Ahmedabad. He had two brothers who were looking after family business. Tribhuvan was the youngest who took interest in sanskrit and philosophy. His father was getting old. He loved Tribhuvan. He had divided the property and kept in his name Rs. 8 lakhs.

"Tapa"

She was browsing through the racks of the library. She turned towards the direction of the sound. Tribhuvan stood in a dilemma having called her name for the first time.

Tapaswini was curious to see his plight. She corrected him. "My name is Tapaswini, not Tapa."

It was the name by which her parents called her.

Tribhuvan stood gaping nervously.

"Is there something?"

"I want to talk to you."

"What is it?" she took pity on him. He looked around suspiciously. Some students were coming inside.

"Please come out" he pleaded.

She became alert. "Is it important?" She asked.

He nodded and started moving out.

She had seen him a number of times and spotted him because he was not in the crowd, not chitchatting, not seeking the company of girls. Tapaswini slowly walked out of the library Tapaswini came and stood at a safe distance.

"Yes, what is it? I have work to do, be quick, Tribhuvan," she told.

"Will you accompany me? We will go to the river."

"Why?" she asked severely.

He was panicky. Trembling for words. "Tapa, I love you. I want to talk to you. Nearly two years..." words failed him. With his palm turned to heaven, he looked at her pathetically.

Tapaswini stood in her track staring at him. Tall, handsome, quiet, innocent, studious and suddenly romantic! She restrained for sometime and then arrived at a crucial decision.

"Okay, what do you want to talk?"

"Not here, please come."

Tapaswini went to the car. He requested her to sit in the front. He started driving cautiously. He was all attention to driving, not prepared to talk. On nearing the favourite spot, near the river, he stopped the car. He did not come out but sat quietly listening without talking, the breeze with the ancient sound, the moving river, the swaying coconut trees, the aimlessly flying birds, the distant chatter of men and women caught in the daily grind and the intermittent silence. He was totally absorbed. Tapaswini looked at him, he was sitting spellbound, lost in eternity. Has he forgotten his mission? She thought of shaking him up.

"Tribhuvan, are you sleeping?"

"It's so quiet here Tapa, sorry Tapaswini. I often come here. Perhaps I will come here one day to die. You are not in the proper frame of mind; you have not listened at all."

"Is that the purpose why you brought me here?" she asked sarcastically.

Innocently, he smiled and told, "Yes."

"Will you drive me back? Or shall I walk all the distance?"

He started laughing, "Do not take me as crazy. I love you Tapaswini, I want to marry you."

He looked at her puzzled.

"Are you employed? How would you support me?"

He looked at her with a naughty smile.

"You are employed no, that would do."

"You do not wish to work?"

"Of course, I would eventually after my post-graduation."

"Can we not wait till you complete your studies?"

Having spoken, she wondered whether she was also a party already and consented.

"No" He was emphatic.

Tapaswini jocularly asked, "Why?"

It was becoming funnier.

"I cannot explain you. Tapaswini, for the last two years I have thought over. I have decided, soon we must be married."

"We will require a house. How do you propose to maintain your car?"

He took out from his pocket three bank books and gave them to her.

Tapaswini was flabbergasted. "Did you rob any bank recently?"

"Not quite. My father is an Industrialist. This is my share."

"Do you really propose to marry?"

"No joke Tapaswini, what do you say?"

"On what subject?" Tapaswini laughed.

"Marriage."

"There is a problem. I am an inmate of a hermitage."

"Are you not allowed to marry?"

"My parents had no issue. A sanyasi blessed them with children. But she insisted that the first baby should be given to her."

He was disheartened and asked, "Are you the eldest?"

"Yes, the sanyasini came when I was thirteen and took me away."

"Do you propose to become a sanysini?"

"I am not yet sure what I would do. In the meanwhile you are here."

Tribhuvan was sad. "Tell me Tapaswini, your decision."

He appeared crestfallen, desperate. Tears welled up in his eyes. She was greatly moved. Tapaswini unexpectedly took his palm in her hand and declared, "Tribhuvan, you have won. In the name of this Ganga, the sky, the wind and the Unknowable God, I swear, I will marry you!"

She started laughing. Unbelievably really ecstatic. He became serious, "Do you make fun of me?"

His voice was trembling; She placed her head on his shoulder and closed her eyes.

The parents of Tribhuvan made discreet enquiries about the background of Tapaswini, and were satisfied. The marriage was performed in Ahmedabad.

They had decided to postpone children till they completed post-graduation. It was a happy period. Tapaswini forgot about the hermitage and all the past commitment.

Before completion of her post-graduation, she became aware of a recurring dream. The meaning of the dream was not clear.

Dream :

She is walking by the side of a tall mountain. Occasionally she looks up and wonders whether she would one day reach the top. She becomes diffident. She wants to get away from the mountain itself. Then she becomes aware of something, some body at her back, very near! She turns around. A person with an ochre robe! He is neither male nor female. A crown with the symbol of the rising sun on his forehead. She is unable to stare at the luminous face. She starts walking swiftly. He starts pursuing. She starts running and comes near the river at the same place where they had decided to marry.

The red car of Tribhuvan is there. She is glad, now confident, he must be inside. She reaches the car with her breath quickening. No, he is not there. But the keys are there. "Tribhuvan, Tribhuvan" she shouts, starts running towards the river. The strange apparition is still at her back. Now very near. She looks far into the river. A boat is moving away from her towards the distant horizon!"

Every fortnight the same dream. The same sequence of events kept her guessing at the possibility of an actual confrontation with the sanyasi. She did not tell Tribhuvan. It was her life, her secret.

The rain had stopped. The sky had become clear except for some dark clouds hiding on the parameters of the horizon. Tribhuvan had taken bath and was towelling his hairs. The doorbell rang. Tapaswini came from the kitchen. In the meanwhile, Tribhuvan had already opened the door. A telegram was delivered to him. "Father expired, start at once."

He stood like a statue. He was totally benumbed. She shook him up.

"Tribhuvan take it lightly. We are not permanent residents of the earth."

He went and sat on the sofa. He was staring outside. Tapaswini prepared a cup of tea and brought. He looked at her as if looking at a stranger.

"No, I do not feel like."

When he was going out, Tapaswini asked, "Are you coming soon?"

"I am not in a mood Tapaswini. I will drive to the point near the river, spend some time," he told.

"Alone?"

"What is wrong?"

She waited patiently for four hours expecting him to come at any time. When the clouds regrouped and cold wind started, she was afraid.

The car was there. She ran and found it empty. He had not taken the key. She looked around. Already it was raining. There was a storm. It was awful. She remembered the recurring dream and the words of Tribhuvan : 'I will come here one day to die.'

Suddenly she looked around. The apparition of a person wearing an ochre robe dissolved before the minds eye!

(iii)

Tapaswini was heartbroken. Sorrow struck a deep blow so hard, she was disillusioned. She knew she had erred having taken Tribhuvan for a ride so far when she was actually not destined to lead a married life. At the back of mind stood the mysterious image like an archaic shadow but alive. It was becoming real. She was sure of it. The time was nearing.

She was scanning through the newspaper. It struck as odd when she read a column in small letters: 'A farm in a valley for sale. Surrounded by hills. Not very far away from the city. Probable price Rs. 8 lakhs.

She took her things in two suitcases and drove the car. After three days, she reached the destiny.

She was concerned with a tremendous task. The first it was to delve on the mind, the known, the unknown and unknowable. In her deep meditation, she was aware of the frontiers of the unknown, a thin wall seemed to separate her from the other dimension. However much she tried, she could not break it. The key was not with her. The second, it was to make the farm self-sustaining. She wanted the farm to keep on changing and getting beautiful for a hundred years. She realised on her part that a commitment was necessary to will, devote her life to exploration of Truth. She had taken a solemn vow as a child. She prayed constantly, God to give her the key that would let her into that dimension.

At last it happened during night time when she was sleeping meditating naked on the floor. She was released like an arrow from the body and mind, the 'self' and involuntarily taken to Akasic heights where there was no gravitational pull. She felt like an apparition of ether. She comprehended the identity of the person who had all along stood behind her as her Guide and benefactor. She became aware of others; she was not alone in her mission, she was only a novice!

This was a crucial time for her. She was deeply involved in the other dimension. She was convinced that a mission awaited her. Secretly she worked day and night. She knew by insight that she should not be obsessed in her spiritual quest, not be carried away by the grandeur of that dimension, Deliberately she took abiding interest in the management of the farm. From there to here, she had to plunge a chasm. Often she felt that the 'here' was an illusion. She sought harmony, reconciliation of opposing forces. She knew otherwise her psyche would revolt; eventually become lopsided.

The Master taught her by signs, an interplay of light and shade, a language without spoken words. She was slowly imbibing a new culture. She became aware of the mental state of human beings. They were not free. They reacted as if programmed without thought. A person born of Hindu parents was conditioned to worship Hindu deities, observe Hindu rituals, festivals and conventions; conditioned to hate others. Tolerance was postponing hatred, violence. So also others born in other communities, following other religions. No one was prepared to think. The state was lethargic, heavy and dull. It was a slow monotonous circular movement without any creativity. The tenets preached by the great Masters were not understood. A sham culture with redundant rituals and obstinate practices had come up. The springs of religion had dried up.

The Master showed Tapaswini the thought structure of the human race; dull, mechanical, vibrating in circles, not free, raw. Very few luminous points were visible.

The Master was hinting at the possibility of a new way. He wanted to assign her new role, to guide the world remaining in that dimension. A mission was assigned to her to build seven Tapovans with solely women who comprised half of humanity. They were suppressed since immemorial times. Women's quest for social justice and equality had still not been realised. It was necessary to bring vast changes in the laws governing their social and economic status. Unfortunately their rights came from relationship to man. They were dependent on male members, wife, daughter, mother etc. Not self respecting individuals. She was told to strive for setting right the imbalance. Opportunities would come on her way; she had to grasp and move ahead. Her disciples would be like warriors who were expected to make themselves fit not only to attain liberation but to forgo the ultimate fruits of liberation in order to serve humanity. They had a vision to create a new world with enlightened women so that the world would be a guiding star.

The Master showed another cross section of the dimension where time was fluid and future and past mingled in the present. It was a mysterious culture as if developed in the spiritual laboratory with images of distant future happenings. Fixing gaze between eyebrows, Tapaswini was taught to foresee minute details of the future. This power was to be used sparingly so that the natural laws were not slighted.

Once when the Master took her on an unusual expedition, Tapaswini became aware of blind forces. They were the forces released by the deceased. It was the natural outcome of superficial living without discrimination, moving slowly by impulses and urges. The monstrous 'self' became ultimately a blind force. The constituents are naturally greed, lust, hatred, anger, jealously and so on. These forces had not attained any identity with the death of the individual. They remained in the consciousness creating disharmony, causing confusion and sorrow.

Tapaswini asked, "Are they harmful to us now?"

The Master told doubting, "It depends on you."

Tapaswini had rightly guessed; a dark throbbing force came hurtling like a torpedo very near Tapaswini who stood without fear in quiet defiance. Just then a miracle happened. A benevolent force resembling a human being intervened and charged the demoniac force away. Tapaswini felt an instant attraction to this force. In the meanwhile, a bond was being established between the force and Tapaswini with a string of luminous beads. Tapaswini was surprised. The Master explained. "It's inevitable Tapaswini. This is your Ally, with you as protector, as long as you need it."

"Does this Ally benefit from me?"

"Naturally. Whatever understanding you gain will be shared by the Ally. The relationship is reciprocal. The Ally evolves more quickly than by taking births. The Ally has unique power over the blind forces strewn around. It can pick up a force at your bidding and do impossible deeds even kill or maim another. The Black magic begins here."

Yogini prostrated at the feet of Tapaswini. There was a peculiar silence. No movement. She got up and stared blankly around. Tapaswini was not there. The door was closed from inside. Obviously she had become invisible.

Morning. She woke up and looked at the cot hoping that the night episode was a dream. It was not. What should she tell Bhairavi and Shivaranjani? She came out. They were waiting for her to come for breakfast.

"How is Tapaswini Ma?" Bhairavi asked.

Yogini became serious. She did not talk.

"She is all right, very fit, great."

Shivaranjani thought that Yogini was talking humorously. They were a little annoyed. They became serious. Yogini held both of them in her arms and told calmly, "Tapaswini Ma was not ill any time."

"Today, you are not your usual self. Is there any problem?"

"After breakfast, we would meet in the Chamber of Tapaswini."

They were exhilarated. It was the first time in many days that they were asked to meet in the chamber of Tapaswini. They thought that there was something urgent and important. They finished their breakfast soon and followed Yogini.

Yogini opened the door. Tapaswini was not there. She told them to be seated. She sat opposite them cross-legged. Slowly, confidently, she started talking.

"I want to make an important announcement. Tapaswini Ma has attained supreme state of non-being."

They were confounded. One night, she tells about a state of non-being. There is no body. No help was sought for the disposal of the body either. Suspiciously, Bhairavi asked seriously, "What has happened to Ma? Don't use cryptic syllables."

Yogini was helpless. "If you do not believe I don't mind. I can't do anything. Listen carefully. Attaining Truth is not the end. It's an archaic myth that Mukti is the end. It's not such a feat as supposed to be even though very rarely men aspire for it and very few make concerted efforts to realise the futility of life on earth. Truth might come to a few. Tapaswini held the view that after attainment of Truth, another Path is open to a dare devil soul, to revert back to earth and build a new body and carry on a new mission to bring down that light on earth : to don the miseries of the secret life!

Bhairavi who had widely studied scriptures and Tantra wondered whether Yogini was not stupefied by some delusion in talking like that.

Yogini continued. "We are making a small beginning. We do not seek popularity. It's a secret work requiring not only patience but all the energy at our command and all ingeniousness. We must have nerves of steel to undertake this mighty task. Even though there are very few who are prepared for this work and there are benevolent forces who bless us, there are also evil forces who would certainly strive to subvert our future progress. Tapaswini would help us from that dimension."

Shivaranjani was skeptical about the statements made by her. She asked the most relevant question.

"Where is Tapaswini?"

"She has purified the gross body and its constituents in that light so that the visible frame has become invisible. She has made great sacrifice. She has decided to remain on that plane to become a media for that light to reach us. She has not yet disbanded her body which might take some years, probably even beyond our death. The new body can survive longer; it has better adaptability; it has greater capability to serve, act; it's divine. The small step by men into this other dimension with new body is a mighty step, a giant leap for humanity; it's like the emergence of a new species."

Bhairavi asked, "Are there others who are engaged in this work before Tapaswini and where are they."

"Tapaswini mentioned that there are a few. You remember she has been often talking before us that there are others. She meant on that plane."

Shivaranjani asked to clear the doubts. "Will that Light emanate more meaningfully than verbal communication?"

"Yes, I think so."

"Is it your belief? Do you have any personal knowledge?" Shivaranjani asked pointedly.

"Personal Knowledge."

"Can you plead on our behalf to Tapaswini to come and meet us at least once. We were initiated by her."

Yogini looked at them wondering. They were not believing. They wanted to verify the facts.

"Still doubting? Okay. I shall make her a request on your behalf. My credibility is at stake."

It was midnight. Yogini sat meditating. So also others, Bhairavi and Shivaranjani, in their rooms. At the back of her mind, Yogini felt that a concept was being formed gradually clothing itself in words. An idea flashed in the mind of Yogini that she should call them.

She opened the door and called them, out of their meditation. They came and sat leaving a place for the guest and started meditation. Silence descended on them. It was becoming unbearable. So they simultaneously opened their eyes. Tapaswini sat before them. The door was locked from inside. No one had opened the door. She was ethereal with a luminous garment. The face was clearly visible, eyes like beaming stars, strange!

"Ma, where were you?" Bhairavi and Shivaranjani asked in one voice.

She smiled at their question. They could not commune any longer; the harmony was getting lost because of anxiety. They wanted to understand through the media of spoken words and the apparition dissolved.

They sat wavering among a thousand dimly imagined possibilities.

2

A young woman was approaching the Ashram. She was tall, fair, brown hair, cut at the level of neck, bob-style. She was beautiful and the saree, the way she behaved showed that she came from a well-to-do family. She was carrying a small suitcase.

After tea Bhairavi asked her, "What brings you here? Who are you?"

The young woman was hesitating to disclose her identity. "I have come from the south. I am bored. I want to spend some time in the Ashram. Is it not possible?"

"This is not a pleasure resort, a hill station or some valley of escape."

"I want to meet Yogini Ma."

"How do you know Yogini Ma?"

"I have read about her in the 'Tapaswini' magazine."

"You may meet her in the afternoon."

Without further enquiry, she took her to the Guest House where visitors were allowed to stay for three days.

After lunch, Yogini invited the young woman. Looking at her Yogini felt that she had seen her before. She recollected but could not place her.

"Who are you?"

The young woman maintained discreet silence and pleaded "Will you permit me madam, to stay here for some time?"

"Before we permit, you may have to satisfy us regarding your personal bonafides. What is your name?"

After much hesitation, she told in a trembling voice.

"Suma."

"Your residential address?"

"Is it necessary?"

"Yes."

"I am your grand daughter Suma."

Yogini was puzzled. "Why have you come here."

"There isn't a moment of joy in my life."

"Why?"

The question baffled her. "I am disappointed I do not feel like living. Will you allow me some time to think. Live?"

"This is not place for drop-outs."

Then she remembered that Kumudini had once attempted suicide. She became cautious. She also recollected the words of Tapaswini that Kumudini's daughter would be an enlightened soul.

"You may stay here for some time till you become balanced. You will be my guest."

She smiled compassionately and patted her cheeks. "At this young age, what made you so desperate?"

"I want to learn at the first disappointment alone; life may be such; other escapes might not be also worth. I would rather think and find out."

"But I am not taking you as an inmate." she told firmly.

Suma was not the type to accept without logic. "You took away Kumari and educated her. For what purpose? She is going to marry."

Yogini was unable to defend herself. She told, "Kumari was helpless. She was brought here at the instance of Tapaswini. I do not know why she brought her here. It's a mystery. In all probability to get her married to Harsha." Then she thought, 'Perhaps to chase another to the Ashram where she rightly belongs!'

A week passed. Suma realised that living with Yogini, Bhairavi and Shivaranjani was not a boredom. The food was wholesome and good. One month was over. Kumudini had written a letter.

"Suma,

Kumari is marrying after a few days. The invitation card will reach the Ashram shortly. She is not likely to attend office after marriage. She had come with her mother and Harsha to invite us.

The job is good. He enquired about you. I do not know why you should continue in the Ashram. You are still young.

Convey my reverential pranams to my mother.

Yours loving Ma"

"Ma

Your letter. I feel convinced now that life has a purpose. Not making money, not marrying a rich man. I am surrounded by educated enlightened persons who are not superstitious. They spend their time questioning, meditating. I want to live here the rest of my life. Yogini Grand Ma is not willing. I will prove it to her that being her grand daughter is not a disqualification.

Tapaswini Ma has become invisible it appears. She works on another plane. Strange things are happening here. I want to continue.

Do not write. Assure Daddy, I have found at last my heart's desire. The purpose why I am born!

With love Suma"

As days passed Suma had undergone a remarkable change. She assisted Shivaranjani in bringing up the magazine. She kept the clothes of Yogini Ma, Bhairavi and Shivaranjani neatly arranged at their places. She called them for breakfast in time, carried messages between Yogini Ma and others. She took interest in the management of the farm. By her own volition, she had found work that would keep her busy whole day that would relieve others of extra work and give leisure. Everyone praised her. She became an indispensable person.

Even after one year, Suma did not express any intention to go back. A time came when Bhairavi requested Yogini Ma to choose a name for Suma. I shall not name her. Let Tapaswini decide," Yogini told.

Yogini Ma announced that Tapaswini Ma had proposed to meet the inmates at 12 p.m. in the meditation hall. Suma was also instructed to be present.

When they came to the meditation hall, ten minutes earlier, to their surprise, Tapaswini was already there. She appeared to be her original self. Her face was luminous, eyes shining. It was frightful to stare into her eyes continuously. Otherwise she was quite normal. Bhairavi, Shivaranjani and Suma wondered at the possibility of a transmutation which defied all explanation. Yogini sat on the same cot but apart.

She talked in her soothing voice. It appeared she was not in a hurry; eternity was on hand.

"Do not be surprised, this is not an illusion. When you reduce yourself, mind and body to finer elements, regrouping and reorientation can begin under divine intervention leading to the creation of a new body. It's capable of becoming invisible. What is necessary is naturalness or innocence."

"What do you mean by innocence?" Suma asked out of curiosity.

"To recogmise your naturalness. You are greedy, jealous, sexual; to be aware, not struggle to change. When you struggle, nothing is changed, there is only restlessness. When there is no struggle, there is innocence, humility, preparedness to let go the self. This state of being is the basic raw material."

"You have mentioned about Divine intervention. This introduces an element of chance, fortune. Therefore, it would lose relevance." Shivaranjani cautioned hesitantly.

"Shivaranjani, the moment you realise the actual state of your being, you are already transcending the parameters of this dimension. The Divine intervention is not found by chance nor by accidental trials. Not by casual experiments. To find, it requires the whole of woman. When you find, it possesses you. Unless the mind is kindled by a beam of Divine light, you cannot penetrate this hidden science and lay hands on the secret of transformation."

"Please tell us about the doctrine of transformation. We assure you, we would devote our whole for this great task with all our heart," they pleaded.

Tapaswini looked at them with great compassion which was a unique feature with her after attainment of invisibility. "I know you are eligible souls, therefore you are here. The search would begin at the level of yourself. If you intend to take up exploration on this psycho-spiritual path, you should have an inclination to lead a virtuous life. You must have the inherent faculty of culture. Because you are intent on transforming the dross of worldly life, the mind and body into Mystic Gold."

They were learning the language of symbol and allegory for the first time. Tapaswini continued. "You must have the gift of wonder. Through this gift alone you will reach above the cares of life and contemplate on the causes of manifestation."

Pointing to Suma, she asked, "Do you desire anything from the world?"

She was thinking. She told slowly doubting her own voice, "I am not sure Ma. I am praying to that Supreme Light to enlighten me. Lift me from the prison of self, free me from the temptations that lead me astray. I am aware that I am greedy, jealous and sexy. Out of this chaos which is my life, desires have ceased to storm my mind. I want to go beyond. Find out Truth."

"You should learn your own nature and coming upon innocence, grasp the meaning of the original manifestation. This is the first step."

Shivaranjani asked, "The basic fibre of innocence appears to be imperfect. How do you propose to start with it?"

"When you are aware of your natural state which is

imperfection, the qualities are in virtue and near power. Such a state can be easily dissolved."

Shivaranjani asked doubting, "Dissolution implies a solvent and a solute?"

"The solvent and the solute are in yourself. Self is the amalgam, unless you examine closely, look at the contents, you are likely never to come upon the ingredients for a very long time; why, perhaps never. You should wake up gathering all your energies."

"How is awakenment achieved?"

"Suma, 'How' is not the way to set about it. Rather we examine our background, the natural state. There are two sources of power, the male and the female. The self appears to be the outcome of the interplay of these forces. You cannot do anything about it despite the dire need to get out of it. When you are in this state and realise that in desiring to do something about it, you indirectly strengthen it, silence in the form of humility descends on you. This is the beginning of the dissolution of self. It requires great skill, constant observation, absolute discipline to reach the point of dissolution. Unless the stream enters you, it is not accomplished."

"What is the nature of this stream, you refer?"

"It's the primordial source of life, the soul of the Universal Phenomena. This water has stupendous virtue. When it comes moving, it can easily pass through body but the brain cells with the embedded memories and images act like impediments. Therefore understanding yourself is the first step. To understand, you should observe the snaky movement of self."

"Who observes?" Yogini asked puzzled.

"Awareness is a strange entity. It's not quality. We are caught up in duality, the object and the subject. Awareness, as we practice is in the fist of sensations. When this state of sensations no longer gives understanding when one realises intensely that all escapes are closed, when it's suffering, it is suffocating, it faces annihilation. Then if you are destined,

‘Awareness’, that beam of light takes over restructuring the functional self.”

“Who observes? My question persists.” Yogini repeated.

“It cannot be verbalised. That Ray is aware. It acts on the stream.”

“From where does this stream of yours originate?”

Tapaswini, with a smile lingering on her lips answered, “You are questioning the primordial beginnings of creation. It would appear that it’s born out of male and female. When there is deep harmony like the symbolic Shivalinga, Ardhanarenateswara, the ‘self’ gets extinguished. Energy comes into being, clear, crystalline, mercurial, moving, conscious and purposeless! Body and mind are brown, ruddy and not bright. The art of transmutation cannot be learnt unless light and energy come to you.”

“We are talking about dissolution of ‘self’. Is sperm a motive and their fusion, creating a homo sapien, a motive? The ‘self’ seems to have been born with the body, deteriorates and dies with the body. It’s the entity in each one of us striving to become somebody, afraid of so many things. It builds institutions, invents laws for it’s survival and stresses the importance of respectability, conventions, traditions, religion and God. Self becomes the target, of instability in relationship and experiences self-pity, self-humiliation and self-aggrandisation. The image about oneself nurtured since ages doesn’t die automatically; time doesn’t destroy it nor any effort, any sadhana. It’s invincible; it’s time; it’s the Satan! It’s rarely exterminated. In death it continues; the hurts, the tensions are not relinquished behind burning embers; it remains as part of human consciousness. And when the time is ripe, it reincarnates!”

“How does it sustain itself? What should be done to dissolve it?”

“The passage of visual forms, sounds, flavour, taste, thoughts through eyes, ears, nose, tongue and mind result in sensations. It appears there is a strange chemistry in the human psyche. The mere sensations turn into a passionate reaction when there is contamination with the past images. These images feed on an entity at the centre, the self which keeps on jutting its tongue like a reptile eating through the sensations. It's survival is based on the horde of images, the vortex of memories."

"Is it possible to take stock of oneself?" Bhairavi asked.

Tapaswini sat quietly for sometime, told, "A cashier at the end of the day takes stock of all transactions. He arranges the stocks denomination-wise the ones, fives, tens, hundreds etc. In the investigation of oneself, the denominations are very few, the images evoking pleasure, pain, lust, security and fear."

"Is there a way of life in which 'self' is totally absent?" Yogini doubted.

Tapaswini closed her eyes, meditated momentarily. "Yogini, meditate deeply. There is no way. Observe the movements of self, the worthless ignominious life. All the contents represent only one value, the 'self' which is a mere pin-point of an image."

Bhairavi was excited. Remembering her experiences, she asked, "In the strange silence, the pin-point self of yester-years undergoes a mutation. In its place, a glow of understanding appears; the body and everything of me and mine turns into a shadow. Ma, is it the Divine intervention you refer?"

Tapaswini questioned, "Why do you want to recognise? If it's true, it brings its own authority there is no need to seek confirmation. The point of light would not remain silent. It would grow till it's a conflagration and you are transmuted into a flame of understanding. Perhaps then the way is open to learn the art of transmutation of body. It's part of the evolutionary plan and eventually man will come to it."

After this she told them to retire to their rooms. Yogini and Suma waited. Suma came involuntarily and touched the feet of Tapaswini. The touch of that solemn body which was an embodiment of Energy invoked in her a magical spell. She closed her eyes. She murmured, "Ma, bless me. Let me remain faithful to the Tapovan, to the search, to the unknowable."

Tapaswini lifted her. "Suma, you have a great future. From today, you shall be known by the name, "Maheswari.""

3

The memory of the past experiences is the cause of suffering. The hand of action moves the Wheel of Life. Perhaps those who have sown the seeds of pleasure are destined to reap the harvest of sorrow.

Kumudini was suffering. Suffering, not caused on account of dearth of money but because of the unfulfillment of desires. She was remembering the days when she became conscious of herself as a woman. In her eyes, Chandra took the role of an elder brother but he married her under exceptional circumstance, Before marriage, she craved for the company of a married man and wanted him to be her life partner. She suffered when she realised that his wife with two children had better chance of winning back her husband and he, her paramour was a confirmed womaniser. Marriage with Chandra and the first pregnancy: doubts whether the baby in her womb was legitimate; her suicidal attempts and Chandra's sacrifice. Sanath's untimely death, Yogini Ma's departure to an unknown destiny added to her grief. Suma struggling to get married to Harsha and Kumudini's realization to her utter dismay that Kumari, according to her a servant's daughter should win over and marry one of the richest men. Suma's departure to the Ashram, to become a sanyasini came as a severe blow to her psyche. She wondered whether life had any meaning for her; she was afraid of the coming events!

Often in her loneliness, the past amorous interludes with Surendra came back with renewed vigour. She went back to those days in her memories and lived those sensual precious moments. She used to deceive Chandra whenever she visited Surendra who was a charmer for her. 'How bold and cunning he was! Totally shameless as far as I am concerned. He never hesitated begging for revealing a part of my body. He would start with a touch at places which he alone knew for certain would be remembered by me. Talking in whispers with short breath as if he had run a hundred miles. Himself blushing while moving his fingers on my breast. He took it for granted that I wanted him. He Provoked me to do so many things which as a wife I had not taken liberty with Chandra. He drove me to such a frenzy! I was not bothered whether he would marry me or not, whether he would look after me or not; I, in fact wanted him more and more. Enjoying him with abandon; Who restrained me? Chandra. Not by coercive methods, simply by loving. So great his love; Never minding when I doubted my first pregnancy to be by Surendra. Even after birth, showing the maximum consideration, more than the actual father. At last when he realised that Deepak belonged to Chandra, not expressing excess excitation but remaining balanced.'

She condemned herself. She was glued to the past. Her vices had taken shape, dragged her down. 'How ugly is my mind; why do I remember those episodes? Why do I touch myself, squeeze my breast the way he would do, remembering his thrust?'

Whenever she touched her left breast, she felt a lump underneath but there was no pain. Yet it was there for the last two years. 'Oh, Chandra, lover, aged only 55 has become a boy of 13. Never bothers about his wife sleeping by his side. Did he get any sexual thrill with Laxmi who was attractive, a virgin for nearly two decades.'

Another thought occurred, 'Why should I bother? At his age, perhaps he is platonic, 'loving a poor girl;' Girl! Why he should call her a girl? Does she look like a girl? Probably yes. The looks are deceptive. She had also two children like me but in quick succession, and then death of her husband and then she remained active; where as I remained a snob wasting time. Of course she is also a decade younger than me. Now she is rich even without the wealth of her son-in-law. How hard work makes for fortune? An ordinary worker woman raped by four men in possession of unlimited wealth! Stars, lucky stars! Does getting raped by four bring luck?' She laughed at her thought.

Deepak had gone abroad. He was now a Director. Harsha had proved to be a friend. Kumari had two sons in quick succession. Both lovely children like made to order. Laxmi had lost her father and was living with her daughter. But she kept the house for making sweaters.

Every day on the bed, they talked till they fell asleep. Even when it was once in six months, he did not go beyond the preliminaries. Rarely removed her clothes. 'Fearing perhaps that he would be tempted to molest me; good friends, a brother!' Kumudini spent time brooding when she was alone. 'What is the basis of husband and wife relationship, if there is no sex? Am I ugly? Of course hairs have become grey here and there. He doesn't recommend hair dye. I have put on fat but not much; that is again his opinion. Should it discourage him from having occasional sex? He talks lovingly like talking to his mother, daughter or sister. Even hugs tenderly. But that touch is barren. I hate. Rarely it touched my sexual depths. Why? Why should he force me to remember him? Crave for the memories of Surendra. Better forget sex like him. Not so easy for me. So bored at home. I should have completed my medical education. As a doctor, so much of fun!'

She walked on the verandah reading some books. Again she remembered Laxmi. 'What a thoughtful person! How busy she looks! Works and earns even though her son-in-law would throw a million if she lifts a finger. Should I join her as an apprentice?' She laughed. Crazy Kumudini, she thought. 'Should I renounce Chandra, hand him over on a silver platter to Laxmi and tell. "Take care of this boy, sleep with him, fondle him, feed him with your milk.' Then go over to Ashram of Yogini Ma. 'Ma, your good daughter, now a sinner wants to be a sanyasini, like you; like my own daughter Suma.'

She walked to the kitchen, felt like eating but resisted as her digestion was affected of late. She went to the terrace. The sofa where Sanath sat meditating was still there, cleaned and polished, where Yogini sat with him talking, laughing and flirting making great love! Affecting and bringing two generations together, high and low, turning everything topsy turvy. Thinking she came down. Already it was getting dark. She felt like walking in the farm, alone. Some workers were seen still sitting below the trees chitchatting. Cool breeze from, beyond the hills evoked bygone memories. 'Only if Yogini Ma and Suma were with me!' She mumbled. Life had lost its meaning, for her again and again.

Time. Dr. Chandra's car came inside. "Kumud, why are you outside?" He came and took her by the hand and walked to the house.

"Are you bored Kumud?"

So concerned about me, my husband, she thought.

"Do you remember me?" she asked.

"No chance at the hospital. So busy, Kumud."

"Can I be of any use for you there?"

He thought over, remembering Laxmi dropping in at tea time and demanding brief romance, he asked a tentative question, "What work can you do?" Then he shook his head and told, "You will be more bored Kumud. Farm management can be a full time work. If you take real interest, there is work, very interesting work like new seedlings etc."

Kumudini also felt that there was scope to think, plan and work. Brooding over is suicidal, she thought.

In the bedroom, Chandra was unusually loving. He was looking at her, all over her body. "My dear Kumud, I feel we have become brother and sister."

She laughed. "We have two children, do not forget."

Chandra smiled. "May be. Is this not better relationship?"

"Are you bored with sex? Are you grandpa? In foreign, it's the age for remarrying."

"They are a crazy lot. They have no culture. When they reach a stage of non-response, they think of another."

She slept turning her back to him. Chandra pulled her to his side. "Are you angry?" He asked.

"Trying to be moral! Why should I be angry? You are not having another woman?"

He placed his hand on her breast. She asked humorously,

"Doctor, have you cared to examine? Two years! You have not cared to uncover and fondle."

She withdrew.

"Kumud, come on."

"No, there is a lump in my left breast."

Chandra sat up. "Since when?"

"For the last two years."

He removed her blouse and brassier. Her left breast was swollen. There was a hard lump. He lifted her shoulder already there was a lump in the armpit. He was shocked.

"Anything serious?" she asked apprehensively.

Chandra maintained the seriousness of the Doctor but he could not conceal his emotion. Kumudini was not only his wife, but a playmate from the tender age. He suddenly realised that he had become indifferent to her during the last two years. Laxmi had taken his time and enveloped his life. Played a havoc in his heart.

"Kumud, we will tomorrow go to the hospital. Is it painful?"

"Only when I squeeze."

"Do you have good appetite?"

"Asking today, so busy otherwise!"

"No Kumud, I realise now, I have not looked at you. I was not a good husband."

"I have no good appetite; sometime headache. I brood over being alone; no enthusiasm. Sometime I feel I should join an Ashram. So bored!"

He came near her, embraced her, kissed her tenderly "My beautiful girl, let us sleep today," he told.

She slept for the first time in many years soundly in his arms. He was awake. If I had sustained interest in her, the interest I evinced in Laxmi, I would have known long ago. Why did she ignore? Perhaps she did not know. He was offended by his behaviour. Was he flirting with Laxmi? Unknowingly he had got himself involved. What is the price? Laxmi a passing fancy, probably a sexual diversion. But I love Kumud. My heart now breaks when I see her. During this period, a few hours, I discovered my love. Oh God! What a tragedy! Already two years. Only six months at the most!

Kumudini underwent detailed examination. It was breast cancer. It had already affected the lymphatic system. The left breast was removed. Vigourous radium treatment followed. Chandra wrote a letter to Suma. Reply came promptly. 'I pray almighty my mother will bear this illness with courage! No mention about Yogini Ma. No intention expressed that she would like to come.

Kumudini was losing her hairs. She blamed none. Perhaps I am paying for my sins, she thought. Within only six months, she had grown like a skeleton.

Laxmi volunteered to stay with Kumudini. This was the time when there was need of a daughter but Suma had stayed away. Chandra wanted to appoint a Nurse but Laxmi refused. She wanted to share the suffering of Chandra. Kumudini was in need of affection; somebody who would not mind sharing her feeling of sorrow; somebody who would lift her from the cot and walk with her supporting her tenderly to the toilet; somebody who would give her food, mostly liquid and ice-cream, hold a tray for her vomits, then rub her face, listen to her moanings, look at her compassionately, fondle her like a baby. Kumudini felt that she should not bother Chandra about her requirements; he should not feel nauseated by her deteriorating body.

"Laxmi, do you know, you are my sister? In the previous life, you were my mother, not Yogini. In next life, I want you to be my daughter. Not Suma!"

With tearful eyes, Laxmi murmured, "You have done so much to me. My little help is no match."

"Laxmi, I want you to do a little more service to me. Promise that you will not fail. You will not ignore, fearing."

Laxmi was curious. "What is it? I promise I will do it at any cost." She assured.

Kumudini dragged her near and whispered. “You live here after my death, love him, my husband. He is a good man.”

Laxmi tried to withdraw but Kumudini had held her in her steel like grip using all her force. “Promise me, stupid girl.” Tears filled her eyes, Laxmi cried. “Why should you make this sacrifice?” she asked.

It’s not a sacrifice Laxmi, my selfish need. My husband should be looked after properly. No one would be here. Deepak has gone abroad, Suma in the Ashram, Yogini lost. Laxmi he would not live in this house. Save him. Promise me, Laxmi.”

It was 10 a.m. Chandra got ready to go to the hospital. Kumudini sat supported by pillows. Her scalp was bare with only a few tuft of hairs. Face, legs and stomach were swollen.

“Doctor,” she called him in a feeble voice. Chandra came near her. Laxmi got up to go. Kumudini, interrupted her. “Do not go away Laxmi from our life. Be seated.”

He took her and tenderly pressed the fingers.

“Doctor,” she was breathing with difficulty. “Will you promise me to fulfil my last wish?”

He looked at her with his heart beating his ribs; in a trembling voice, he asked. “What is it?”

“Laxmi will remain here with you taking care of you.”

Suddenly she started gasping for breath and fell sideways. Laxmi brought the Ganga Jal. Chandra poured it into her mouth. It came out.

Chandra who was all along craving for an opportunity to have maximum liberty to keep company with Laxmi found that something had happened to him. He was not able to have that freedom which he had before when Laxmi used to come for a few minutes. Though now she lived in the house; sat with him for food, arranged his bed, kept ready his clothes, he felt that he could not be free as before. She slept separately in another room. Both were surprised why there was not that familiarity.

That passionate love was missing. Whether the spirit of Kumudini hovered between them after bringing them together. The past weighed heavily on Chandra who felt mortally wounded, guilty for having neglected his wife for two years. Kumudini as a baby had filled his mind, occupied his heart and become part of his being. With her death, she continued as a phantom chasing him as a shadow. He had to expunge this shadow. Unless he did it, he would not be free; it would endanger his psyche.

Laxmi took care of him. Only after Chandra left for hospital, she went to the showroom and to her house. She sat with him during tea time as before but he was not romantic. They met without even smiling and departed. At times she felt that she should go away and never return. But she remembered the last words of Kumudini and determined to suffer some more time. It was becoming impossible for her to fish him out of the dark whirlpool of the past.

She felt that the previous brief contacts were fruitful than the stay at home permanently. She felt deeply that this was her battlefield and unless she won, there was no salvation for both of them. She wanted to restore him to his original self.

Four months were over Chandra was a corpse stuck up in the childhood days.

Kumudini had requested Laxmi to use all the sarees. She had particularly offered her most favourite saree which she wore on special occasions, telling her, "I would be pleased if you wear it. I won't give it to my daughter even."

It was a full moon day. The balcony outside the bedroom was aglow with the cool moonlight. Wearing the saree, she stood before the photo of Kumudini, offered jasmine flowers to appease her soul and prayed that she would as a last resort try to save Chandra. She took the glass of milk and entered the bedroom. It was 11 p.m. Chandra stood in the balcony looking at the distant horizon counting days when he would also join Kumudini. Life was so fleeting. Listening to the rustle of the saree, he turned around. He was shocked. He wondered whether it was Kumudini because Laxmi had stood with her back to him. Laxmi during the period of four months had not dared to enter his bedroom. Her restraint was shattered not by her desire to claim him back but by the suffering of Chandra. If she failed this time, she wanted to get away permanently. After some time Chandra recognised her and slowly came near her. Her heart throbbed; like a bride she was blushing. Though initially he was shocked he remembered the past, she had access to him. He had loved her, declared his love. He thought he had no right to deny her the minimum having dragged her so long, so far. Taking her face in his palm, he lifted it. She was beautiful. Her eves were closed. Out of fear she was trembling. There were tears in her eyes. He kissed her lightly. She succeeded in retrieving him from the whirlpool and placing him in her virgin heart.

Chandra turned around and looked at the clock. It was 2 a.m. He was not getting sleep. For the last two years, he was affected by high B.P. He looked at Laxmi. She had unwound her hairs; she was naked, asleep. 'How innocent she looks! She kept complete reliance on me. In love.' He embraced her. She cuddled nearer and put her arms around him.

"Not yet sleeping?" she murmured.

"Sleep Doctor, what are you thinking?" In the warmth of his embrace, she found complete solace. He did not disclose the nature of his sickness. 'Why should I not marry Laxmi?' Once when he suggested, she was astonished. She was sitting on his laps, his fingers kneading her nipples.

"Are you crazy, Doctor'? I won't get children. I have undergone tubectomy. Why marry?"

"A wife has status. We love each other."

"Yet, your children...my children, what they would take us to be? No, never, I am happy like this."

"But people would talk."

"True, let them."

"Then why not marry"

"No. I feel we shouldn't. Don't think on these lines. Is this marriageable age?" Chandra laughed and told, "For you it's."

Kumari had objected when Laxmi volunteered to stay with Kumudini, when the later was suffering from terminal cancer. "Chandra can afford to have a Nurse. Why should you go to her? She hated you all her life. Till I was married. Even thereafter because Suma had joined the Ashram."

"My life is not your concern Kumari. As a child you have gone away and returning, you have left me to live with Harsha. You do not know my life, my obligations."

After death of Kumudini, Kumari and Harsha requested her to come and stay with them. Laxmi refused. Kumari realised then, there was a deeper cause and she kept quiet. Inwardly she disliked her mother's affair with Chandra.

Laxmi rarely visited Harsha and Kumari. Only under pressure, particularly of Harsha, she would go and see. The sweater business yielded her good income. It was more a past time. She was imaginative and found out ways to expand business. Promod had joined Harsha and preferred to stay at madras where he worked in one of the companies of Harsha. He was briefed by Kumari to boycot Laxmi. She was leading a life which did not earn her respectability but satisfied her conscience. She detested the conventions, the prevalent morality, the traditional norms and taboos. Economically she was independent and made sufficient provision for the future; vaguely she was aware of a time when she would be leading a lonely life. She loved Harsha who treated her with reverence inspite of the indifferent attitude of Kumari. Harsha held an enlightened view. "Kumari, you were brought up in an Ashram. How is it that you do not consider freedom as the highest virtue. Your mother is not so old. She is having a life of her own. How does it affect you?" "I feel nauseated. Do not talk about her."

Harsha knew why she was having an aversion about her mother. She came from servant's quarters; she worked as a cook in Kumar's house; in love with him; became pregnant before marrying him; raped by four; marriage with Kumar under persuasion of Chandra; death of father and Kumar; affair with Chandra; playing nurse to Kumudini; death of Kumudini and love affair with Chandra. All these events in the eyes of Kumari meant gross immorality. She also did not like her mother to continue in sweater business when she had married a very rich man.

Chandra suffered a mild stroke. Laxmi found him on the bed disfigured struggling to use his limbs. She hospitalised him. Harsha wanted her to take his help. She refused. She wanted to bear the entire burden on herself. It was her last service to a man who she really loved all her life. She sat by his side, nursed him day and night. She stopped visiting the showroom. She avoided the factory, remained at home, fed him, helped him in the toilet, on the wheel chair, listened to his lullaby and deciphered his wants. She managed the affairs of the farm, kept upto date accounts. The staff were instructed long ago that as far as the management of the farm, her words were to be taken as the authority. She knew that Chandra was not likely to recover completely, as his age made the chances remote. His father had also succumbed to the same decease. She wanted to give him the maximum love; make him feel happy. He was her lord; with utmost devotion, she served him. Chandra told her in his feeble voice, "Since ages my tapasya has borne fruits in you. You are my blessings. May you come to me in every life. I will carry your memories for a thousand lives. These loving eyes of yours are pearls found only in heavenly abode!"

Laxmi closed his lips with her soft fingers. "I do not deserve. I am greedy to possess you."

He gave her a pass book. He had deposited Rs. 4 lakhs in her name. She looked at him. Tears in his eyes made her accept it.

Suma arrived fortunately on the last day. Deepak was also informed to come at once. Chandra was not conscious. Suma looked at the frail figure of her father; felt surprised at the sight of the emaciated body; the havoc death plays in the life of man. Laxmi sat with tearful eyes holding his hand, never taking her eyes of his face. The end came in the morning. Deepak arrived in the evening. His wife who was pregnant could not accompany him.

On the fifteenth day, after observance of all the rituals, Laxmi packed her clothes which she had brought while entering the home and came out with the bag.

"Suma, my work is over. Let me go now."

Suma asked tenderly, "Where do you propose to go?"

"To my house where I run business. Good bye."

Tears rushed down her cheeks.

"I am also leaving this place shortly, joining the Ashram permanently. Deepak proposes to settle abroad. We are selling the farm and the house. Why should you not stay here till then?"

Laxmi was shocked. "Suma, this place has a history. Your mother, father began their life, here. Your grand mother came from our house, which is on this farm. Your grand father lived and died here. For nearly a century this farm has fed your family. It's like Kalpataru. Why do you want to sell?" she asked pathetically.

"I am a sanayasini Laxmi. I am not interested in the past. I want to die to all the memories. The past has no hold over me. If it's there, I would try to understand and free myself. Dying to the known is our cult, Tantra! Deepak is not willing to come and take over. Life is movement Laxmi. Sorry. Till we sell stay here."

"How much you propose to raise from the house and the farm?"

"I do not know. We have entrusted it to Harsha."

Laxmi had no sleep. Her roots were there. She was born on the farm as a worker. Her father was buried there. Her children were born there. Her lovers, her business; her life had taken shape and grown there. She counted all the money she had saved in the sweater business including the money left by Chandra to her. She had Rs. 8 lakhs.

She went to the office of Harsha. He was surprised to see Laxmi.

"Is there anything, I can do for you Ma?" he asked.

"Yes, there is." she was nervous.

"What is it?" He asked in all humility.

"I am told Chandra's property is on sale. How much do you expect to get?"

He knew that Laxmi was shrewd in business. "The average income was bout Rs. 1 lakh p.a. The house is worth about Rs. 3 lakhs. It's nearly thirty miles away from the city limits. There are servant's quarters. I think taking into account all the liabilities, it may be worth around Rs. 20 lakhs. But persons are not interested to invest in the farm. It's not a profitable venture."

She placed before him Rs. 8 lakhs and told "You advance me a loan, Harsha, for the balance on the security of the farm. I shall return it within a reasonable time. I want that property."

Harsha was stunned. She continued in her trembling voice. "I want it, not for earning money. My roots are there Harsha. My memories, my love, everything is there."

She started crying. Harsha sat like a statue. 'This woman before me is not an ordinary woman. She would make a history wherever she lives.' He was proud of her.

"No loan. Will you accept the property as a gift from your son-in-law?"

She looked up. She was proud of him. She wiped away her tears and told, "No Harsha, I do not want as a gift. You may be my son-in-law."

"Okay, I will give you a loan."

"On one condition. Do not disclose it to your wife. Nor to Suma till the completion of the transaction."

"Yes Ma."

She got up to leave. Harsha came out of his chair and touched her feet. She lifted him, kissed his forehead, "I am proud of you, son."

4

Laxmi came and gave the keys. Suma took them with certain reserve because she had ceased to be a part of the house for the last twelve years. It was a long duration in the life of a person. So many changes had happened. She was like an alien inhabiting the world of Chandra and Laxmi. Kumudini was dead ten years ago. She thought that she had no right to call them father and mother. She had forfeited those rights the day she went away to the Ashram, the day she declined to come and assist her mother during those critical last days when she was being destroyed systematically by terminal cancer. She was not also moved by the news of her father suffering from stroke and withering away on a wheel chair. Suma did not know perhaps that dying was a painful process with the person undergoing this metamorphosis taking stock of all his past and reminiscing the bygone memories. The loved ones, the blood relations had a role to play. But often, even wife and children shirked responsibilities causing immense grief to the dying person. Suma was no exception. She preferred to remain aloof in the name of Ashram under the excuse of renunciation, which was becoming a ruse to a weakling to stay away from pain and suffering. Who was there to discharge the essential task? Laxmi! She appeared alive not dead like her; dead surely, she thought.

She went and opened the cupboard. It was of Kumudini. Her jewellery in tact with a list written by her hand. She opened the black jewel box; everything was there, shining. She would never use them being a sanyasini. Deepak's wife perhaps would need them; she was not here, away in the States, pregnant. Her father gave her a lot. Suma doubted whether Laxmi had used them. A widow. Why should she doubt her? The sarees, they were not there. Ten years since her death, naturally Laxmi must have used.

She opened the next cupboard, her father's clothes. She fondled them with tears bursting from her eye balls. Clean, ironed and scented! My mother's affectionate work? No, how can it be? Laxmi! She remembered the obscene gesture made by Sabi with his fist and palm. She came upon the two diaries, one of Sanath and the other of Chandra. Diaries with names embossed in gold.

She went and sat on the chair, started reading Sanath. Farm was a treasure trove for him. He loved and nursed the ancient property. She felt sad they had decided to sell. Herself appeared diminished before the giant ancestors. She read the pages: his first encounter with Yogini, his broodings and his passionate love for her till the last day of his death. They belonged to another dimension, totally detached, they were seekers at heart, monks who lived a family life with great discretion.

She took the diary of Chandra. Starting from the day of a ten year old coming to the doors of Sanath. Baby Kumudini he had attached her photo. Lovely baby. Page by page she read. The birth of Deepak, his resemblance to Chandra, the discovery that Surendra had undergone vasectomy, well before the contacts he had with Kumudini, Suma laughed. It was like reading a thriller. The death of Sanath, departure of Yogini after encounter with Tapaswini. Chandra's love with Laxmi.

He wrote : Laxmi touches my feet after her marriage with Kumar. Not as a formality. She holds my feet in her naked palm longer than necessary as if she is touching God. Never she would get that opportunity in life. She lifts her eyes and looks directly into my eyes; tearful orbs of light. That one look would repay all my good deeds in my previous lives. I loved this girl from this moment.

The discovery of affliction of Kumudini by cancer, his suffering. Laxmi's sacrifice. 'Where is Suma my daughter? My heart aches for Suma.' Kumudini suffers. Is it a virtue of a sanyasini? What is the use of sanyasa? Laxmi is a greater yogi, a Karma Yogi. Kumudini loves her. She told her : You were my mother in my previous birth. Not Yogini! You will be born as my daughter, not Suma. You are my sister in this life."

Tears rushed. Suma wiped her eyes. Unable to control cried helplessly.

A para appears 'in the end : 'I must have done a lot of sadhana in my previous life. Laxmi comes as the fruits of this Tapas. I have forgotten Kumud as if she belonged to my previous life. So also my children. How is it I am not related to them!'

The diary ended. Suma closed it. The rest was clear. She must have nursed him like a child. He lived on the wheel chair for about one year. There was cash of Rs. 16,000 and an account sheet of paper. The amount pertained to the income from the farm. There was nothing to reveal about the expenditure incurred on treatment of Chandra.

Slowly she came down after nearly two hours. Laxmi was waiting down with her two suit cases and the wheel chair. She got up and told, "Suma, I am leaving this place. These suitcases contain my clothes. A few sarees of Kumudini. She wanted me to use them. I want this wheel chair!"

Tears trickled from her eyes when she claimed the wheelchair. Suma looked at her, refined, loving, humble as a cow. My father was certainly lucky, she thought.

"Wait for a few days Laxmi, We are also leaving. Till then remain. I beg of you."

Suma took the suitcases and went up. Laxmi came swiftly behind "I will carry them Suma."

"Let it be. You have done so much to our father and mother. Atleast let me carry these suit cases." she laughed. She told her to sit. "Laxmi, I have gone through the accounts. What about the expenditure on the treatment of father?"

"Suma. I am greedy I wanted to spend from my savings exclusively. Excuse me."

The auction was conducted under a shamiana built specially for the purpose. There were about two dozen parties. The highest bid was for Rs. 20 lakhs. On behalf of Laxmi one of the representatives of Harsha managed the bid.

"Who has taken this property?" Suma asked Harsha.

"Do not be surprised Suma. Laxmi has purchased the farm."

Suma was dumbfounded. "So much money!" She exclaimed.

Harsha smiled "She had Rs. 8 lakhs. The rest is loan on the security of the farm."

Laxmi was busy in the kitchen. She was arranging tea and snacks for the participants. Suma went inside. Laxmi was unassuming. "May I also assist you?" She asked.

"I will serve you Suma."

"Let me help you."

After departure of the guests, Suma asked, "You did not tell me, you want the farm?"

She spread her hands helplessly. "Suma, you wanted money. I do not want this farm for my sake. At the same time I cannot think of leaving it in the hands of another. Your grand mother, grand father, mother all were born here. My roots are also here Suma. This is more precious than money to me. This is greater than life!"

Suma sat silently and then asked the most disturbing question. "What would you do with this vast property?"

"I am alone Suma. You and Deepak are away. My children have boycotted me. I have not seen them for about ten years. Believe me. I will build an Ashram here, Suma, in course of time!"

Suma looked at her. Her face radiated a peculiar glow. The woman before me is not an ordinary woman, she thought. It was a problem. What should be done with the ornaments? When she asked Deepak, he categorically mentioned, "Suma, you are the daughter. Keep them with you."

"But I won't use them in the Ashram."

"Do whatever you please. My wife has enough."

Suma thought whether she would offer them to Laxmi who was using them when Chandra was alive. For whose sake, she would wear them? She is a widow once again!

She decided to take the ornaments and the money and place at the feet of Tapaswini.

5

A taxi came and stood at the gate. The watchman opened the door and bowed to the person inside. Tapaswini came out with her brief case. All of them stood up. They were bewildered. "Ma!" they exclaimed.

"Where is Shivaranjani and Maheswari?" Tapaswini asked. Yogini told, "They have completed twelve years. They have gone home."

Bhairavi asked in her excited tone. "Ma do you need a vehicle to travel?"

"Why? I do need when I am in this body. I am like you subjected to cold, heat, gravitation, decease and death. We are not transforming the Nature's laws. Within the parameters of its laws, we work. The parameters have wide scope."

"From where do you come?"

Tapaswini smiled compassionately at Bhairavi. "You consider me as a human being. I need rest after journey, bath, some refreshment."

Bhairavi touched her feet and went inside to make arrangements.

Maheswari and Shivaranjani came in the evening on the same day. They were happy to learn about the presence of Tapaswini in the Ashram.

Morning. They met in the meditation hall. Tapaswini appeared serene. Unlike on previous occasions, she appeared normal. Her eyes were half-closed, meditative. At times she appeared remote not concerned with the present. She asked Shivaranjani to narrate her experiences.

"Ma, I stayed at my place in London for about a week. My mother had expired four years ago. My brothers could not inform me as they had no address. They were making attempts to lay hands on my property. I told them that in the Ashram, we are not dependent on public contributions. We manage by our own resources; therefore my share of property is required by me. I have accepted my share of Rs. 10 lakhs. Please accept it Ma."

Tapaswini turned towards Maheswari, asked her to narrate her experiences.

She sat for some time thinking and felt that she should narrate the whole story which she had gathered from the diaries. Unless she told everything, she felt that her mind would not feel unburdened. She told everything about Laxmi, her beginnings as a worker, her pregnancy, being raped by four men, the help of Chandra, marriage, the birth of Kumari, Yogini's arrival, the prosperity of Laxmi by hard work and luck, the romantic interest of Chandra, Kumudini's terminal sickness, the sacrifice of Laxmi in nursing her, the statements of Kumudini that Laxmi was her mother in her previous life, not Yogini; Laxmi would be born as her daughter in next life, not Suma, Kumudini's pleadings that Laxmi should live with Chandra and take care of him; living as husband and wife for ten years; Chandra's sickness, nursing him on the wheel chair, his death, selling away of property for Rs. 20 lakhs and raising a loan on the security of the farm and finally, her determination to open an Ashram!"

Maheswari added, "I have brought my share of Rs. 10 lakhs and the ornaments for being offered to the Ashram."

Tapaswini sat for a long time closing her eyes. Then she told firmly. "I cannot accept this money and the ornaments. Go back and offer them to Laxmi!"

6

Laxmi sat alone on the terrace and meditated. Silence seemed to pervade around. For the first time in her life, she felt that it had a life of its own. Within her, the thoughts ceased. She had totally resigned to fate; efforts to improve her lot seemed to have taken a break; herself, a mere cipher of no consequence in the face of immensity. To her shock, she came to realise that the silence was aware of herself.

Some one was nearby. She opened her eyes. She could not recognise initially. She was Suma. Who stood there wondering.

"Ma, are you meditating?"

Laxmi was overwhelmed by her humility. She got up, took her in her embrace and shed tears, "Yes, truly you are my daughter."

After narrating the developments and instructions of Tapaswini, Suma pleaded, "Ma, unless you accept the money and the ornaments, I will not be accepted in the Ashram.

"Do you want to go back? Why don't you live with me? We would open an Ashram."

"Ma, I am going to be initiated as a sanyasini by Tapaswini Ma. This is a great event in one's life. Ma, bless me that I will succeed," she touched her feet.

Laxmi caught hold of her, "Not necessary. You will succeed undoubtedly. Please give this money to Harsha. I have raised a loan."

Harsha heard from Suma everything, understood the import of the whole transaction. He refused to accept the money. He told, "Suma, as far as Laxmi is concerned, tell her that the account is closed. But I cannot accept this money which was offered at the feet of Tapaswini once. This is my contribution to the Ashram. Please tell my mother to persuade Tapaswini to accept my contribution."

Laxmi was puzzled. She looked at the vast farm, the coconut trees swaying in the breeze, the enormous silence still hanging around, the distant voices of children, the chirping of birds and her own thoughts. Suddenly she shook herself off and looked at Suma. "Don't go, remain with me."

"Ma, I want to go atleast after two days. Tapaswini Ma is not staying in the Ashram. She comes only when she pleases."

"Where does she go?"

"We do not know. At times she disappears even before our very eyes. She has attained the highest."

Disbelieving she said, "I want to meet her."

She was getting ready to go. She wanted to convey her decision to Laxmi. She was nowhere. Doubting she went to the terrace. Laxmi sat closing her eyes in deep meditation. Her face serene. Suma stood gaping. Laxmi opened her eyes.

"Suma, please come."

"Ma, I propose to leave today evening."

Laxmi placing her hand on her shoulder tenderly whispered, "Tapaswini Ma has promised to visit us."

Suma was surprised. Is she off or telling the truth? Has she attained the insight to meet Tapaswini in the other dimension?

"When?" Suma asked skeptically.

"I do not know. Believe me, soon."

Suma started doubting her sanity. "But let me go today. I am afraid, I will miss her."

"You might miss her, if you leave me today." Laxmi cautioned.

"How do you know she is coming?"

"In the dream, I saw a sanyasini coming to me. I went and prostrated at her feet. She told, 'You wanted to meet me. I am Tapaswini, I am coming to you.' I opened my eyes. She was there in the room, a luminous apparition vanishing in thin air."

Suma kept quiet. Anyway she would be leaving that night. There was ample time to think. "Ma, let us have breakfast."

They came down; Suma silent, skeptical, doubting; Laxmi calm, expectant and happy.

"Suma, why are you serious? Relax, eat properly." her motherly affection reminded Suma of her mother.

"Ma, why are you not eating?"

"I will take with Tapaswini."

Suma was shocked. Is she deranged?

Both of them came out on the verandah. Laxmi sat on the cane chair. Suma standing near her looked on. It was a new development. Another day had begun for Laxmi, a beautiful day. From the distant trees came the koel's voice calling her lover. Silence and then sound of the wind brushing the leaves, the urgency in the human voices from the worker's quarters, the meek cows with the jingling of bells returning home after emptying their breasts and a taxi moving towards their house. Who could that be? It came and halted infront of the gate. A sanyasini came out. Laxmi ran near the gate and prostrated at her feet. Suma also came running wondering at the prediction. Tapaswini!

"Bless me Ma." Laxmi with tears rolling down her cheeks mumbled.

Tapaswini lifted her, watched her face holding it in both the palms and told, "You are truly a beautiful woman." She kissed her forehead. Beauty for Tapaswini meant integrity, both the inner and the outer.

Suma rushed forward, penitent, perplexed. "Ma, excuse me. I was to come to you tonight. Ma stopped me telling that you are coming."

Tapaswini lifted her also. "You are a lucky girl, Maheswari."

Maheswari was initiated in sanayas. Tapaswini initiated Laxmi and gave her instructions on meditation. She told her, "Even though you are also fit as on today for donning the ochre robe which is a great burden, I would allow you twelve years time to continue as before and meditate. Look after the farm which is going to take care of many a great souls hereafter. Your name will be remembered Laxmi. This Tapovan shall be known by your name, 'Laxmi Tapovan'. Bhairavi Ma will come here shortly to help you, Till such time, Maheswari will be with you."

Kumari also prostrated at her feet and murmured, "I have

erred Ma in rejecting my mother. Can I also help the Ashram by opening a Yoga class and running a dispensary?"

"This is Laxmi Tapovan. Bhairavi will come here. We want whole hearted dedication. You cannot be a housewife and the same time, work here. You would fail at two fronts family and Tapovan."

Kumari was hurt; her face was small, she could not look up and stand.

Tapaswini told gently. "Do not get hurt which would reveal that you are still nursing an ego. Relax. You are still young. Learning requires the whole of life Kumari. Do not waste it. You are very lucky, you have a man like Harsha."

Harsha asked in all humility. "Will you come to our house for food tomorrow?"

"We do not accept invitations from householders. So both of you along with your children, come for food tomorrow."

She looked at Laxmi who was glad.

Bhuvaneswari Ma was seriously ill. She had written a letter.

"Tapaswini,

Your mother is having only a few days left. Before I leave. I want to meet you.

I cannot entrust this Ashram to my disciples. There are no male inmates. A few sanyasini's are there. I feel they are dedicated souls.

Come and help me. With love

Your mother Bhuvaneswari Ma."

Tapaswini was not there when the letter was received. It remained waiting for her arrival. She came one day unexpectedly. Before opening the letter, she told, "Yogini, some useful work awaits you."

After reading the letter, she told with concern "You will be incharge of Bhuvaneswari Tapovan."

6

Sophia, a tourist came one day enquiring about Shivaranjani Seeing her, she could not believe her eyes.

"You are a British subject?"

"Yes and no. I belong to the world."

"I am Sophia, a tourist. I have read your magazine. It's quite interesting. I thought of staying here for a few days if there is no objection."

"We entertain guests only for two days. Beyond that, you may stay as a paying guest and that too only for about a week."

"I have already visited four Tapovans. How many are there?"

"Seven."

"I have brought a letter from Bhairavi."

Shivaranjani read the letter. Sophia asked casually, "What are the names of the Tapovans?"

"The seven are located at the seven extremities of the country. Yogini in the North, Bhairavi in the South, Laxmi in the Centre, Shivararjani in the East, Maheswari in the West, Bhuvaneswari in the Northeast and Parameswari in the North West."

Having disclosed, Shivaranjani wondered whether Sophia had not collected these particulars from the four she had already visited. Whether she was trying to confirm, be accurate in her data. She became cautious.

"I would like to stay for about a week."

Sophia was carefully observing everything. She was

impressed by the affluence of the Tapovans. She was curious about the central garden cordoned off by a fence, Her curiosity to get acquainted with the medicinal plants remained unfulfilled as Shivaranjani explained that the garden was jealously guarded by Tapaswini. The visitors were forbidden. Sophia had already visited four Tapovans which were identical with the one she saw there. Her questions ranged from simple like the food preferred by the sanyasinis, the lessons imparted to the students in the yoga and pranayam classes and their effects; and the complex questions like the result of meditation: entry into the other dimension, the methodology used to study the thought, the percentage of accuracy in achieving results, the contents and topography of the other dimension. She was curious about the meditation hall which was constructed with an eye on security. There were no windows to this hall which was very spacious, only ventilators opened to the outside. The ceiling was illuminated with concealed electric lights. The walls were naked painted in subdued colour. The floor was dust-proof. It was well protected by wind and sound. It was very calm. Sophia wanted to participate in meditation, but she was not permitted.

Shivaranjani felt suspicious. Sophia justified her curiosity declaring herself as a feminist.

"We are not involved in feminism. It's convenient to run the Tapovan with only woman devotees."

"Shivaranjani, since how long you are in the Ashram?"

"Twenty years."

"I read some time back that the Tapovan is experimenting to explore the thought structure of the world. What are the results of this exploration?"

Shivaranjani remembered the instructions of Tapaswini on the previous occasion when all the seven Tapaswinis had assembled at Varanasi on the night of the New Moon. They were exploring the thought structure of the two Power Blocks I and II. Tapaswini was very critical about the magazine. As far as possible she advised Shivaranjani not to mention the details of the exploration in the other dimension. She wanted absolute secrecy to be maintained. Already there have been some indiscretions. The unscrupulous persons carried the impression that Tapaswini was interested in Black Magic; they were pursuing a path of Evil; they were Satans disciples. The human race was still immature. It was better to keep the details of exploration concealed. The secret mission undertaken by them on the New Moon nights were of utmost importance for saving the world community from the brink of disaster. Tapaswini had explained that there were two major Power Blocks; for the sake of convenience she named them as P I and P II. Each Block comprised of a number countries under their aegis. They had powerful nuclear, chemical armament capable of annihilation of the human race within minutes. Humanity which took so much time to come to the present stage would be lost before we had time to repent. Who would be the victors, who the vanquished? Who would inherit the earth? It was a natural sequel of the advanced technology; simultaneous development of the mind had been unduly delayed. Under similar circumstances, in the past advanced civilisations were wiped out. Shivaranjani became alert.

She told, "Sophia, I do not know what you are talking about. I am however convinced that we work for the common good."

Sophia was not prepared to give up her efforts to arrive at the bottom of the truth.

"Can any one of you as a possibility, with precision penetrate into the thought structure of another and alter his consciousness so that it strives for peace with greater vigour?

"I do not know," she told nervously. The questions of Sophia indicated that she was in possession of certain secret information about the activities of the Tapovan.

Just then they were aware of an eerie feeling that somebody was present among them. The door was closed. A thin vapour crystallised and suddenly from nowhere, materialised Tapaswini. Sophia was paralysed. She sat spell bound. It was something incredible, her western mind could not grasp. She became certain of her deduction that these were the seven monks who had influenced the President. This could have great repercussions. What should be done? She was shivering with excitation and fear.

Tapaswini asked her direct questions. "Sophia, why are you collecting minute details about our Tapovan?"

"I am a tourist, proposing to write a book on Tapovans in the Eastern Block."

"When are you leaving?"

"Tomorrow."

"How long have you lived in the various Tapovans?"

"Four months."

"Is it not adequate to write a book?"

"No Madam. I am stunned seeing you materialise from nowhere, what is the Tapovan doing for the world?"

"Only those who are willing to devote their life come to know. Do not be curious."

"Can I stay for some more time?"

"How many days more?"

"One week."

"Here?"

"Yes Madam."

"I permit you."

Sophia left the room. Tapaswini waited till she was sure that the visitor reached the Guest house and then told, "She is too much inquisitive. Collecting intelligence." "Yes Ma. She has already collected about the historical background of all the Tapovans. It appears she was fond of our magazine. She claims herself as a feminist. Particularly she was interested in our writings on the possibility of contacting the thought structure of the human race; influencing particular individuals for the good of humanity. Some years ago, we referred to that dimension from where the saviours of the world descended on the earth from time to time. A possibility, we had suggested to create a parallel centre on earth with enlightened souls who could work silently and control the destiny of the world. Sophia was critical of the article and wanted specific details; percentage of success in this exploration."

Tapaswini became serious and told, "The magazine may be closed stating that it is not economical. We have achieved remarkable progress in coming to our goal. I doubt Sophia, her intentions."

Tapaswini recollected. "When all seven of us stood around the supine body of the President, his response revealed that he was capable of carrying the impression on waking. If so, he might have talked to others."

Shivaranjani was puzzled. "Is she a spy?" she asked.

"Why not? If what we have achieved become known to them and they have a definite clue, there is every possibility, shortly, they would plan, initiate action to eliminate all of us. This would mean postponement by a hundred years."

"So great is the risk!" Shivaranjani stood aghast.

"Yes, Shivaranjani. Be careful. Satanic influences cannot be ruled out. We must be on our gaurd. Shopia is not the type who would devote her life for learning pranayam and yoga. For four months she is sticking to our Tapavanas. Careful Shivaranjini. I want you to find out from her room if there are any objectionable material like diary, scrap of paper where she must have thoughtlessly scribbled, any report. Collect every piece of evidence. Let me know immediately. Shivaranjini went through her room. After a through search, a small diary was found below the bed in the centre of the cot sticking to the lower surface of the bed. The diary contained entries for the last one year. She was not an ordinary tourist. Reference to words like 'Mrs.', 'Boss', 'Security' '7Ms', etc. created doubts. There was a mention about the mental condition of one 'P'. The mention of the Tapaswini magazine and mission meant that Sophia had come upon some invaluable information about the cause of the change of attitude of the President.

Tapaswini went through the diary and then closed her eyes.

After considerable time she told Shivaranjani, "Let the diary remain with me. Where is she now?

"She has gone to the park an hour ago."

"Do not rely on her."

Tapaswini had suspected long ago that President of P1 was capable of remembering his dream. If he had written down in his diary, there is a possibility of leakage. Or the President might have disclosed to his psychiatrist. The Intelligence Agency might have doubted Sophia. The information collected by her was invaluable. If she was allowed to go back, there was likelihood of grave repercussions. The work so far accomplished would be nullified. It was certain that they would try to eliminate the seven sanyasinis. Therefore Tapaswini activated the Ally to destroy Sophia. To submit to the machination won't work. A novel methodology was being invented.

Sophia on return searched for the diary. When she realised that her room was subjected to search in her absence, she packed up her things and decided to leave the Tapovan. After lunch, she came and told Tapaswini "I am leaving Madam. Sorry, I troubled you."

"Take your diary." Tapaswini gave her without any reaction showing on her face, "Goodbye Sophia."

Sophia was thunderstruck. Terrified, when she extended her hand. A cold icy wind had surrounded her with an iron grip. She, with difficulty, moved out, forgot even to greet Shivaranjani who stood there watching. She took her car drove on. After one hour, the car had travelled up a hillock and fallen in a ravine.

When this incredible thing was happening, she was terrified. The vehicle was not under her control and how could that be, she failed to visualise; her sanity was endangered at the queer event. She took out her watch and scribbled "Time 1.7 Ms." Those who looked at the car were astonished and reported to the Police.

Tapaswini knew that the work they undertook was not an

easy one. She expected all these possible results. She appreciated the acumen of Sophia who had sensed rightly and had collected invaluable particulars to build up a plausible theory. She felt that utmost secrecy was necessary hereafter in the execution of their work. It was also necessary to find out a way by which the person on whom the experiment was carried out, would not be in a position to know or carry the impressions beyond the confines of the dream.

During the emergency meeting which was attended by all the seven sanyasinis, Maheswari asked doubting, "Ma even though we held implicitly that this work is for the common good, why is it that it took the toll of three lives?"

The others were also curious to find out the answer. Tapaswini told calmly. "True. If we had remained passive, it would have taken the toll of millions of lives. The destiny of the whole world was involved. Therefore our action is justified. We have as you are aware succeeded beyond expectation in affecting the thought structure of the Presidents P I and P II. If we had neglected, they would have ultimately annihilated the whole human race! Therefore we were concerned about curing them of their malady. Our intentions were clear and I believe our work was looked after by the Masters. Unfortunately the President of P I was an advanced soul who carried glimpses of the dream in the wakeful state and consulted the psychiatrist. Not so the President of P II. President of P II dismantled the entire socialist structure. He strove towards world peace and development of the third world. Both of them together would have created a new order but they were eliminated. They were working for us. Let us pray for their souls."

They stood up in silence for two minutes. Tapaswini continued. "New persons have assumed power. They cannot suddenly do away what has already been done. There is some time available to us to think and devise new ways. In the meanwhile, I want to alert you all. The Intelligence Agency is not to be slighted. Sophia came and lived unassumingly for nearly four months. She had collected considerable material. I am baffled by going through her diary. She might have already given these particulars to the Agency. It was unfortunate we have been naive thinking that she was interested in becoming a sanyasini and supplying her all the particulars. She was a spy. Do you know under severe strain when inspite of herself the car was climbing a hillock and plunging any moment into the ravine, she had the presence of mind to leave a clue to the Investigating Agency. The watch is in their custody. It would tell many things which we would have preferred left unsaid. Therefore in future, no disclosure about your prowess, dreams, about the possibility of bringing about transformation in the psyche of man. John, the Baptist was beheaded by Herod because he had promised with an oath to give the daughter of Herodias whatsoever she would ask. Remember Jesus, the Son of God, he was not spared. They did spit in his face, buffeted him; smote him with the palm of their hands. They set up over his head his accusation written. Two thieves were crucified with him, one on the right, and another on the left. People who saw him, reviled him wagging their heads. They challenged him to come down from the Cross. 'He saved others, himself, he cannot save. He trusted in God; let him deliver him.' And about the ninth hour, Jesus cried with a loud voice saying, 'My God, my God why hast thou forsaken me!' No doubt, he experienced and expiated the sins of the world on the Cross. But it created doubts in the mind of common man that Jesus was unable to stand against the forces of Evil even though he was the amalgam of the Natures of Father, the Creator, and the Holy Ghost, the Inspiring Breath! Perhaps he revered the parameters of Nature and preferred death and gave up the Ghost in deepest agony like any other mortal; then chose to rise in the other dimension as Son of God. It was unique but dismal; man celebrating humiliation and murder and creating a saga of religion! Our legendary Avatars, Ram, Krishna, were different. They survived under gravest threat to their lives; model heroes who are worshipped for their valour, invincibility, wisdom. There is a rethinking. Why should a saviour be left to the mercy of the fragile humanity? Is there no honourable way to restructure the human world? Our work was chosen with the greatest care and much thought. We are here to bring out a new culture."

Shivaranjani demurely asked, "You have given us an astute evaluation of the gaps in our knowledge of how God as an Avatar evolved. Are you the latest Avatar?"

Tapaswini sat quietly musing and then told, "Single handed you can't do anything. We have undertaken this hazardous task."

The Intelligence Agency prepared a detailed report and referred to the parapsychology Department for opinion. It was marked Top Secret.

Resume of the report :

The State is watching with concern and apprehension the latest shift in policy of P I. The President has consistently rejected the advice tendered by Experts who have felt that there is a dangerous tilt towards philanthropism, third world emancipation, upliftment of Black population. The Defense expenditure has been cut drastically sacrificing National interest. The National pride is no longer a virtue.

These developments have synchronised with certain psychological developments in relation to the psyche of the President. He has suffered a shock by a recurring dream. From his diary, it is revealed that an year ago, seven sanyasinis appeared in his dream; they were like luminous apparitions surrounding his supine body, injecting in him beams of light. They have appeared to him to be benevolent forces aiming at his all round development. These dreams have recurred on New Moon nights continuously for the past one year.

Sophia, one of our staff members had undertaken a preliminary investigation and had revealed the existence of seven Tapovans in the Eastern Block. There are seven Tapaswinis who run these Tapovans. She had collected nearly one hundred magazines of the Tapovan. On the basis of the writing she had prepared the following report.

It's the belief of Asians that God incarnates on earth to regenerate Dharma (Righteousness) and destroy Evil. The theosophists have also propounded a theory, that there is a higher dimension, the White Brotherhood from where the world has received its share of saviours. The Tapaswini magazine independently refers to the existence of a dimension of liberated souls who had forgone the fruits of liberation and preferred to stay back on earth for the good of humanity. They have developed a new ethereal body luminous and fairly permanent which can travel in and out of that dimension. They claim that the thought structure of humanity can be fairly accurately viewed from that dimension. Those who control the destiny of mankind are very few. The have also evolved a technique perhaps to recognise the thought structure of these individuals and influence them to change their attitude. In other words, they have hinted at the prospects of reorienting their brain cells so that they behave like responsible citizens.

A doubt arises whether the seven monks had anything to do with the change of attitude of our President. It appears in P II also there have been an upsurge of democratic trends.

Unfortunately, Sophia who was investigating into this phenomena for the last four months was killed under mysterious circumstances near a Tapovan in the Eastern Block. She had furnished us invaluable information. The seven Tapovans are financed by big Industrialists. The sanyasinis are highly educated, some of them are foreign trained Doctors. We are puzzled and are inclined to infer that the East might have made a dent on the other dimension and come upon a way to influence the thought structure of man.

Her untimely death is another puzzle. After leaving Shivaranjani Tapovan (Shivaranjani is an English Lady, her original name is Eileen), Sophia had driven the car for about an hour and then a strange thing appeared to have happened. According to eye witnesses, it was stunning scene to find the car climbing a steep hill and plunge in a ravine. The car had exploded and nothing had remained except the back of the steel frame of her watch on which she had scribbled with the penknife the words and figures, "Time 1.7 Ms.' The handwriting reveals that she was seized by a terror; perhaps she was aware of a demoniac force lifting the vehicle. The onlookers have given various versions. The car was lifted slowly in the air by a mysterious force and thrown into a ravine. Is it possible that the sanyasinis came to know of her mission and eliminated her by invoking a force from that dimension?

The crucial question that haunts our mind is whether these sanyasinis who call themselves as the legendary Sapta Rishis (Seven sanyasinis) are capable of bringing about a change in the thought structure of politicians by remote control? Make them behave according to their whims. Whether there is a possibility to invoke a force from that dimension to destroy another?

The Parapsychology Department after a detailed examination held the view that such an eventuality could not be ruled out. Perhaps it was a distant possibility in future. They were however skeptical about the seven sanyasinis accomplishing the task referred to by Sophia. The claims of the Vedantins and the seers that the entire creation could be held on the stretch of a palm was an academic hogwash. However our knowledge of the mind is very limited. It appeared there was a higher dimension; its nature, we have not known. Perhaps, if the sanyasins proved to be genuine in their claims, it is likely such individuals were structured on a different wavelength; their atomic constituents biologically might be totally different. It might be possible if a thorough study is undertaken to identify them by a device and corner them. If they are intent on altering the thought structure of man, it would amount to a gravest offence, more than murder. Therefore it would be prudent to eliminate them by a legislation.

Huge funds should be provided for this investigation."

2

The death of Sophia was a challenge to the Intelligence Agency. To resolve, it was the most bizarre event. She was not addicted to drinks or drugs. She was moderate in habits. She exercised the highest discretion in her activities. She was alert, confident and clever. She grasped many problems with an uncanny insight. On the date of her departure, she had ensured that her car was in fit condition. It was got checked up, repaired six days before. She was not sentimental, suicidal type. She had not lost control of her mind. She had left a clue even though she was under greatest stress. The available clues pointed out to a mysterious end. Probably the sanyasinis became aware of the Sophia mission and succeeded in eliminating her. They had done it in an inexplicable way. Their scientific mind failed to grasp the modus operandi.

They were not prepared to give up so easily. They had set up an independent fund for the purpose manned by personnel who had an aptitude for mystery and occultism. Captain Margaret was the head of this organisation.

In the backdrop of highly sophisticated technology, they were aware they had neglected the inner dimension. In the face of reliable data collected by Sophia they were not prepared to set aside her findings as figment of imagination. They had decided to keep the mind and heart open. They were willing to investigate and learn. They deputed Margaret to investigate into the death of Sophia. She brought a letter addressed to Shivaranjani by the State Department.

Margaret was received with all affection by Shivaranjani. She was allowed to stay in the Guest house. Fortunately Tapaswini was also available. Margaret asked questions directly without reservation; it was an official visit by a State representative.

"Madam, Sophia was deputed by us to find out whether the seven monks who had visited our President in the dream were in any way connected with the Tapovan? I have come to ask the same question."

Tapaswini smiled and told lovingly "I assure you Margaret, we do not work to the detriment of any individual."

"Sophia died under mysterious circumstances. Are you in any way responsible for the death of Sophia?"

Tapaswini became serious but gently told undisturbed, “I am sorry for the untimely death of Sophia which I read in the Newspaper. We are of the view that in this life every action has a reaction. No one can be held responsible for the death. She alone is answerable.”

Margaret felt that Tapaswini was an adept in evading direct answers. “What is the purpose of the seven Tapovans?”

“Since ages East is seized of a purpose. We are obsessed of a work to probe and map the unknown dimension. Unnamable! To understand oneself.”

“Are you working for altering the social value?”

“I have not understood your question.”

Margaret felt that it was another way of evading answers.

“Are you seized with the task of changing the mind of man? Influencing his brain, altering the thought structure?”

Tapaswini answered with a smile.

“Perhaps the mind brought up in western culture cannot grasp the intentions of the liberated mind. I am not creating a chasm between East and West.”

Margaret became more and more specific. “Sitting at the Tapovan, can you hope to influence the brain of any particular individual who might be thousands of miles away?”

“I do not know. It was only a coincidence perhaps, dreaming of seven monks by your President and your presumptions.”

“Is it a possibility?”

Tapaswini asked pointedly, “What is it you want to know?”

“Influencing another through space?”

“Margaret anything is possible.”

“Is it within your reach?”

“Why should you know? We do not waste energy on unproductive works.”

“Can you destroy another from a long distance?”

“How irresponsible it looks, killing?” Tapaswini laughed.

"I want to see your medicinal plants."

"We do not take strangers inside the garden. The plants need some privacy. Moreover these plants have only medicinal value, no magical powers."

"Can I participate in your meditation session?"

"There is no meditation session. It's not a subject to be taught, Margaret. That is why I mentioned about western culture. That is you want to do something about meditation even!"

"How is one to start, what is it to arrive at meditation?"

"When you understand yourself, there is a beginning of meditation. It's not preached for influencing another." Margaret asked, "Are you the cause and the world effect?" Tapaswini smiled and replied, "Why not this way? I am the effect, the world is the cause."

"I am puzzled. It's against theological concepts."

"Right you are. We do not challenge concepts or authority. We are carried away by names. You should examine every issue and not accept anything blindly. The world is the cause. The earth moving round the sun, on its own axis revolving, creating days and nights, seasons, affect me. Essentially I am the effect. I cannot do anything."

"You mean caught up in a wheel which keeps on ruthlessly grinding!"

"You are right."

Margaret asked astonished. "Is there no salvation for man so imprisoned by the cause and effect?"

"No, it's impossible."

Margaret sat thinking for a long time. She was speechless. Then she told slowly, "My thinking seems to come to an end."

"That is a good beginning, Margaret."

"Then what happens?"

"We point to the end of Path. Ending is the beginning of meditation."

She sat puzzled. The eyes of Tapaswini were half closed. They were looking like streaks of light. She was looking into the eyes of Margaret, searching, seizing the helpless victim.

She asked spell bound, “I am the effect. The world is the cause. Cause and effect. In the ending of ‘Me’, what happens to the cause?”

“How can you end me?” Tapaswini asked.

“I do not know, really I do not know.”

“That is when the ‘me’ faces its end!”

“In ending ‘me”, will the cause also come to an end?”

“If nothing is left, on what cause will operate? When you move deeper, the world, the cosmos, appears to be the effect acting on the spur of an Unknowable Cause!”

“What is the Unknowable Cause you refer?”

“The Other.”

“What is the Other?”

“The Unknowable.”

“What is the Unknowable?” Margaret was puzzled.

“The Unknowable is Unknowable.”

Margaret remembered the Eastern philosophy of Brahman, Nirvana and God!

Tapaswini retorted at once. “Not Brahman. Do not compare Margaret. You cannot recognise the Unknowable!”

Margaret was perplexed. Tapaswini was capable of reading another’s mind! Probably she could probe into the thought structure of another.

Thus more confounded, much impressed by Tapaswini, recognising that the charisma of her presence had already set in motion a perceptible change, she decided to leave the Tapovan the next day. She however confessed before Shivaranjani, “I felt that I am coming to the end of human cycle in the presence of Tapaswini. I felt as if I am near the precipice. There was only one thing to do meditate.”

Shivaranjani smiled and told sympathetically, "You are fortunate, Margaret to grasp the truth. I think you received Initiation!"

The Intelligence Agency had lost another of their best Agent, not physically but psychologically. Margaret on return refused to talk about the Tapovan. This was another case of suspense. She repeatedly asserted "I could not grasp anything in the Tapovan."

She resigned her assignment and it was learnt she had travelled to Shivaranjani, Tapovan. Shivaranjani asked Tapaswini "You have not harmed Margaret. Whereas Sophia."

Tapaswini smiled and told, "In both the cases, there was action. In the case of Sophia, she was not so advanced; she had to be eliminated. Margaret, she arrived at the point in listening when her 'self' was annihilated. The later was a profound action!"

GLOSSARY

Ally	: A Disembodied force.
Ardhanareeswara	: Androgynous state; being both man and woman; an explosive state coming into being with the confluence of male and female potentialities
Arhat	: The one who has reached Nirvana.
Avatar	: Descent or incarnation of the divine
Brahman	: Absolute one without a second
Chaya Brahma	: Shadow Being; with the coming of Truth, the self, the body and the phenomenal existence transforms into a shadow, grows into Truth attaining immeasurability and dissolves into nothing.
Eternity	: It stands for the hundred years of Brahma, the duration of a Mahakalpa or a period of 311,040,000,000,000 years.
Great Bird	: AUM. The syllable A is considered to be its right wing, U, its left, M, its tail and the ardhamatra (half meter) its head. A yogi who comes to it is not affected by karmic influences.
Hierophant	: The great Initiator.
Initiation	: It brings the disciple on the sacred path leading to Truth.
Jivanmukta	: Liberated soul

Karma	:	Action or retribution
Kundalini	:	The fiery power or Fohatic power, world mother, the great pristine force; it's presumed to be dormant in human body.
Linga	:	Symbol of Universal God where male and female principles are in confluence eliminating 'self', leading to an explosive state; it's the symbol of creativity; Shiva.
Om	:	AUM The syllable A, U and M and the ardhamatra symbolize a great mystery; it's the essence of consciousness and beyond this soundless sound, the unknowable abides!
Point of light	:	Bindu Brahma; it's the Universal God as comprehended by the seeker through a minuscule opening in consciousness; in occult parlance, the elimination of 'self' that reveals the true nature of being.
Sadhana	:	Spiritual striving
Sahasranama	:	Thousand names of the Goddess, Energy; it's a futile attempt to describe the indescribable.
Sanyasin	:	The one who has renounced the worldly life to lead a life of contemplation and search of Truth.
Secret life	:	The Adept enters a new body, 'Nirman kaya' and remains throughout the cycles helping mankind.
Shadow	:	The body is held as a shadow in mystic schools.
Shavasan	:	Corpse pose in Yoga.

Stream of life	: The primordial state of energy that ultimately leads the seeker to Truth.
Tapas	: Austerity or asceticism
Zodiac	: A band of celestial sphere that represents the path of the principal planets, the moon and sun.